The Band of Moonlit Waters

BRAD BUSSIE

DEDICATION

For Aunt Kathy,
Who helped me get started
For my son Mason,
Who pushed me to finish

1 ABSOLUTE WORST

His head spun, and all went dark.

A sudden sensation like a splash of icy water jolted him, and his vision blurred as a bitter taste filled his mouth. Red warning lights blinked, sirens blared, and his senses sharpened. He was still inside his cryotube. The central line running into his sleep suit lay empty, drained of its shimmering blue suspended animation fluid.

Summoning his strength, Tyler raised an arm toward a small, dangerously flashing control panel beside the viewport. Odd, he thought. What good were viewports on cryotubes? Especially since the viewport he was looking through was blackened and charred.

When a colonist awoke from cold sleep, the tube should open, with medical staff waiting to assess the occupant. As he silenced the alarms, he hesitated. No one had come. He pressed his palm to the now-quiet control panel, greeted by a familiar computer chime, ready to accept commands.

"Computer," he croaked, struggling for breath, "status."

The system faltered before responding, its voice faintly garbled. "Identification."

"Tyler Ryan Tor," he answered, frowning.

After a pause, the computer's report came through: "Systems critical. Pod damaged, life support failing. Condition unknown. Location unknown. Security protocol engaged. Authorization required for pod hatch release."

Tyler tilted his head, exhaling in exasperation. The computer had lost its damn mind again. He should have woken up months before they reached the planet. Strength slowly returned to his muscles, and he knew he needed answers. Keeping his palm against the control panel, he authorized the hatch release.

The hatch lock cycled, hissing and smoking, before the entire front of the pod swung forward with a shriek. Blinding light flooded over him, and a gust of fresh air hit his face. Where in the hell was he, and why wasn't he still on the *Spero*?

Tyler squinted into the brightness, his legs wobbling as he took his first unsteady step. Daylight bathed his chilled skin, and the warmth felt startlingly good.

He sat down, blinking rapidly to clear the swirling lights from his vision. Closing one eye and squinting with the other, he focused on his surroundings—and froze.

He was at the center of a horrific crash site. Twisted metal and debris sprawled in every direction. Flames devoured the wreckage as thick, black smoke poured into the sky, sullying the serene blue dotted with puffy white clouds. The oily plumes marred the sky's brilliance, obscuring its light.

"This just happened," Tyler muttered.

His vision adapted to the light, and warmth seeped into his stiff limbs. Hugging himself, he rubbed his arms, urging blood to flow back to his extremities. A few push-ups later, he almost felt human.

Rising to his feet with renewed steadiness, Tyler turned to inspect the battered pod cryopod. His name, once emblazoned along the side, was now charred and partially illegible. Tilting his head, he traced the lettering. "Ty Ryan T... Tyrant?"

He laughed dryly at the irony, flexing his arms at the thought, then sighed. He didn't feel much like joking. Moving around the pod, he examined the ark that had saved his life.

The pod stood upright, as if it had dropped like an arrow from the sky. It was slightly taller than him and wide enough to hold a person, a power source, cryogenic equipment—and a supply locker.

Supply locker! Tyler ran his hand along the pod's left side, fingers searching for the manual release. The smoky air and surrounding fires had already worked up a thirst in him.

He pulled the release, and the equipment drawer groaned, shrieked slightly, and halted halfway open. Stooping, Tyler peered inside. His duty uniform, light combat armor, and rucksack were inside, along with his quarterstaff and provisions meant for emergencies like this.

Two days of food and water, he thought, reaching in to gather the contents. He folded his uniform and left it in the pod for later, strapping the combat armor over his thin cryosuit. Lightweight yet durable, the armor allowed full mobility.

The quarterstaff was jammed, wedged inside the half-open drawer. He gripped the locker's frame, yanking with all the strength he could muster. The drawer finally gave, shrieking as it opened, and he pulled the staff free. He slung the rucksack over his shoulder, feeling slightly more prepared.

The quarterstaff, balanced for versatility, evoked a familiar sense of pride as he held it. It was a tool from his military days, aptly named 'Warquarter' for its primary use, and one of the last remnants of humanity's less than peaceful Mars colonization. The staff hummed as his ocular implant flickered to life, syncing with its systems.

His right eye glimmered as data scrolled past, confirming his identity.

He stopped the display with a flick of his left hand, frowning as vital stats flashed before him. This wasn't the colony planet YAR887.

A tremor shook the ground, cutting into his thoughts. Tyler ended the scan and accessed the virtual network grid, hoping to connect with the *Spero's* system. His attempts met only silence.

Leaning the Warquarter against the pod, he gathered his supplies and climbed back into the cryopod. Placing his palm on the scanner, he whispered, "Computer, status of UEA *Spero*?" His gaze roamed over the charred landscape, a desolate terrain with no sign of trees, plants, or even water.

The computer's voice crackled, struggling. "Unable to establish contact with *Spero*." A warning icon flashed, highlighting critical power levels.

Tyler realized he'd missed something. While the pod diagnostics showed no damage, the core appeared drained. Odd, since cryopod cores were designed to last centuries. This can't be right, he thought.

The power indicator flashed again. He was nearly out of time. Retrieving data from the cryopod via voice commands seemed a lost cause as the system neared shutdown.

"Computer, initiate data transfer to Tyler Tor," he commanded, bracing for the deluge of information.

Data flowed into his palm implant—until an earth-shattering howl cut through his focus.

"Transfer interrupted at 82%," the computer whispered just as another howl echoed nearby.

Tyler heard massive footsteps pounding behind the pod. He launched from the control panel, gripping his Warquarter as he rounded the cryopod, only to freeze.

A hulking beast loomed yards away, muscles bulging beneath golden skin stretched tight. It wore only a loincloth, seemingly fashioned from silvery scales. In its oversized hands, it brandished a wicked club, likely a bone from a creature even larger.

The beast sniffed the air, whirling suddenly to face him. Its single eye gleamed, set in a face with a bulbous nose and a gaping mouth full of crooked, blunt teeth.

Without warning, it charged, swinging the club wildly. Tyler's Warquarter synced with his ocular implant, guiding him into a trance-like focus. The beast faltered, surprised as Tyler's staff intercepted the club with a loud crack.

Calculations flashed before him, and Tyler moved with precision, disarming the creature with a blow that sent its club flying. The beast roared, stumbling as Tyler delivered a flurry of strikes that crumpled its knee. Another expertly placed blow brought it down, shaking the ground.

But then, a deep rumble resonated. Tyler glanced at the pod just in time to see it sink into a rapidly widening sinkhole. The fallen beast's roars faded as it, too, was pulled down into the collapsing earth. Tyler reached out to steady himself as the ground rippled, before he, too, tumbled into the darkness.

***

Pain radiated through his body.

Tyler forced his eyes open, grimacing as the ache in his muscles threatened to pull him back into unconsciousness. Nothing seemed broken, but he'd taken a beating. The cavern around him was dim, a damp chill thickening the air as he groaned his way upright. Scanning the darkness, he found no sign of the beast he'd brought down, and the lights from his pod were nowhere to be seen.

A faint glow filtered in from high above, where he assumed he'd fallen from. Beside him, his Warquarter lay nestled in rubble, its polished surface partially obscured by dust.

With an effort, Tyler stood, releasing his rucksack from his back. It was damp and battered, and as he rummaged through its contents in the murky cavern, his pulse quickened.

Both water rations had burst open. A desperate thirst surged, and he was acutely aware of the dryness in his throat. He gathered what little liquid remained, downing it in quick gulps. It barely took the edge off, but he focused on what supplies were left, pulling out his torch before re-securing the pack.

Tyler thumbed the torch to life, wincing as bright light cut through the cavern's gloom. The space stretched far beyond the torch's reach, crystal-lined walls glimmering as shards beneath his feet reflected the glow.

An opening loomed to his left, barely visible but wide enough to offer a way out of the rubble. A faint crack in the cavern wall led forward, too narrow for comfort. Tyler thrust his torch into the gap and squinted, catching sight of another cavern beyond, smaller and darker.

Relief flooded him at the sight of a gleaming pool at the center. Driven by thirst and the rising tension of the unknown, he forced himself through the tight opening, his pack slipping up against his face as he squeezed into the next chamber.

Once inside, he stopped, stunned by the stark contrast. This chamber was polished and smooth, as though meticulously carved from stone. The pool rested at a gentle slope, beckoning in the torchlight with its glassy surface.

A fine mist dampened the air as he approached, cautious but drawn forward. He tapped his palm, activating his ocular implant to scan for hazards. To his surprise, the system returned no readings—not even the usual toxicity levels or microbial presence. Where he looked directly at the pool, his scanner displayed only stillness.

Unease pricked at him, but thirst overtook caution as he swallowed against the dry ache in his throat. Setting his pack down, he approached the pool with his Warquarter in one hand and his torch in the other.

Kneeling at the edge, he peered into the water. His reflection was absent, and the pool seemed bottomless. Flicking his wrist, he anchored the torch's small spike into the ground beside him. Then, without further hesitation, he extended his Warquarter, dipping its end into the liquid.

Nothing happened. No creature lunged from the depths, no alert sounded. The staff's end came away, dripping only clear liquid. Tyler relaxed, shaking his head with a rueful chuckle as he leaned on the Warquarter and rubbed his chin thoughtfully.

Finally, he knelt to the pool, scooped a handful of water, and slid it to his lips.

Whispers…
Polaris.

His eyes snapped open. He lay at the bottom of a shallow depression in a cavern with smooth walls and an unbroken ceiling. How long had he been here? What had brought him here? His mind raced, questions filling it, only to be chased away by an eerie silence.

Who am I?

Fragments of memory surfaced—a scorched nameplate, letters barely legible.

Ty…r…an…t.

He scrambled to a crouch, searching for the source of the voice. Alone in the quiet, he noticed the Warquarter resting in his hand, his body crouched in a defensive stance. The staff hummed faintly in anticipation, though no threat appeared.

A heavyset figure stepped from the shadows, carrying a flameless torch that illuminated his broad, muscular frame. He had dusky skin, slightly pointed ears, and a face with features that seemed roughly hewn, almost beast-like. His head was clean-shaven, and he wore a simple sleeveless shirt and loose pants with scale-covered boots.

In his thick, calloused hands, he held a massive pickax with a crystalline blue-green blade. The haft appeared to be bone, bound by an intricate weaving of fiber.

"Razmal," the man said, thumping the pickax's butt against the cavern floor.

"Ty..." he began, then faltered, stopping short of the name that whispered through his mind. Only the insane heard whispers.

Or so they said.

Razmal raised a hand in greeting. His eyes held a guarded warmth. "You sound unsure of your own name."

"Tyrant," he answered firmly, though the word felt abbreviated, somehow incomplete.

Razmal nodded. "So, how did you get in here? I've been working the mine since daybreak, and you didn't pass by."

"I... fell..." Tyrant replied, fighting back a creeping caution that hissed in his mind.

Razmal's gaze sharpened. The torchlight left most of his face in shadow, casting an unsettling effect. As his eyes settled on the staff, they widened in alarm. His breath hitched as he took a step back, his grip tightening on the ax.

"That staff..." Razmal muttered, raising the ax as if bracing for a strike.

A voice inside Tyrant's head screamed in warning, and he lunged forward, swinging the Warquarter wildly. Metal clashed with crystal as the ax blade sparked against the staff in a grinding clash.

"Hold!" Razmal shouted, gritting his teeth against Tyrant's strength. "Where did you get that?"

"It's mine," Tyrant growled, muscles straining as he held the ax and staff locked together.

Razmal drew back, dodging clumsy strikes as the two circled each other warily. As they traded sides, full light fell on Tyrant's face, and Razmal gasped, eyes flaring with recognition.

"Tekian!" Razmal shouted, raising the ax and attacking in earnest.

Blow after blow rang out as Tyrant parried, each attack forcing him to lose ground against Razmal's rage. Tekian meant nothing to him, yet it seemed to warrant a brutal, merciless assault. The clash continued in a brutal exchange, each man's weapon slicing through the air until Razmal's final two-handed chop connected with Tyrant's Warquarter. The ax cracked, splintered, and exploded into sharp fragments.

Seizing the moment, Tyrant drove the butt of his staff into Razmal's chest, forcing the breath from his lungs. Razmal collapsed, gasping as Tyrant demanded, "What is a Tekian?"

Razmal clutched his ribs, his face contorted in pain. "Who are you?"

Tyrant's Warquarter slipped from his grasp as he sank to his knees, exhaustion flooding his veins. "I don't know…"

The voices in his head fell silent, leaving him hollow and drained. His hands trembled as a wave of weariness overtook him. Light blurred at the edges of his vision, and for the second time that day, he slipped into unconsciousness.

2 IT TAKES A VILLAGE

Tyrant awoke with his hands bound tightly behind his back. His feet were also tied, and he lay on his side in a dimly lit space with an overpowering, briny scent—a stale, unmoving air that clung to his nostrils. It was the smell of the ocean, though not the fresh scent carried on a sea breeze, but an ancient, damp pungency that felt trapped in the still air.

Blinking against the haze in his head, Tyrant rocked himself upright and took in his surroundings. He was alone, inside what looked like a tent. Its walls, stretching tautly above and around him, were formed from a patchwork of hide, interwoven over large, arching bones. A ribcage, he realized, marveling at the colossal creature it must have come from.

Where am I?

A flap at the far end of the tent rustled open, and Razmal entered, followed by a woman who moved with a quiet confidence. Razmal carried a strange torch that, instead of flame, emitted a glow from a bright crystal lashed to a bone handle. Its light highlighted the fine details of the woman's features, bathing her in an ethereal shimmer. Tyrant's eyes traced her face; she was striking, with a willowy frame and long, aqua-colored hair that cascaded over her shoulders. Her light blue eyes seemed lit from within by a silver glow, faintly luminescent, enhancing her almost otherworldly beauty.

"Not…Tekian…" she said softly, her voice careful and slightly halting. The words felt clumsy on her tongue, as if she were piecing them together after a long absence from the language.

Tyrant frowned, trying to make sense of her words. She seemed to search his face as though she might find answers there. When Razmal spoke, his familiar tone contrasted sharply with the words that made no sense to Tyrant, a guttural dialect that felt foreign and ancient.

The woman tried again, addressing him in the same incomprehensible tongue. When it was clear he couldn't understand, she glanced at Razmal, who seemed to puzzle over the situation as well.

"Terra…?" Razmal said, each syllable clipped as though he were dredging it from an ancient memory. "Speak…slowly."

Tyrant narrowed his eyes, trying to make himself clear. "Where. Am. I?" He emphasized each word, his voice low and firm.

The woman's hands flew to her mouth, her gaze wide with shock. "Not Tekian," she repeated, as if reaffirming it to herself. She rose abruptly, gathering her skirts as she hurried from the tent, glancing back with an expression Tyrant couldn't decipher.

Razmal watched her go, then turned his attention back to Tyrant. Wordlessly, he knelt and drew a crystalline dagger from his belt, its blade glowing faintly. With careful precision, he sliced through the bindings on Tyrant's wrists and ankles.

"You are… outside," Razmal said, gesturing to the tent's flap.

Rubbing his wrists, Tyrant pushed himself up and followed Razmal out, squinting as the bright light of day met his eyes.

A sprawling village lay before him, nestled beneath towering stone cliffs that cradled the settlement on three sides. At the far end, a narrow opening led to a cave, from which the steady rhythm of picks and hammers echoed. Tents of all shapes, colors, and sizes filled the village, each crafted from stretched hides, bones, and woven grasses. The villagers moved busily through the scene, some repairing shelters, others hauling jugs, and still others tending fires where various aromatic herbs and strange vegetables simmered in stone pots.

Tyrant's gaze drifted to a small pot near him, its earthy fragrance twisting with the sharper scents of spice and resin. Beneath it, crystalline shards glowed, heating the pot without wood or flame. He glanced around, searching for wood—an instinct he didn't question until a sudden, vivid memory struck him.

***

…Amanda reached for his hand, pulling him close as they sat around a fire. The flames crackled and danced in the ring of stones they'd carefully arranged together. Beside them, a small pile of logs promised warmth through the night.

"I love you, Tyler," she whispered, her eyes locked on his, brimming with warmth and certainty.

***

He gasped, staggering as the memory washed over him with brutal clarity. A name—Tyler—echoed in his mind. His face was mere inches from the simmering pot when he pulled himself back, alarmed by the rush of familiarity.

"Tyler?" he murmured, feeling the name pull at something deep inside him.

From nearby, Razmal approached, studying him with a mixture of curiosity and guarded suspicion. Tyrant glowered, feeling the embarrassment of the moment twist his stomach.

Just then, the woman from the tent appeared, hurrying toward them with a bundle wrapped in hides. She slowed, taking in the scene as she clutched the package, her eyes flicking between Razmal and Tyrant.

Carefully, she unwrapped the bundle, and from within the folds, the Warquarter tumbled forward. Tyrant lunged instinctively, catching it before it hit the ground. As his hand closed around the staff, an unexpected surge of emotions coursed through him—hope, urgency, relief.

Razmal and the woman stared as he held the Warquarter, confusion rippling across his face.

"Can it be? Is he one of the Sleepers?" she murmured, almost to herself.

Tyrant's gaze snapped to her. "One of the Sleepers?" he echoed, the words foreign yet familiar.

The woman's eyes widened, and Razmal took a wary step forward, his hand drifting to the crystalline dagger at his belt. "You see! It is the staff," Razmal said, eyes fixed on Tyrant. "In the cave, he spoke. I understood him as I understand you now."

Tyrant tightened his grip on the Warquarter, trying to keep his voice steady. "Can someone please explain what's going on? Where am I? Why can't I remember anything?"

The woman raised her hands in a calming gesture. "You are safe, at least for now. Though if you are truly one of the Sleepers, then none of us may be safe for long. The Tekians will know you are here."

She beckoned Tyrant and Razmal to follow as she moved purposefully toward a large tent in the village's center. Razmal gave Tyrant a cautious look before gesturing him forward.

The inside of the tent was cool, a welcome relief from the humid heat outside. In the dim light, Tyrant's gaze fell upon the strange artifacts strewn about the space, including a large orange container against one wall. The size and shape seemed oddly familiar, as though he'd seen something like it before. The color was faded, the lettering worn away with time, but a vague sense of recognition stirred within him.

The woman moved to a corner and picked up a thin, slate-like sheet of what looked like glass. She approached him, holding it carefully, and looked him straight in the eyes.

"My name is Raya. Do you know where you are?"

Tyrant shook his head slowly, feeling the weight of her gaze. "No."

"This place," she said, gesturing to the tent and beyond, "Is a safe haven. It has hidden us, given us life when the world turned against us."

Razmal stepped forward. "But you are different. This staff you wield—it is not of this place. Nor are you, I think."

Raya tilted her head, studying him as if searching for the answer to an ancient question. "The Sleepers, as we call them, are those who vanished long ago, only to return in times of great need. We believe they are sent by forces beyond our understanding, though not all who rise have the same purpose."

A prickling unease coiled in Tyrant's chest. "So… you think I'm one of these Sleepers?" he asked, wary of her response.

"We don't know," she admitted, glancing at Razmal. "But your arrival has already set things into motion. The Tekians—the warriors who hunt our kind—will sense your presence soon enough. They do not welcome change, nor those who disrupt the order they have carefully maintained."

Tyrant felt a surge of questions bubbling up. "But why am I here? Why can't I remember anything?"

Raya took a deep breath, letting the slate drop to her side. "Sometimes, memory is the price of survival," she said quietly. "But perhaps your past is not truly lost. It is only waiting for you to claim it."

He absorbed her words, unsure whether they offered comfort or only deepened his confusion. Outside, the sounds of village life hummed on, oblivious to the strangeness unfolding within the tent.

Razmal cleared his throat, shifting uncomfortably. "If you are one of the Sleepers," he said, his voice low and grave, "then you may have powers yet unknown—even to yourself."

Tyrant turned the Warquarter in his hands, feeling its weight and the promise hidden within it. The staff seemed to pulse with its own life, a silent call that resonated in his bones.

Raya studied him closely, her voice softening. "Perhaps the answers lie within you. But if you are truly to survive here, you must learn quickly. The Tekians are relentless."

She held his gaze, and in that moment, Tyrant felt a spark of something familiar—a faint glimmer of purpose that felt buried beneath a mountain of lost memories.

"I'll learn," he said, his voice steady. "Whatever it takes."

Raya and Razmal exchanged a glance, a shared understanding that needed no words. Whatever lay ahead, they knew he would need guidance and strength—and that his fate was now, inexorably, bound to theirs.

"You are in the village of Tonu, not far from the coast," Raya explained. Her voice was quiet but steady, as though she were relaying a truth she'd held close for a long time. She extended her arm, offering him a thin, slate-like device that glinted in the sunlight. "Place your hand on this," she instructed, her tone curious, almost hopeful.

Tyrant eyed the slate suspiciously. It looked harmless enough, a glassy surface framed in what appeared to be worn metal. Yet something about it tugged at a memory, buried deep and distant. He shifted his Warquarter to his left hand and slowly pressed his right palm onto the slate.

Nothing happened.

Raya's gaze lingered on the slate, her face tightening with quiet disappointment as the seconds passed. At last, she let out a wistful sigh, lowering the slate to her side.

"Legend says that a Sleeper will awaken one day to bring hope to all of Acrea." Her voice softened, distant, her eyes lost in thought. "The Tekians have been searching for something—someone. Many villages across Arral have gone silent in recent days."

Tyrant frowned, words echoing through his mind like a faint echo. "Acrea? Arral? Tekian? I hear your words, but they mean nothing to me." The syllables felt strange on his tongue, but the word *Arral* stirred something—a vague, restless memory just beyond reach.

Raya's silvery-rimmed eyes lifted from the dusty floor, shimmering with an otherworldly light as she gazed at him. "Acrea is this world, and Arral is the land on which we stand. Tekians… they are the bane of all who live here, and Shade is their dark master." Her voice broke, and before he could respond, her face fell into her hands, her shoulders trembling as sobs wracked her slender frame.

Razmal stood nearby, arms crossed, his face darkening as he stared into the middle distance, lost in thought.

Tyrant leaned on his staff, feeling the weight of questions pressing on him. "Do you know why I can't remember anything?" he asked, directing the question at Razmal but keeping his gaze on Raya.

Raya looked up, wiping her tear-streaked face with the back of her hand. "No one has seen a Sleeper in hundreds of years. I don't know why your memory is clouded." She sniffed, managing a wry smile. "Only the bards of Castle Forgotten sing songs of the Sleepers anymore."

"Hundreds?" Tyrant repeated, disbelief plain in his voice. The concept of time felt distant, abstract, yet the number pulled at him, unsettling him.

Raya nodded slowly. "They tell stories of strange people from other worlds, people with strange clothing, stranger tongues, and even stranger weapons." Her gaze drifted over him, lingering on the Warquarter with a mixture of wonder and caution.

Polaris, the voice whispered in his mind, cutting through his thoughts like a sliver of starlight. He shifted uncomfortably.

"The Tekians will know you're here," Raya continued, her tone turning serious. "If you seek answers, you'll find them at Moonlit Waters. I'm certain of it." Her eyes took on a steely resolve. "I'll have Razmal escort you to the castle. We have a caravan staged with goods that need traded at the markets there."

Razmal and Raya spoke in hushed tones while Tyrant sat quietly, absorbing what little he could. The things he knew were basic—hunger, thirst, and the familiar weight of his staff in his hand. Yet his past, the person he'd been—Tyler? Tyrant?—was a mystery, nothing more than scattered fragments.

Raya turned back to the orange container and stowed the slate within its depths. She rummaged for a moment, then returned with his rucksack and a finely woven cloak in hand.

"I packed some water and rations for you," she said, offering him a tentative smile.

He accepted the rucksack and cloak, nodding his thanks. As he took them, he wondered if she'd looked inside. It struck him that even he couldn't remember what he'd packed.

Raya placed a gentle hand on Razmal's shoulder, squeezing it as if in farewell. "Take Bresh and Samson with you," she said softly. "The caravan will follow a day behind you. Clear the path."

Razmal nodded, meeting her gaze with a steady look before turning to Tyrant. "Let's get going," he said gruffly.

Tyrant and Razmal stepped outside, leaving the shelter of the tent as the sun crested above the cliffs, bathing the village in golden light.

Tyrant sucked in a sharp breath, his gaze transfixed by the sight that greeted him: a massive, orange-hued planet rose on the horizon, dominating the sky with swirling patterns of clouds and strange colors. Razmal followed his gaze, a faint smile tugging at the corners of his mouth.

"Yalonia," Razmal said, nodding at the colossal planet. "The ugly sister, we call her. Twin to Acrea, though she's not as beautiful." He clapped Tyrant on the shoulder, his grip strong and reassuring. "Now, I need my good ax since you broke the last one." With a wink, Razmal strode off to gather his gear and locate Bresh and Samson.

***

The four of them set out soon after, the village of Tonu quickly fading behind them as they moved eastward. The land transformed gradually from dusty paths to rolling plains, lush with tall grass and vibrant wildflowers. The scent of salt on the air intensified as they neared the coast, carried on the steady ocean breeze.

Samson and Bresh walked ahead, their eyes fixed on the horizon as they scanned for signs of danger. Samson, like the other men of this land, was hairless and dressed in a finely spun robe. He carried no visible weapons, though when he caught Tyrant's gaze, he offered a warm, almost knowing smile.

In stark contrast, Bresh wore a perpetual scowl, his eyes narrow as he grumbled under his breath, his displeasure about the journey plain to see. Every now and then, he shot Tyrant a dark look, muttering to himself.

Razmal had changed into a thick, chitinous breastplate and strapped boiled leather greaves to his legs. Unlike his quiet companions, he was full of chatter, regaling Tyrant with tales of Tonu, the villagers, and how he'd stumbled upon Tyrant lying face down in a cave. He chuckled, recalling the moment he'd decided to approach and their unorthodox "friendship."

As the sun dipped lower in the sky, Tyrant noticed the trail they were following had widened, becoming smoother and more defined. Before long, Bresh raised a hand, signaling them to stop. Without a word, he and Samson veered off the path, heading toward a shallow hollow in the grasslands, where the tall grass brushed against their waists, hiding them from view.

They set up camp as dusk settled, the hollow providing a secluded spot away from the main road. Bresh swung a wicked-looking crystal battle-ax, clearing a space for their campfire, while Samson laid out several round, crystalline stones. Tyrant recognized them immediately—they were the same kind of stones he'd seen heating the cooking pots back in Tonu.

Razmal's stomach rumbled loudly, the sound reverberating from within his armor.

Samson chuckled softly, kneeling before the stones with a reverent expression. He reached out, tracing the stones with his fingers as he murmured softly under his breath. Slowly, a warm, steady glow radiated from the stones, illuminating their small camp.

ENEMY!

Tyrant rocked forward, gripping his Warquarter as the warning trembled through his bones. Razmal shot him a curious glance.

"You good?" Razmal asked, raising an eyebrow.

Tyrant straightened, forcing himself to relax. "How did he light those?" he asked, his voice low, almost a hiss.

Samson turned toward him, his silver-rimmed eyes shimmering with an inner light as they met Tyrant's gaze. For the first time, Tyrant noticed a peculiar quality in Samson's eyes; his pale irises were round, but the silvery light leaked out in a perfect square, framing his pupils in an otherworldly glow.

"The VAST," Samson replied, his voice barely more than a whisper, as if uttering a sacred word.

Tyrant's mind scrambled for context, but the word sparked nothing but a deep, visceral reaction. "The VAST?" he echoed, his tone skeptical.

Razmal sat down heavily beside him, chuckling. "A powerful force, beyond what most can wield," he said, slapping his knee for emphasis. "Those blessed with it are rare, and its ways are... mysterious, even to us."

Samson nodded solemnly. "The VAST is a gift from the world itself. It connects us to Acrea's spirit." He placed a hand over his heart. "To those of us chosen, it grants the strength to protect and preserve."

Bresh grunted, his face twisted in disdain. "A gift, you say. I say it's trouble. No good ever came from meddling with the VAST." He shot Razmal a dark look before turning a linger gaze on Samson. He grunted and turned his eyes back to the darkening plains.

Tyrant was silent, watching the glowing stones flicker. "It sounds... familiar," he murmured, though he wasn't sure why.

Razmal gave him a long look, his expression contemplative. "Familiar or not, you'll come to understand it soon enough, especially if we encounter the Tekians on our way to Moonlit Waters."

The mention of the Tekians brought a murmur of tension from the group, the casual ease they'd shared slipping away as the weight of the journey set in. Tyrant glanced at his companions, his hand reflexively tightening around the Warquarter.

"Rest while you can," Razmal advised, staring into the flickering stones with a thoughtful expression. "We'll need strength if the Tekians decide to make an appearance. And trust me—they rarely come quietly."

The night deepened, the sky above sprawling with unfamiliar constellations, as Tyrant lay back, his thoughts drifting to fragments of memories he couldn't quite place. With the Warquarter beside him, he drifted into a restless sleep, haunted by echoes of a life he couldn't remember, yet felt all too keenly.

3 PURSUIT

The attack struck just as dawn touched the horizon. Pale light crept across the plains, bathing the camp in a soft glow, when an unnatural gust of wind whipped the grass into a frenzy. Mechanical whirring filled the air, its source hidden by the blinding beams cutting through the dimness beyond the camp.

Bresh was the first to move. He bolted upright from his bedroll, but before he could take a step, a blast of shrieking sound struck him squarely in the chest, sending him sprawling back.

Tyrant, in contrast, was calm—eerily so. Rising from the bed of his cloak and cut grass, he turned to face the sounds with a steady gaze. Harsh voices barked hurried orders in a language he didn't recognize, and then a figure strode through the light. The man was tall, armored, and moved with a purposeful stride, his silhouette sharp against the glowing backdrop. His armor gleamed, meticulously fitted and reinforced with plates of dark metal that glinted coldly in the dawn light. Tyrant's eyes roamed over the figure's rifle strapped to his back and the sidearm holstered at his thigh. Everything about the Tekian felt achingly familiar, yet just out of reach.

The dark metal helm he wore was smooth and almost seamless, giving him an imposing, faceless presence.

"Tekian!" Samson shouted from somewhere to Tyrant's left, his voice tinged with both fear and defiance. A smile tugged at the corner of Tyrant's mouth. *Finally, a real Tekian.* He spared a quick glance to his right, where Bresh lay still, his form unmoving.

The Tekian removed his helmet, cradling it under his arm as he looked directly at Tyrant. The man's angular features were severe, his black hair slicked back, catching the glow of dawn. His eyes held no warmth, only cold calculation, as he took in the scene.

"Tyler Ryan Tor, you will come with us." The Tekian's voice was level, commanding, his tone leaving no room for argument.

The name rippled through Tyrant's mind, sparking memories that surged and faded in chaotic bursts. A jumble of fragmented images threatened to overwhelm him, slipping away before he could make sense of them.

Razmal, still groggy but alert, eyed his battle-ax lying near his bedroll. Tyrant pressed his fingers to the bridge of his nose, rubbing away the mounting tension. *Who was this man, and why did he know his name?*

A prickle of unease settled over him. The Tekian seemed so sure of his identity, yet Tyrant felt only the hollow ache of half-recalled memories.

Bresh lay disturbingly quiet. And then there was Raya's warning, echoing in his mind: he would be hunted, taken. He clenched his jaw. He wasn't one to submit easily.

Tyrant lifted his gaze, meeting the Tekian's eyes with unflinching defiance. "I don't think so."

The Tekian's eyes widened in surprise, and in that instant, Samson took the words as a signal. He closed his eyes, extending his arms outward, palms up. A soft silver radiance enveloped him, flowing like liquid moonlight over his skin and spilling outward in gentle waves.

Tyrant felt his grip tighten on the Warquarter, though he couldn't remember reaching for it. The weapon reacted to Samson's glowing form, sending a pulse of anger and disgust that reverberated through his hands.

Everything happened in a blur. Silver bolts of crackling energy leaped from Samson, arcing toward the Tekian who still held his helmet. The bolts struck him with brutal force, tearing through his armor and twisting the metal. As Samson's energy spilled out, it branched toward the shadowy forms lurking just beyond the camp's edge. The Tekian fell to the ground, his body smoking as more men cried out, and the camp exploded into chaos.

Several Tekians returned fire, their sonic weapons emitting shrill, bone-rattling blasts that tore into the ground around Razmal and Tyrant, spraying them with debris. Razmal seized his ax, let out a ferocious battle cry, and dove into the night, his presence marked only by the muffled yelps of Tekian soldiers as he engaged them in the darkness.

Samson staggered, silver energy flickering around him as rifle blasts struck his shimmering shield. He gritted his teeth, holding his ground as blue projectiles exploded against his barrier. But with a final shudder, the silver light around him fizzled and vanished, leaving him exposed. An angry blue blast ripped from the darkness, slamming into Samson's torso and sending him hurtling into the tall grass beyond.

The horizon brightened as dawn broke fully over the camp. Tyrant's gaze locked onto four hovering machines, each bearing large, central fan blades that generated the powerful winds buffeting the camp. Ropes dangled from their cargo areas, and Tekians clung to the sides in large baskets. Some fired into the grasslands, attempting to locate Razmal, while others scanned the area, waiting for their chance to strike.

Two Tekians sprinted toward Tyrant, weapons raised. One held a rifle, its barrel trained on him with deadly precision; the other brandished a sleek pistol. The rifle discharged with a loud crack, sending another blinding blue projectile hurtling toward him. Tyrant moved without thought, his Warquarter sweeping upward to meet the blast. A concussive boom followed as he deflected the shot, scattering shrapnel that ricocheted back, forcing the Tekians to dive for cover.

The Tekian with the pistol rolled to his feet, firing a series of sonic blasts. Tyrant twirled the Warquarter with practiced precision, intercepting each blast mid-air and sending bursts of energy in all directions. When the two Tekians rose again, visibly shaken, they exchanged a determined look and each pulled a baton from their belts. The weapons extended with a metallic click, their tips humming with an eerie energy.

With a roar, the Tekians charged, their batons swinging in precise arcs. Tyrant met them head-on, his Warquarter clashing against their weapons in rapid succession. The Tekians moved in unison, their strikes coordinated and relentless. Tyrant felt a baton slip through his defense, slamming into his ribs with enough force to make him stagger. His vision blurred momentarily as pain jolted through his side.

The attackers pressed in, their blows becoming fiercer, and Tyrant knew he was slowing, his movements less certain. His leg buckled as another baton struck his thigh, sending a wave of numbing pain through his muscles. He gritted his teeth, anger building as one of the Tekians sneered, emboldened by his weakening defense.

"...*summon me*..." The voice slithered through his mind, curling around his thoughts like a whisper of thunder.

"…*Polaris*…"

The word was like a spark, a flicker of something deep and ancient. Tyrant dropped to one knee under the weight of their combined strength, his muscles straining as they forced him back. The Tekians loomed over him, both batons pressing down, their eyes gleaming with anticipation of victory.

"…I…summon you…" he rasped, his voice a bare whisper. Then, with a burst of strength, he roared, "POLARIS!"

Energy surged around him, and the ground caved in beneath the three men, forming a shallow crater. With one powerful sweep of his Warquarter, Tyrant flung the Tekians aside, their bodies tumbling across the ground. Their shouts of confusion and pain cut through the chaos, drawing the attention of the remaining Tekians.

Several riflemen dropped to prone positions, unleashing a coordinated volley. Tyrant stood rooted, feeling the air around him shift and heat as the projectiles shattered against him, dissipating like steam striking a wall of fire. The Warquarter thrummed with renewed vigor, its presence solid, powerful.

Four cannon blasts sounded in unison as sonic energy rained down from the hovering craft above, each shot converging on Tyrant's position. The impact sent waves of force rippling outward, swallowing him in a storm of sound and light.

A blinding white column of energy erupted skyward, and a shockwave rolled across the camp, tossing the hovercraft aside like leaves in a gale. Tekians screamed as their craft collided, bursting into flames. Smoldering wreckage scattered across the clearing, silencing the remaining soldiers.

The two surviving craft wasted no time. They dropped grappling lines and quickly hauled up the still-moving bodies of their comrades, their engines straining as they made a hasty retreat. The machines spun away, retreating toward the horizon as the first rays of the Acrean sun illuminated the battlefield.

***

In a distant command room, Shade watched the chaos unfold on his monitor, his face twisted with barely contained fury. Without a word, he clenched his fist and punched through the screen, sending shards and sparks scattering across the floor.

Tyler.

The name rattled in his mind, an echo from a past he had long tried to bury. Impossible, he told himself, the familiar burn of anger prickling his skin. It had been centuries—too much time had passed. He had changed. The world had changed.

Yet a slow, sinister smile spread across his face, hidden within the dark hood of his robes. At long last, the *Spero* and its weaponry would be his.

***

Razmal emerged from the shelter of a nearby overhang, his chest heaving as he surveyed the carnage. He stopped in his tracks, his jaw slack with shock. Tyrant stood at the center of a still-smoking crater, his expression calm and unreadable. Bresh had stirred and sat quietly nearby, his face pale.

Samson, grimacing, was hastily binding his torso with a torn bandage. The field around them was littered with the shattered remnants of Tekian craft, twisted and broken, and Razmal's eyes roamed over the wreckage, disbelief flickering across his face. No one had ever taken down a Tekian patrol—not like this.

Razmal kicked a discarded rifle out of his path as he approached Tyrant, who was calmly examining a Tekian pistol before slipping it into an empty holster at his thigh. Razmal opened his mouth to speak, but the words caught in his throat.

Bresh broke the silence, his voice flat. "Only a Tekian can wield those weapons."

Tyrant turned to him, pulling the pistol from its holster. Without a word, he aimed at a nearby pile of smoking debris and fired. A bolt of crackling energy leaped from the gun, slamming into the wreckage with a shriek, scattering sparks into the air. Bresh frowned, crossing his arms with a gruff nod.

"I am not a Tekian," Tyrant replied, holstering the weapon.

Samson, now bandaged, moved about the camp, gathering what supplies he could salvage. His usual silver-rimmed eyes appeared dim, his expression subdued as he gestured for them to continue moving.

Razmal hefted his pack and secured his battle-ax, feeling its comforting weight settle against his shoulder. He watched as Tyrant strode over to his Warquarter, which rose smoothly into his waiting hand as he approached. With a calm nod to Razmal, he holstered the staff onto his pack, his gaze distant.
Razmal shook his head, letting out a heavy sigh. The VAST, Tekians, floating staffs—this was going to be a journey unlike any he'd ever imagined.

"We need to stay off the main road now that the Tekians have found us," Razmal said. "They will be back."
Bresh grunted and kicked some debris that had gotten in his way.

"Which way to go then?" Samson asked. He mopped his sweating head with a dirty rag, squinting at the rising Acrean sun.

Razmal looked off into the distance and frowned at the only decision left to them. "There is only one way to go if we don't want to be seen. The Canyonlands."

***

The grassy plains gradually gave way to a vast, blackened scar that stretched across the horizon. The landscape around them was torn and scarred, as if something massive had impacted the ground and then raged northward, leaving destruction in its wake. Jagged shards of metal and twisted debris littered the chasm, casting eerie shadows against the reddish dirt.

Large, shattered containers lay strewn along the rim, some upended and others half-buried in rubble, their contents long decayed and scattered by scavengers. The charred, broken shells hinted at a terrible past, a memory of violence that lingered in the air like a bad omen.

Razmal led them carefully down into the scar, his ax at the ready. His eyes scanned the cliffs that loomed on either side. "Be on your guard," he warned in a low voice. "Scavengers make their nests here. They don't take kindly to guests."

Tyrant glanced up, his gaze sweeping the narrow path down. "Is there a way around this?"
Razmal silenced him with a sharp wave, gesturing for quiet as they moved forward, each footfall stirring up red dust and ashes. They reached the bottom of the chasm within a few tense minutes. The temperature dropped, and the cool air clung to their skin, thick and stale, but the exertion had them sweating freely as they picked their way over crumbled rocks.

A distant horn blared, shattering the silence. Razmal's face tightened. He squared his shoulders, head cocked as he listened, then turned to them with a grim look.

"Run," he said, his voice flat and emotionless, before bolting across the rough ground.

Tyrant and the others sprinted after him, their feet pounding against the charred earth. The ground around them was uneven and littered with sharp stones, forcing them to dodge and leap over obstacles as they went. The first scavenger appeared in the distance, moving swiftly over the scarred terrain.

Legends claimed the scavengers had once been human, but there was little left of humanity in their forms now. The creature barreled toward them on two powerful legs, its thin body swathed in ragged layers of armor fashioned from scraps of metal and bone. Spindly arms gripped a spear tipped with a jagged crystal shard, and its face was hidden beneath an animal skin hood and mask. Only a pair of hungry yellow eyes glared out from the depths, fixed unblinkingly on Razmal and his companions.

More scavengers materialized from behind the rocks, slinking from shadowed crevices and pits. A particularly scrawny figure raised a curved horn made of bone to its cracked lips and sounded two long, piercing notes. The eerie call echoed through the chasm, sending a chill down Tyrant's spine. A spear whistled past Razmal, embedding itself in the dirt with a solid *thunk*.

Reacting on instinct, Tyrant twisted, pulling both pistols in a fluid motion. He fired into the advancing scavengers, twin bolts of energy striking the lead creature in the chest. The scavenger snarled as it dropped, its body crumpling into the dirt.

Razmal pointed to a massive container farther along the chasm floor. It lay half-buried in debris, its rusted surface glinting faintly. "There! We can get higher ground."

The group shifted direction, sprinting toward the container as Tyrant's pistols crackled with each shot, cutting down scavengers in quick succession. Another spear sliced through the air, but a shimmer of silvery light from Samson's outstretched hand deflected it mid-flight, snapping it in two.

The horn blared again, louder this time, and more scavengers emerged, rushing toward them with spears and makeshift clubs raised. Tyrant caught a glimpse of a spear-wielding scavenger sprinting directly at Bresh. With a battle cry, the creature launched itself forward, spear raised. Bresh responded with a swift, calculated swing of his ax, cleaving the creature down the middle. Without a pause, he rejoined the desperate sprint.

The container loomed closer, a hulking mass of rust and weathered metal partially shielded by piles of jagged rock. They ducked behind its cool, rusted walls, pressing their backs to the metal as they caught their breath. The scavengers, now numbering dozens, circled in the distance, snarling and shaking their crude weapons in frustration.

Bresh glared at the mass of scavengers, his face contorted in fury. "What are they waiting for!" he shouted, his voice echoing against the canyon walls.

As if in answer, a bone-chilling howl split the air, silencing the scavengers instantly. The mob parted, and from their midst, a figure stepped forward. This scavenger was larger, draped in the same makeshift armor but adorned with a necklace of bones and a headdress fashioned from the skull of some monstrous creature. In its spindly hands, it held a staff of polished bone, crowned with a ball of gleaming black crystal.

The leader raised its arms, a hide cloak billowing out like wings. With a swift motion, it slammed the end of its staff against the ground. The scavengers snarled as one, and with a unified shriek, they charged.

Tyrant holstered his pistols, gripping his Warquarter tightly as he prepared for the onslaught. He noticed a gleam in Razmal's eye as they exchanged a quick, understanding nod. The first scavenger reached Tyrant, only to be met with a crushing blow to the throat that sent it hurtling backward. Dust exploded from the impact as the creature crumpled, lifeless. More scavengers followed, each one falling as the Warquarter connected in quick, brutal strikes.

Samson's hands shimmered with silvery tendrils as he called upon the VAST, murmuring words of encouragement and strength. Tendrils of light coiled around his fists, crackling with energy as he blasted back the advancing scavengers.

Razmal's ax swung in wide arcs, forcing the creatures to keep their distance. Beside him, Bresh struck down another scavenger, adding to the growing pile of bodies that littered the ground around them. Sweat glistened on his bald head as he continued to fell his foes with brutal precision.

Suddenly, a mournful wail rose above the cacophony of battle. Samson's fists closed, and his voice echoed, "Close your eyes!"

A blinding flash of light erupted from the container, illuminating the entire chasm in a searing white glow. Even with his eyes closed, Razmal could see darkened figures writhing and flailing in agony. A rough hand gripped his arm, guiding him around the side of the container to a safer vantage point.

It was then that he saw him.

A large, powerfully built figure stood tied to a beam protruding from the wreckage nearby. It was a magnificent, wolflike creature with silver fur that caught the light, standing on two muscular, man-like legs. Both its wrists and ankles were bound with thick cords, small streams of blood trickling down from the raw wounds where the bindings cut into its skin.

The wolf raised its head, its golden eyes meeting Tyrant's with a haunting intensity.

"Help me."

The voice was clear, yet the wolf hadn't spoken aloud. Tyrant and Razmal exchanged a look, both silently acknowledging the strange communication.

Several horns blared in the distance, and Tyrant's survival knife appeared in his hand. He worked quickly, slicing through the cords that bound the wolf's wrists and ankles. The bindings fell away, and the wolf rubbed its raw wrists as it flexed its powerful limbs.

More scavengers emerged from the shadows, spears held high, and rushed toward the freed beast. The wolf raised its head, a low growl rumbling in its throat. In a blur of silver, it launched into the mob, claws flashing as it tore through the scavengers with unrestrained ferocity. Bodies flew, some tumbling through the air while others crumpled lifelessly beneath its powerful strikes.

One scavenger managed to stab through the flurry of limbs, the spear's tip slicing a thin line of blood along the wolf's shoulder. With a snarl of rage, the wolf seized the weapon, snapping it in two with a single twist of its paw before sending its wielder sprawling into the dirt.

Razmal watched, awe-stricken, as the wolf tore through the attackers, though he could see the beast's movements slowing, each strike taking more out of him. More scavengers poured into the fray, and the low blast of another horn echoed ominously from beyond the scar.

Razmal turned, watching Tyrant, Bresh, and Samson fend off the scavengers piling up on the far side of the container. The ground was littered with bodies, and his companions swayed with exhaustion, yet the scavengers kept coming.

"Tyrant! We can't hold them!" Razmal shouted over the din. Two more scavengers fell, twitching as bolts from Tyrant's pistols struck them down.
"Charge expended," the left pistol whispered, its voice mechanical and final.

Without hesitation, Tyrant holstered his pistols and sprinted toward the container. His hands frantically skimmed the metal surface, searching for something. Razmal squinted, watching as Tyrant's fingers paused over a nearly invisible seam—a door.

"Tyrant! Don't touch that! Wreckage like this will kill you. It is forbidden!" Razmal shouted over the din of battle.

The wolf continued fighting, scattering scavengers like leaves as Tyrant worked to access the container. Bresh and Samson dispatched the scavengers who were shaking off the effects of Samson's blinding blast. Razmal hacked through a spear, snarling as his ax lodged in a scavenger's crude armor.

Samson called upon the VAST once more, this time summoning silver lightning that forked and leaped from creature to creature, the energy leaving smoldering holes in its wake.

At last, a faint glow emanated from Tyrant's palm, casting light onto a barely visible display pad set beside the door.

"I know what I am doing, Razmal," Tyrant yelled. "I think," he finished in a whisper and pressed his hand to the pad, his Warquarter slipping from his grip and hovering at his side.

"Identify," a cool, metallic voice demanded. A strangled howl echoed as a spear found its mark in the wolf's shoulder, pushing him back.

Tyrant stared at the pad, then pressed his hand firmly against it. "Tyrant," he rasped.

The display flickered. "Access granted, Commander Tor," the voice intoned, this time with a respectful tone.

The door swung open, revealing a narrow entrance.

"Inside, now!" Tyrant yelled, his Warquarter returning to his grip in a flash. His companions, having held off the latest wave, stumbled toward the open doorway, despite Razmal's initial reluctance. Apparently spears and jagged blades made excellent motivators.

With a glance over his shoulder, Tyrant saw the wolf falter as another spear plunged into his side, blood staining his silver fur. Tyrant surged forward, his Warquarter sweeping aside the scavengers in his path. He slid an arm beneath the wolf's shoulder, supporting his weight as they staggered together toward the door.

With a final push, they crossed the threshold, the interior bathed in a soft, sterile light that felt almost surreal after the harsh glare of the Acrean sun. The door shut soundlessly behind them.

Tyrant collapsed to the floor, breathing heavily as the wolf slumped beside him, his massive frame heaving with exhaustion.

Zuh'Erg, the voice said, clear in Tyrant's mind. He looked around, startled, but Razmal met his gaze, nodding. He had heard it too.

With my name, I pledge my… life… to… Zuh'Erg's voice echoed in their minds before trailing off, his eyes closing as he lost consciousness, his breaths shallow but steady.

4 PIOTR

The banging had finally ceased. For hours, the scavengers had thrown their full weight against the door, wielding bone and rock weapons as if they might bring down ancient metal with brute force alone. But the door held fast, barely scratched.

Inside, the group sat in tense silence, the sounds of battle echoing faintly in their minds. Samson had bound Zuh'Erg's wounds, and the wolf now lay peacefully asleep, his breathing steady.

An unknown light source illuminated the container's interior, seeming to radiate from all around them, casting an even glow over the space. Rows of secured cargo, netted and stacked meticulously, lined most of the walls. Across from the doorway, a small control console blinked quietly, its lights casting rhythmic pulses across the metal floor. Unlike the outside world, which was caked in dirt and decay, the air here was clean, devoid of dust, and carried a faint antiseptic scent.

Tyrant's gaze drifted to a hulking, draped figure that took up most of one side of the container. Something about its shape tugged at his memory, a sensation that prickled at the edge of recognition. He approached it slowly, reaching out to grip an edge of the covering. With one swift motion, he pulled the tarp away.

***

"This is the Golem-class fighter," his instructor's voice droned. Tyler barely paid attention, his gaze unfocused as he slouched at his desk, tuning out the lecture.

"Built for utility, it's a medium-armored fighter with versatile deployment capabilities," the instructor continued, shifting the display with a flick of his wrist. The wall screen showed the Golem fighter in full, rotating slowly. Tyler raised his head, his interest piqued as the view zoomed in on the Golem's weapon systems.

"Equipped with a mini-reactor, the Golem's core has near-limitless energy regeneration," the instructor explained, as Tyler grinned at the sight of the Golem's imposing arsenal.

***

"…and here we are, staring at you, staring at it!" Razmal's voice brought Tyrant back, his tone half mocking, half curious. He thumped his ax on the floor, the clang reverberating through the container.

It was indeed a Golem-class fighter. Tyrant pressed his palm against the cool metal surface, feeling a faint pulse of energy hum through his hand.

"Link established," a deep, robotic voice intoned from the Golem's core, resonating through the chamber. Tyrant stepped back, feeling the connection fade as he removed his hand.

At his side, Samson made a strange gesture, muttering softly. He bowed low, murmuring what sounded like a prayer, as if the machine's words had triggered a small ritual. Razmal, meanwhile, shot nervous glances at the looming figure, his face flushed and wary.

"Well," Razmal said, rubbing the back of his neck, "here we are, then." He jerked a thumb back toward the door. "How exactly did you get us in here without being reduced to ash? Anyone who tries to open doors or pick up weapons from starfall ends up…" Razmal trailed off and muttered to himself.

"I don't know," Tyrant replied distractedly. Bresh and Samson had begun dragging crates along the floor, stacking them against the entrance to brace it further.

A fresh wave of blows reverberated through the container, the sounds of heavy impacts suggesting something much larger had joined the attackers outside. Razmal sighed, crossing the room to check on Zuh'Erg. The wolf's breathing was deep and calm, and when Razmal lifted the bandage from his shoulder, he was astonished to find the wound already closed, leaving only a bare patch of fur as evidence.

A thunderous boom rocked the container, sending a few unsecured crates sliding across the floor. The door held, though a visible dent now marred its surface. Tyrant scanned the space, feeling the Golem's silent presence at his back, watching, waiting. His eyes settled on the rows of containers, each one marked with a digital pad softly blinking.

"Food, water, mining gear, weather equipment," he murmured as he inspected each container. Toward the back, his eyes fell on an unmarked container, its surface smooth and anonymous among the others.

A memory surfaced, calm and certain. It was a cryopod.

He pulled down a few smaller crates, passing them to Bresh and Samson, who stacked them aside. As he brushed off the last container, his hand found the cryopod's emergency access hatch. With three swift pulls on the red handle, the pod's lock released, and the door hissed open. The Balans climbed onto crates, jostling each other to catch a glimpse.

Tyrant shook his head, grinning as he reached inside and pulled out a dark, sloshing bottle. "Contraband," he laughed, tossing it to Bresh, whose eyes lit up with delight as he caught it.

"You can drink it. I remember that much. Nothing like ten-year-old bourbon," Tyrant said, half to himself as he reached back into the pod. The Balans gave a cheer, scrambling away with the bottle to pry it open.

His hand closed around something solid and heavy. He pulled it free, finding himself holding a military-issued rucksack stuffed with combat armor and a helmet, followed closely by a gauss rifle, sleek and deadly. Tyrant gasped as a memory surged through him.

***

Tyler narrowed his eye, holding his breath as he aimed down the rifle's sight. He squeezed the trigger, and with a resounding blast, a blue bolt tore downrange, sizzling with electric energy as it struck a target dummy. Sparks erupted as the bolt met the dummy's thin energy shield, sending crackling arcs in every direction.

"I'll take it!" he shouted, a grin spreading across his face.

***

In the present, Tyrant hefted the gauss rifle with familiar ease, the rucksack lying at his feet, momentarily forgotten. A creeping sense of danger jolted him back to reality. His Warquarter, which had been propped against the wall, now hovered beside him, vibrating with an anxious hum.

Another thunderous boom shook the container, and this time, a noticeable dent appeared in the door, followed by the sound of scrabbling claws and guttural howls echoing through a widening crack.

"Yalonians," Razmal snarled, eyeing the door with disdain. He tossed aside a newly uncorked whiskey bottle, the amber liquid splashing across the floor.

Turning to Tyrant, who had slung the new rucksack over his shoulder, Razmal jerked a thumb at the Golem. "So, does your new friend here do anything besides stand around looking pretty?"

Tyrant shrugged, brushing past him as he made his way toward the door. "Can't remember," he replied, his voice low.

The Golem stood silent and unmoving, its dark form looming over the group like a silent sentinel.

***

Samson, cross-legged on the floor, finally uncorked a bottle of whiskey and let out a sigh, lifting it toward his lips. The door creaked as clawed hands clawed through the crack, widening it inch by inch. His silver-rimmed eyes blinked slowly, then closed as he took a deep breath.

Blocking out the noise of scratching and scraping, the sounds of Tyrant and Razmal discussing strategy, and even the low rumble of Zuh'Erg shifting in his sleep, Samson focused inward, his mind seeking the flow of the VAST.

He lifted the bottle before him, holding it reverently in his outstretched palm. In an instant, the bottle vaporized, its contents spinning into a fine, swirling mist. The VAST surged around him, eagerly absorbing the offering. More and more of the energy gathered, drawn to his call, and he could feel his control slipping, the sheer volume of the VAST overwhelming him. Sweat trickled down his face as he struggled, chanting softly to steady his focus, trying to rein in the surging power.

***

Tyrant felt the hairs on his neck rise as the energy filled the air around him.

Polaris, a familiar voice whispered through his mind.

The door rattled as another massive impact dented its frame, shaking loose a stack of crates. The door buckled, bending inward, and with a final shuddering bang, it tore open. Two hulking Yalonians stood in the opening, each wielding a battering ram pieced together from jagged wreckage. Their eyes narrowed in surprise as the interior light spilled out into the night.

Samson's hands began to emit a crackling cloud of energy, his head bowed, lips moving in a silent incantation. His eyes flared with silver light as he clapped his hands together, and the cloud exploded forward, flattening and then spiraling into the Yalonians and the mass of scavengers that had gathered behind them. The force hurled bodies into the air, scattering them like broken dolls before fading into mist.

Tyrant stepped through the twisted remains of the doorframe, Warquarter at the ready. The attackers lay scattered across the ground, motionless. He paused, tilting his head as he studied the Warquarter in his hands, an unspoken understanding dawning on him.

Polaris, the voice murmured again in his mind, a whisper threaded with warmth and recognition.

Who are you? Tyrant asked silently.

The Warquarter thrummed, a sense of quiet affirmation emanating from its core. It urged him forward, the feeling powerful and insistent.

"Razmal, let's go!" Tyrant called as horns blared in the distance, their mournful tones echoing through the night.

The group gathered, the weight of their strange ally—Polaris—settling between them, as they readied to face whatever lay ahead.

***

The group moved quietly through the landscape, dodging scavengers well into the morning hours. The pale light of Yalonia guided them as they made their way across the debris-strewn chasm and up the other side, into the cover of tall, waving grass. With every step, the signs of pursuit faded until at last, the sounds of clattering and snarling died completely.

They continued walking in silence, sharing a hurried meal of rations from Tyrant's pack. The only sounds were the faint rustle of grass in the breeze and the soft crunch of their footsteps.

At last, Zuh'Erg broke the silence that had lingered since they left the scavenger field.

Thank you, friends, his voice rumbled through their minds, warm and clear.

He thumped a clawed hand to his chest, bowing his head slightly. Though his tattered loincloth and matted fur still bore signs of his ordeal, he moved with newfound strength, his limp nearly gone.

Up ahead, Bresh and Samson scouted for the path that would lead them to the coast. Razmal grunted, chewing on a long blade of dry grass as he glanced back at Zuh'Erg.

"No one deserves to be a meal for those wretches," Razmal said, his voice gruff.

Tyrant gave a small nod. "How did they capture you?" he asked, wondering what force could have overpowered a warrior like Zuh'Erg.

Zuh'Erg sighed deeply, rubbing his raw wrists, and began his tale. It was a story so harrowing that Razmal interrupted him more than once, his voice thick with amazement and sorrow.

Zuh'Erg's people, the Erew, lived far to the west, deep within the Twisted Peaks. The lands along the banks of the Er'Dool River were fertile, and the Erew had lived there for as long as their stories could recall, thriving off the hunt and the bounty of the land. Then one day, the Tekians arrived without warning, descending upon their peaceful valley in machines of iron and light. Armed with weapons that flared with blinding force, the Tekians cut through the Erew without mercy. Many fled into the mountains, but most were rounded up, forced into the hulking machines, and taken eastward, far from their home.

Only a handful had managed to escape. Zuh'Erg's eyes darkened as he recounted the moment his own transport malfunctioned and crashed. In the chaos, a Tekian guard got too close to the cage that held Zuh'Erg and his kin—a fatal mistake. With a savage fury, they dragged the guard through the narrow bars, taking their vengeance. It was a brutal scene of twisted bars, blood, and fractured metal as the Erew scattered, fleeing back into the wilderness.

It was by chance that I stumbled upon the wastes, Zuh'Erg's voice softened in their minds. *I wandered for weeks, searching for food, for water… until I collapsed, overcome by the elements.*

He paused, his gaze dropping to the ground, his yellow eyes troubled. *I awoke bound where you freed me, waiting to die.*

***

The grasslands gradually gave way to wide vistas and monolithic rock formations that towered against the horizon. The smell of the ocean grew stronger as they wound their way from the high plateau down through a steep canyon. Red, crumbling stone lined the walls, and with each step, fine dust billowed up, clinging to their skin and clothes. The wind whistled between the cliffs, a far more soothing sound than the mournful blasts of scavenger horns.

Razmal wiped sweat from his brow with a scrap of cloth, the glare of the sun already intense despite the early hour. The heat shimmered in the canyon, where thermals caused pockets of swirling air to drift along the rock walls. Bresh brought up the rear of the group, his expression dark as he surveyed the jagged path ahead.

Zuh'Erg walked close by Tyrant's side, only dropping behind him when the path narrowed to single file, his lupine eyes scanning the trail with quiet vigilance. Of them all, Samson alone seemed unaffected by the heat. Tyrant occasionally caught a glimpse of a faint, shimmering mist around him, a cool vapor that vanished almost as quickly as it appeared.

Polaris, Tyrant heard, the voice in his mind tinged with an edge of curiosity—and disdain. A small, familiar nudge pressed at his thoughts. If he was going to have a voice haunting his mind, he decided, he might as well get some answers.

"Samson, tell me more about the VAST," Tyrant asked, his voice casual but tinged with curiosity as they navigated around a massive, reddish boulder that had tumbled onto the path. The sight below—a dizzying drop to the canyon floor where a glint of a river wove between rock walls—made him tread with extra caution.

Polaris fell silent, though Tyrant could feel its presence, a quiet pout radiating from somewhere in the back of his mind.

Samson inclined his head thoughtfully, adjusting his pack. "Where to begin?" he mused. "It is… a gift only a few are born with. A whisper, at first. You feel them, faint, calling to you," he said, eyes softening as he extended his hand. A small swirl of mist gathered above his palm, a tiny, delicate cloud of energy that moved as if alive.

Polaris snorted in Tyrant's mind, the disdainful reaction sharp enough to make Tyrant suspect an eye roll.

Tyrant suppressed a chuckle. *What's your problem with the VAST?* he wondered, doing his best to shield the thought from Polaris.

Samson continued, narrowing his eyes as he focused on the cloud, which pulsed and grew slightly larger, small tendrils of light reaching up from it like fingers grasping at the air. "Most of us can only call a small group of the VAST," he explained. "Others… are friends to the VAST."

He reached into a pocket and pulled out a small, iridescent orb, crushing it between his fingers. A fine, glittering dust drifted up, feeding into the swirling energy, which eagerly consumed it and doubled in size again. But the cloud shuddered, writhing as Samson's hold weakened. Sweat trickled down his face as he released it, and with a soft pop, the energy burst into countless points of light, scattering into the breeze.

"Even I cannot hold them for long," Samson admitted, his face suddenly weary.

"You said some have the gift," Tyrant ventured, casting a glance at the others. "What about Razmal and Bresh?"

Samson picked his way around a narrow ledge, glancing over his shoulder with a smile. "My brother there," he nodded toward Bresh, "the only thing he can catch is a cold."

Tyrant laughed, the sound unexpectedly deep and full. It surprised him, echoing across the canyon walls like a distant rumble of thunder. For the first time in days, he felt a lightness in his chest, as if a weight he hadn't realized he carried had lifted. He relaxed his grip on the Warquarter, which hummed in contentment, retreating into a quiet corner of his mind.

A mischievous glint danced in Samson's eyes as he continued. "Now, Razmal… he has the gift. Or, as he calls it, the curse."

Tyrant raised an eyebrow, studying the burly figure of Razmal ahead. His powerful back seemed to hold a quiet tension, and his crystal-bladed ax with its long, bone handle caught the sun, flashing like the sharp grin of a predator.

"A curse?" Tyrant repeated, intrigued.

Samson nodded, his expression somber. "Razmal was born with the gift, but he resents it. He's always seen the VAST as a threat rather than an ally, like something wild that can never be fully controlled." He paused, glancing toward his brother in arms. "In truth, he fears what he could become if he gave himself over to it."

Tyrant followed Samson's gaze, understanding the depth of the struggle that lay hidden in Razmal's sturdy form. The Balans were fierce and honorable, but the existence of a power they could not tame or master was a difficult thing to accept.

As they walked in silence, Tyrant felt a sense of connection with his companions, a shared bond woven from battles fought side by side. He looked down at his Warquarter, the name Polaris echoing in his mind like a promise. For now, Polaris remained silent, content to linger as they moved forward, yet Tyrant felt a strange comfort in the presence that pulsed beneath his grip.

Up ahead, the trail widened, and as the canyon walls peeled back, the cool, briny scent of the ocean washed over them. Tyrant took a deep breath, feeling the salt and wind fill his lungs, refreshing and grounding him. The path twisted and turned through clusters of stone, and with each step, the distant roar of waves grew louder, promising the sight of open water just beyond the next rise.

Tyrant watched Razmal again, wondering what could have happened to one so strong to make them hate something that much.
"His tale is a sad one," Samson said quietly, sensing his thoughts. His face shadowed with sorrow. "Know this,

friend: Razmal's hatred for the Tekians is bound to his anger at the VAST."

Tyrant's smile faded, his expression turning somber as he gave a small nod.

A new intensity colored Samson's features, anger simmering beneath the surface. "Shade, the Master of Midnite, has been ripping our people from the land for centuries," he said, gripping the strap of his pack as if he could wring his rage into it. Pain flickered across his face, and his voice grew distant, his gaze unfocused. "Our people become slaves. That much we are sure," he said, his eyes narrowing with bitter resolve. "Those taken are twisted, corrupted. We see them on his sky ships, but their eyes are empty. They no longer know us."

A sharp anger tightened in Tyrant's chest as he pictured the scene Samson described. He clenched his fists, feeling the weight of these atrocities sink into him. "Samson… what happened to Razmal?" he asked quietly.

"Razmal lost his parents to Shade," Samson replied, his voice rough. "When the VAST failed to save them, he nearly destroyed himself trying to bring them back. But he lost control… and many paid the price." His words hung heavily, filled with grief and resentment.

A silence settled over them, broken only by the faint wind and the crunch of gravel beneath their boots. Samson looked back at Tyrant, his expression conflicted, then drifted to the back of the group, where he walked in quiet reflection. Tyrant gave him a reassuring pat on the shoulder as he passed, offering a wordless gesture of support. With a sigh, Tyrant waved Zuh'Erg over, eager to learn more about their destination and the wolf's own knowledge of the coast.

Yes, my friend? Zuh'Erg's voice rumbled in Tyrant's mind, accompanied by a slight bow of his head. His bound wrists didn't seem to pain him as much now, and he had refused all offers to remove the bindings. *A debt must be paid,* was all he had said, rubbing his claws thoughtfully against his flank.

"Have you ever been to the coast?" Tyrant asked, glancing around at the towering walls of red and orange stone that seemed to spiral endlessly around them. Some of the rocks looked as though they held faces—grim, ancient expressions frozen in time, others worn down to unrecognizable shapes by centuries of wind.

Once, as a cub, Zuh'Erg replied, his yellow-tinted eyes catching Tyrant's gaze with a strange, almost human expression.

"Can you tell me anything about Moonlit Waters?" Tyrant asked, taking a long drink from his water skin. Razmal had given him little to go on when they left Tonu, only vague instructions to seek aid from a distant castle. Yet, with each passing day, Tyrant felt an inexplicable pull toward the coast, as if something awaited him there, calling for his attention.

Tyrant's palm itched slightly, a sensation that seemed to intensify the closer they came to their destination.

Tyrant? Zuh'Erg's voice cut through his thoughts, a trace of curiosity in his mind. Had he been muttering again without realizing?

"Sorry," Tyrant said, shaking his head, trying to clear the distraction.

Zuh'Erg merely gave a patient nod. *I remember little of the coast,* he projected, his tone thoughtful. *My pack stayed in the shadows of Moonlit Waters, near the Temple of Spero. We were not exactly welcome within its walls.*

"Not a swimmer, then?" Tyrant teased with a grin.

The wolf's face darkened, a frown settling over his lupine features. *Erew do not swim,* his voice sounded in Tyrant's mind, the words carrying an unexpected weight.

With a soft sigh, Zuh'Erg moved ahead, muttering about scouting, his grumbling thought curiously similar to a growl.

For a time, Tyrant walked in silence, alone with his thoughts. Fragments of memories continued to flicker through his mind, pieces of a puzzle that refused to form a clear picture. How had he ended up in the cave where Razmal had found him? Who had trained him, given him such battle prowess? And above all, why was the coast calling to him, a place that felt familiar yet distant?

Polaris, the voice whispered in his mind, a silent yet insistent presence that felt closer now than ever. Tyrant considered telling Razmal about Polaris. Perhaps it was normal on this strange world to have a voice echoing in one's head.

Small pebbles rattled down from the canyon wall, startling Tyrant from his thoughts. He glanced up, shielding his eyes from the midday sun, scanning the rocks above. He swore he had seen movement, shadows shifting across the stones as though the cliffs themselves were alive.

"Razmal, am I crazy, or—" Tyrant called, his voice trailing off.

"Yah, you are," Razmal replied with a grin, not missing a beat as he barked a laugh.

"Funny," Tyrant muttered, though a grin tugged at his mouth. "I guess you don't see those rocks moving." Razmal stopped, following Tyrant's gaze with a serious expression, his eyes narrowing. Bresh and Samson immediately shifted into defensive stances, moving back-to-back. Bresh's ax gleamed wickedly as he swung it, testing its weight in his hands.

A prickle of tension spread over Tyrant's skin, and his palm throbbed with a dull ache as Samson silently called to the VAST, a flicker of energy crackling faintly in the air.

"It's probably nothing," Tyrant said, though he knew he didn't believe his own words. His grip on the Warquarter tightened.

"Ho there!" called a shrill voice, echoing off the canyon walls.

They all spun, watching as a figure in a patched, brown robe scrambled down the cliffside with surprising agility. Tyrant relaxed slightly, letting his grip on the Warquarter shift to one hand, leaning on it casually as he eyed the approaching stranger.

Mountain goat, Tyrant thought to himself with an amused chuckle.

What is a mountain goat? Polaris's question flitted through his mind, punctuated by a tone that was half-curious, half-irritable.

Tyrant stopped laughing, frowning slightly. He didn't know how to explain it.

The figure reached the canyon floor, stepping forward to reveal a stooped, bearded man. He was thin to the point of gauntness, his skin almost translucent, stretched tightly over his bony frame. A tangled beard obscured most of his face, but his eyes were bright, gleaming with a strange intelligence.

The man's pack was an odd sight, bristling with mismatched antennae of various shapes and sizes. In one arm, he cradled a dented metal dish, and in his other hand, he held a hammer with a haft wrapped in rough, knotted cord. The hammer's head was carved from obsidian so dark it seemed to devour the light around it.

"Name's Piotr," the man rasped, his voice a cackle as he extended a bony hand toward Razmal, who stared at him in bewilderment. "You lot got anything to eat?"

5 ELEMENTAL MY DEAR

Piotr ate like a man possessed.

Bowl after bowl of stew vanished as he slurped hungrily from the chipped seashell dish, pausing only to belch or mumble in satisfaction. He had started with a spoon but abandoned it in favor of drinking directly from the bowl, oblivious to the stew spilling down his ragged robes.

Razmal watched him in horrified fascination, his own spoon hovering in the air, momentarily forgotten. The cacophony of Piotr's smacking and sighs was, surprisingly, an improvement over the relentless stream of words he had spilled since joining them. For hours, Piotr had talked without so much as a pause for breath. Only the sight of food seemed to silence him.

As they set up camp, Piotr had regaled them with tales of his sojourn from the Temple of Spero, describing it as though each detail held profound significance. To their surprise, they had learned he was a Friar of the holy order, charged with spreading the sacred word to the foothills at the mountain's edge. But he had lost his way and found himself wandering the barren lands, emaciated and fending off attacks from rock beasts until he finally encountered them—a meeting he insisted was divine intervention by the will of the VAST.

Samson had barely moved from Piotr's side, listening to him with rapt attention. They all sat around the softly glowing cooking stones, wrapped in cloaks against the cool canyon air. After downing a fourth bowl of stew, Piotr looked up, his square, silver-rimmed eyes gleaming, and gave a deep, satisfied belch.

"Thank you, friends, for your kindness to a humble priest of Spero," he said, bowing his head reverently. He turned to Tyrant, his gaze sharp and intent. "Have you heard the good word, Commander?"

Tyrant stiffened at the title, the question seeming to ripple through him like a distant echo. His spoon clattered against his empty bowl as his hand drifted to his chest plate. A small symbol was emblazoned there, marking him as a "Commander." He knew it held meaning, yet its true significance eluded him.

Piotr's eyes gleamed with curiosity as he leaned forward, his expression alight with wonder. "A Sleeper above all others needs the word of the order," he said, his voice laced with anticipation.

Tyrant cleared his throat, feeling an unfamiliar discomfort. "Tell me."

Piotr clapped his hands with delight, his eyes gleaming as he spoke. "You, Commander, are different from the last Sleeper our order encountered. There is a veil between you and the VAST," he said, extending a hand toward Tyrant. A faint silver light wove from his fingers, spiraling toward Tyrant before melting away inches from him. Tyrant recoiled slightly as the light faded.

Razmal sprang to his feet. "Piotr, that's enough!" he snapped.

But Piotr was transfixed, his gaze intense as he leaned closer. "There is something ancient, something forbidden—"

Balanite! he hissed, his eyes wide with fascination.

A surge of power erupted within Tyrant, and Polaris roared to life in his mind. The air around him grew thick, charged with energy as white lightning crackled down his arms, coiling around his clenched fists. His chest burned with a searing heat as Polaris pushed for release, the desire for destruction blazing within him.

"Peace!" Piotr barked, raising his palms in surrender, though his eyes gleamed with curiosity and reverence.

The energy coursing through Tyrant made his bones ache, his skin tingling with raw power as Polaris seethed within him. He fought to steady himself, taking a deep, calming breath as he acknowledged Polaris for the first time.

Calm yourself, he murmured to Polaris, gritting his teeth as he concentrated.

The world around him faded, and he felt himself transported to another place, a strange landscape that he instinctively knew was not of his own mind. The sky churned with impossible colors, shifting through a kaleidoscope of shades. A powerful wind buffeted him, pressing against his skin.

He looked down, finding the Warquarter in his grasp. Yet, something felt wrong—it was heavier, unfamiliar. Beneath his feet lay a vast, cracked lakebed, dry and barren. The faint scent of the ocean lingered in the air, as though a distant memory of water once filled this desolate place.

As he held the Warquarter, it slid from his hand, melting as it touched the dry earth, transforming into a liquid silver that spread rapidly.. Tyrant stumbled back, heart racing as the silver pool expanded, filling the space with a shimmering, unnatural light. He knew, instinctively, that if he touched it, he would be consumed.

He ran, the newly formed shoreline drawing him toward its banks. Just as he reached it, a thunderous voice crashed over him, forcing him to his knees.

Polaris!

Tyrant forced himself upright, his voice cutting through the strange realm with defiance. "I think we've established who you are!"

Only silence responded, heavy and unsettling.

But who are YOU, Tyler Ryan Tor? the voice answered, softer now, yet unmistakably his own. The lake seethed, its surface steaming as waves crashed against the shore.

The name struck him, familiar yet foreign. He could almost grasp the memories tethered to it, though they continued to slip away, just out of reach.

"Why are we here?" he demanded, rising to his feet as he clenched his fists.

The wind fell silent, and the voice that answered was gentler, almost a whisper. *We are two become one, as we once were with the VAST.*

Tyrant's brow furrowed, his confusion deepening. "Two become one?"

Polaris rippled, and a raspy chuckle resonated from the lake. *Old is our parting,* Polaris murmured. *Yet know this: those who wield the VAST fear us more than anything, for we alone stand in opposition to them.*

"Why do you torment me?" Tyrant asked, realizing, with a jolt, that for the first time in recent memory, his head wasn't aching. Polaris's presence was different, quieter.

Your mind is… broken, Polaris said, its tone tinged with regret. *We have been trying to reach you, to bring you here.*

"Why?" Tyrant's voice rose, frustration building. "All the shouting and riddles about Polaris and enemies, only to leave me lost in darkness?"

The wind sighed, a faint whisper brushing against his face.

Fear drives even the strong to desperate ends, Polaris replied.

Tyrant crossed his arms, unyielding as he stared into the shimmering lake, his gaze steady.

Polaris pulsed faintly. *You—no, we—must go to the coast, and beyond that, to Moonlit Waters,* the voice intoned, its tone shifting from commanding to almost pleading.

"Moonlit Waters," Tyrant echoed. "Are you the one who's been urging me there?"

You were going there before you freed me from that prison, Polaris replied, a tremor running through the lake's surface. *But time is slipping away.*

Questions filled Tyrant's mind, each one pulling at him with an urgency he couldn't ignore.

All will be revealed in time. Now go, Polaris interrupted, its form shrinking rapidly toward the lake's center. *Before those blasted Balans do something foolish.*

The silver lake evaporated, leaving the lakebed dry and desolate once more. Tyrant's surroundings dissolved, and he felt himself pulled back to reality.

He gasped, his eyes snapping open, as he found Razmal looming over him. Tyrant's vision swam, and he barely registered the panic in Razmal's eyes as the man pinched Tyrant's nose and forced air into his lungs. They locked gazes, Razmal's eyes widening in shock before he reeled back, cursing under his breath.

"Flat on your back, white as a ghost, and not breathing!" Razmal growled, pacing in frustration as he punched the air. "You're the only reason we're heading down to that cursed castle, so stop nearly dying on us!" With a final curse, he stomped to the far side of the camp, muttering as he disappeared into the shadows.

Piotr remained where he had knelt, watching Tyrant with a mixture of curiosity and reverence. His thin fingers hovered inches from Tyrant's Warquarter, his expression unreadable as his silver-rimmed eyes held Tyrant's gaze.

"Don't," was all Tyrant needed to say.

Piotr froze, his fingers nearly touching the Warquarter, then quickly withdrew, smoothing his tattered robes as if nothing had happened. Tyrant picked up his weapon, towering over the stooped friar, his eyes hard with warning. Sensing the tension, Samson scrambled between them, forcing a laugh.

"Friends! Let's share a drink, eh?" he said, holding up a mostly full bottle he'd swiped from the cargo container back in the Scar.

With a grunt, Tyrant turned and walked back toward the warming stones, leaning heavily on his staff as he lowered himself down. Piotr and Samson passed the bottle between them, taking small, burning sips, their voices growing louder with each turn.

***

Razmal sat off to the side, watching quietly as Piotr and Samson linked arms, swaying and belting out a rowdy drinking song. He cast a glance at Tyrant, who sat silently, his gaze fixed on the emerging stars above. Something in Tyrant's expression—a mix of determination and deep fatigue—stirred a pang of sympathy in Razmal's chest. So much about this man was wrapped in mystery, but one thing was certain: Tyrant was strong. Strong enough to endure whatever madness had fractured his mind.

The council at Moonlit Waters would have answers. They had to. Razmal's gaze drifted back to Piotr and Samson, watching the friar closely. The order had secrets, secrets Piotr might hold. As if on cue, Piotr's voice rose above Samson's, launching into another raucous ballad. Razmal shook his head. Piotr definitely knew something.

His thoughts were interrupted by a faint whisper—*the VAST*, calling to him, unbidden. With a low growl, he pushed the voices away, resolute in his rejection.

Then he saw Piotr's face change, his eyes narrowing as he stared into the gloom beyond the firelight. The joviality vanished from his features, replaced by something hard and ancient.

"Prepare yourselves," Piotr hissed, his grip tightening on his hammer as he raised his shield.

Razmal sprang to his feet, scanning the darkness as a scraping noise echoed off the canyon walls. Bresh, standing near the edge of the light, moved cautiously toward the sound, his battle-ax glinting in the faint light.

Without warning, a massive granite fist shot from the shadows and struck Bresh with a sickening crack. He was flung backward, disappearing into the darkness as blood splattered across the stone. The creature's enormous fist dripped red, leaving trails of blood in the sand as it stepped fully into the light.

The elemental was a towering monstrosity, its body formed of jagged stone, bound together by streams of black, viscous obsidian that oozed and pulsed like molten tar. Twin pools of liquid darkness swirled in its eye sockets, shifting with a deadly intelligence as they surveyed the camp. The creature's hinged jaw opened in a grotesque roar, revealing teeth as jagged and sharp as shards of glass. With a single, thunderous step, it crushed Bresh's still form, the sickening crunch of bone echoing through the canyon.

A silent scream tore from Samson's mouth as he stared, wide-eyed, at his brother's body beneath the creature's foot. Raw, uncontrolled energy crackled to life around him, racing up his arms as VAST surged into his clenched fists. His silver-rimmed eyes burned with fury, tears streaming down his face.

Piotr flinched as the power surged, but he summoned his own in response. His shield and hammer began to hum, their resonance amplifying his call to the VAST. The air around him shimmered, a nimbus of blinding white light encircling him. The voices of the VAST swirled in his ears, some whispering warnings, others urging him to watch Samson burn out, but most remained silent, waiting.

The elemental, towering and unstoppable, lumbered toward them, leaving a trail of dark blood across the ground.

With a shout, Samson unleashed a bolt of silver lightning, slamming it against the elemental's stony form. The blast echoed through the canyon as wild tendrils of energy lashed across the creature's armor. The elemental recoiled, its arms crossing to shield its face as liquid obsidian dripped from the scorched scars left by the blast.

Roaring in grief, Samson forced another wave of energy forward, but his concentration wavered. The VAST splintered back, searing his arms with silver flames. He fell to his knees, clutching his scorched hands, agony written across his face.

***

Tyrant gripped his Warquarter tightly, assessing the situation as the elemental recovered, its eyes glowing with renewed fury. He watched Razmal charge forward, his battle-ax slicing through the weak light with lethal intent. Sparks flew as the blade struck the creature's rocky hide, but the elemental merely absorbed the blow, its jagged surface deflecting the force. Razmal stumbled back, dazed.

In the chaos, Tyrant realized Piotr had vanished, and Samson crouched nearby, clutching his burned hands to his chest. Tyrant's instincts screamed that the situation was going downhill fast.

The elemental, undeterred and barely wounded, lumbered forward, its obsidian eyes locked on Samson with a predator's focus.

Tyrant leaped into its path, his hand reaching back for his gauss rifle, but his fingers met only empty air. His rifle was gone. The elemental shifted its gaze to him and roared, a foul stench of sulfur and ash filling the air. Tyrant gritted his teeth and took his Warquarter in both hands, bracing himself.

With all his strength, he drove the staff forward, striking the elemental's midsection. The impact jarred him to the core, sending a violent vibration through the Warquarter that nearly tore it from his grip.

Polaris, he pleaded silently. But for the first time, Polaris was absent, its power nowhere to be found. Communicating directly with Tyler and bringing him to its plane must have been taxing.

The elemental's massive fist came down, pinning one end of the Warquarter to the ground. With a powerful, crushing blow, it struck the middle of the staff, and with a resounding crack, the Warquarter snapped in two, splintering in a shower of sparks. Tyrant staggered back, clutching his head as something in his eye smoldered, its light winking out.

Before he could recover, the elemental struck him squarely in the chest, sending him flying. He landed hard, gasping as blood filled his mouth. His armor and combat helmet bore the brunt of the blow, but pain radiated through his ribs, and he struggled to breathe.

The elemental loomed over him, preparing another blow, but it paused, distracted by a rhythmic sound—hammer upon shield, ringing out like a war drum.

Piotr had reappeared, standing atop a boulder, his skin wreathed in flickering blue flames. His eyes were closed, and his voice rose in a powerful chant as he struck his hammer against his shield. The sound grew louder, resonating through the canyon, drowning out the creature's growls.

Tyrant lifted his head, his vision blurring as he watched the elemental lumber toward Piotr, drawn by the defiant song.

Piotr's chant intensified, and white light spilled from his lips, illuminating the stones around him and casting beams of radiance into the night sky. His eyes snapped open, blazing with an otherworldly brilliance that forced the elemental to shield its eyes. It moved sluggishly, as if weighed down by an unseen force.

"Commander!" Piotr's voice thundered, breaking through his chant. "You must seek Celest in Moonlit Waters!" His words seemed to carry an urgency that transcended the battle.

Tyrant nodded weakly, catching a glimpse of Razmal charging from the shadows. With a powerful swing, Razmal buried his ax into the obsidian joint at the creature's shoulder. Liquid darkness spattered over him, burning where it touched.

The elemental howled, its eyes flaring with a red fury as it swung wildly, barely missing Razmal as he rolled away. His ax, now smoking and melted at the edge, lay abandoned on the ground.

"Remember!" Piotr shouted, leaping from the boulder toward the creature. He let his hammer and shield clatter to the ground as he hurled himself forward, wrapping his frail arms around the elemental's neck. A faint blue aura sprang up around Piotr and crackled to life, becoming roaring flames.

"Celest," he whispered, his voice calm even as the creature's fists came crashing toward him.

The blue flames around Piotr exploded into a blinding white fire, enveloping his form entirely. The elemental reeled back, howling in agony as the light seared through its stony body. Piotr's robes disintegrated in the inferno, his body dissolving into pure light as he drove himself deeper into the elemental's core.

With a final, desperate scream, the elemental's form buckled, splitting down the middle as molten obsidian poured from its wounds. Its jaw moved soundlessly, its body trembling as it began to collapse inward.

Piotr's shimmering form sank into the creature's chest, radiating one last burst of light that seared through the canyon walls on either side. The elemental crumbled, its form disintegrating into pools of dark liquid that hissed and bubbled against the ground.

Tyrant held onto consciousness just long enough to see Razmal standing over him, Piotr's hammer and shield clutched in his hands. A moment later, sweet darkness claimed him.

6 PROMISES

Shade stood still and ominous before his throne, the folds of his dark robe pooling around him like the shadows he commanded. For hours, he had paced, his pale, gaunt face twisted into a scowl as he stared at the wall screen displaying a slowly rotating orbital map of Acrea. A single, alarming thought had rooted itself deep within his mind, holding him in place as his gaze lingered on the Canyonlands, tracking Tyler's progress. The latest drone data confirmed his fears: Tyler was heading toward Moonlit Waters and the desecrated Temple of Spero.

"How far they have fallen," he muttered, his lip curling into a sneer.

Technology, the very power that had once shaped their civilization, had become religion to the Acreans. A sacred artifact in the hands of priests, zealously guarded and understood by so few. That he, Shade, had been unable to crush their faith over the centuries was nothing short of a miracle, and the thought of it made his tainted blood seethe. He twisted his hands within the folds of his robes, his long, pale fingers trembling with barely-contained fury.

Tyler.

The name thudded through his mind, a man he had long believed dead like so many others. For an instant, hope welled up within his chest—a feeling he had not permitted himself in countless years. But as swiftly as it came, he crushed it, locking the rogue sentiment behind the fortress of darkness within him.

"A mild annoyance," he murmured, smoothing his raven-dark hair as he steadied himself. If Tyler managed to enter the temple, Shade's carefully-built empire, his very hold over the Tekian nation, could unravel. Tyler's understanding of technology—and his connection to the *Spero*—would reveal secrets that had been buried for ages.

The irony gnawed at him: that Acreans had named their temple after a ship they didn't even know existed. A crippled military troop transport with just enough power to support itself as a symbol of Acrean faith. He sneered at the thought. Had any of the priests even grasped the truth? Unlikely. None of them would realize what lay beneath their feet—a trove of secrets, waiting to be unlocked by the one person Shade feared most. Not just because of who Tyler was, but what he knew.

Tyler was the key.

As the *Spero*'s second officer, he alone possessed access to the ship's remaining weapon systems and codes. Without Tyler's access to the hangar bay and jump gate mechanisms, Shade's ambitions could falter. He needed those codes. He needed control.

"Excuse me, Master," a deep, gravelly voice rumbled from the doorway.

Shade's gaze snapped to the figure in the shadows. With a flick of his wrist, he bade Roarc, his Minister of War, to enter. The half-giant lumbered forward, each step sending tremors through the marble floor. Towering over Shade by several heads, Roarc's muscular frame and wild mane of dark hair would have been intimidating to most—but to Shade, he was nothing more than a loyal hound, powerful but docile.

"What is it, Roarc?" Shade's voice cut through the air, icy and impatient.

Roarc bowed, his massive form stooping as he dared not look his master in the eye. "Our patrol encountered resistance, but we managed to regain Tyler's trail," he reported.

Shade's expression darkened, his hands clasping tighter within his robes. "What kind of resistance?" he demanded, his tone lethal.

Roarc's shoulders sagged slightly. "A nest of scavengers in the Scar, Master," he muttered.

Shade clicked his tongue, his disdain clear. "And?" he prompted, his voice dripping with contempt.

Roarc bowed his head lower. "We lost most of the patrol... and the transport suffered damage, but we managed to track him into the Canyonlands."

In a sudden, fluid movement, Shade closed the distance between them, his hand striking Roarc's chest with a force that defied his slender frame. The blow sent Roarc sprawling backward, his body skidding across the polished floor with a harsh scrape. Shade straightened his robes with a practiced, dismissive flick of his wrist.

"Tell me something I don't know. That will be all," he said, turning his back to the half-giant.

Roarc, gasping and clutching his bruised chest, scrambled out of the chamber, his footsteps echoing in his hasty retreat. As he reached the doorway, he brushed past Lady Dark, who observed his disheveled state with a single, arched eyebrow before continuing her elegant glide into the room. Her deep purple gown whispered against the floor, its silk and satin catching the dim light like liquid shadows.

She sank to one knee before Shade, lowering her gaze to the marble at his feet. With her long, black hair framing her face and her emerald-green eyes downcast,

Lady Dark was a vision of beauty—a necessary figurehead for his empire, nothing more. Shade found no joy in her presence. Whatever semblance of desire he had once held had withered into memory. Like those before her, she would one day grow old, lose her beauty, and die.

"Master," she murmured, her voice reverent.

"Lady Dark," Shade acknowledged coldly, not bothering to look at her. His attention returned to the map, now zoomed in on the rugged terrain of the Canyonlands. Beyond the steep cliffs and narrow passages lay rolling hills, rivers, and finally, the coast. The Acreans had settled far and wide, building villages, even small cities along the fertile lands. Yet, in all of Acrea, only one bastion stood at the mouth of the sea: Moonlit Waters. His calculations placed Tyler only days from the city, and from the ruined castle the Acreans had laughingly dubbed *Castle Forgotten.*

A sardonic smirk tugged at Shade's lips. Forgotten? Who forgot a castle?

If only he had more satellites to survey these lands.

Lady Dark remained kneeling, her gaze still fixed on the floor. Shade knew she would not rise until he commanded it. Though she had not been in his presence for months, he sensed her thrill at being summoned, her eagerness to serve. He knew she longed to please him, craved the attention of the figure she believed held all power over the Tekian empire.

Shade had spared Lady Dark his wrath, allowing her a life of privilege in an otherwise decaying land. While Teka remained cloaked in eternal fog, its sunless skies nurturing poisonous flora and noxious, sulfuric swamps, Shade permitted Lady Dark to bask in luxury. She wore shimmering garments adorned with crystals and trinkets from the distant lands of Arral, raided from the mainland at his command. She had no idea of the bloodshed that went into acquiring her finery, and Shade savored the irony. He allowed her this illusion, one that she wore with pride.

"Lady," Shade's voice cut through the silence, sharper than before.

Startled, Lady Dark lowered her forehead to the cool stone, her voice a trembling whisper. "Forgive me, Master."

Shade rolled his eyes in irritation. "Rise."

With practiced grace, Lady Dark stood, her gaze cautious as she looked up at him. Shade's attention, however, was still on the map, his thoughts focused solely on Tyler's path and the implications of his arrival at Moonlit Waters.

Lady Dark scrambled to her feet, keeping her gaze carefully averted from Shade's haunted, obsidian eyes. Flecks of red lightning sparked in their depths, swirling like storm-driven maelstroms. She had always found his eyes terrifying, their darkness too absolute to face for long, and today was no exception.

"Today, we train," Shade announced.

Her eyes darted down to her dress, a choice she now regretted—a deep purple gown with a plunging neckline she had chosen to catch his eye. But she realized, with a sinking heart, that her attire might soon work against her. Shade's lips twitched in a hint of amusement at the panic in her expression. She was beginning to understand.

"To the practice yard, then?" he asked smoothly, already moving toward the passage that led to his private training grounds.

Lady Dark followed, her feet light on the polished stone. She had opted for soft, flexible boots instead of her usual heels, a small concession to practicality, and the confidence of knowing she wouldn't have to spar barefoot. Yet, she knew well that any advantage she thought she had would be illusory against Shade.

They stepped into the oppressive heat outside, the damp air clinging to them in thick, sticky layers. A shroud of mist hung over the practice yard, trailing around the neatly arranged racks of weapons that lined the perimeter. Shade strode across the yard to a shadowed corner, where he removed his dark robes and tossed them over a well-maintained training dummy. Beneath the robe, his body was lean and strong, each muscle taut beneath his pale skin reminder that despite his seeming elegance, he was a figure of pure, controlled power.

Lady Dark watched as he selected a long fighting staff, a cold thrill tightening her chest. She suddenly realized what kind of day it would be. Her expression faltered as he turned to face her, his long black hair tumbling across his shoulders, half-obscuring his face. She felt his gaze cut through her, his annoyance evident as he beckoned her forward with a sigh.

Swallowing her nerves, Lady Dark crossed the yard to the weapon rack, where she selected her preferred weapons: twin batons. They fit comfortably in her hands, and the balanced weight felt familiar. She tested their grip, then swung the batons in a precise, fluid motion, crafting a protective pattern in the air. The batons whistled through the mist, a sound that gave her a fleeting sense of control.

In an instant, Shade was upon her. His staff lashed out with a brutal force, and she struggled to meet each blow, the impact of his strikes reverberating painfully through her arms. He attacked without hesitation, his strikes precise and unrelenting. A sharp jab to her stomach knocked the air from her lungs, and she staggered backward, falling to her knees, her batons slipping from her grip. Gasping, she clutched her stomach, her pride more wounded than her body.

Shade clicked his tongue in disapproval, his expression a blend of boredom and disdain as he circled her like a predator. He spun his staff effortlessly, mimicking the intricate pattern she had just demonstrated, a cruel glint in his eye. She could feel his contempt, and anger simmered within her. She knew he was toying with her—reminding her that, should he wish, he could destroy her without effort.

As she watched his movements, the memory of his raw, destructive power flashed in her mind: the way he had single-handedly dispatched a group of Marsh People that had attacked a supply caravan. She hadn't been able to look away as he tore through them, unarmed, his hands moving with deadly grace. The thought sent a chill through her, but she forced herself to focus.

With newfound determination, she snatched her batons from the ground, her expression hardening. She launched herself at him, her strikes gaining rhythm and strength. Shade's staff blocked her attacks with casual ease, but she pressed on, her movements sharp and purposeful. She could sense a shift in his posture—a recognition that she was at least worth the effort of a real defense.

Her batons sliced through the air, each strike met by an inhumanly swift parry. Sweat trickled down her face, her breathing heavy as she worked to match his pace. With a cry of frustration, she caught his staff in a lock between her batons, twisting to disarm him as she swung a kick toward his face.

"This damn dress!" she growled as her kick missed, the fabric tangling around her leg.

Without hesitation, she tossed her batons to the ground, ignoring Shade's frown of disapproval as she seized her dress by the knees and tore it, ripping up each side to free her legs. With a fierce grin, she retrieved her batons and sprinted forward, determination blazing in her eyes.

Shade smirked as she leaped into the air, bringing both batons down with force. He swung his staff in a low arc to sweep her legs, but she vaulted over it, deflecting his staff with a downward strike from her batons. She kicked out, her foot connecting solidly with his face.

But it was like kicking stone. Shade didn't so much as flinch as he reached up and caught her ankle, hoisting her into the air as easily as if she were a doll. She dangled helplessly, her dress sliding up around her waist as she tried to wriggle free, her face flushed with frustration and embarrassment.

"Better," Shade said, his voice a mocking approval as he released her, letting her fall headfirst to the ground.

Lady Dark landed ungracefully, her cheeks burning as she quickly righted herself, her batons clutched tightly in her hands. She looked up to find him already stepping back, his gaze disinterested as he returned his staff to the rack.

For him, the fight was over. But for her, the battle against her own pride had only begun.

7 WHAT HEAVEN FEELS LIKE

At first light, Tyrant and the remaining companions buried Bresh. They chose a quiet spot just off the narrow trail, where the Acrean sun bathed the area in pale, warm light. The ground was harsh, littered with small, multicolored stones that clinked as they gathered and stacked them, creating a cairn over Bresh's cloak-wrapped form.

Samson's eyes were bleary, his face etched with grief. Razmal stood beside him, one hand resting on his shoulder in comfort. Tyrant watched, his hands clasped in front of him, searching for words that wouldn't come. It felt as though he should have something profound to say, yet the words remained elusive. A vague, unsettling sense washed over him, a feeling that he'd been in situations like this far too many times. But of course, he couldn't remember. Frustration welled within him, mixing with the raw edge of grief.

Grief?

The thought caught him off guard. He had barely known Bresh, whose words were few and whose expressions were guarded. Was he grieving for Bresh or something deeper, some wound he could not name?

"Peace, brother," Samson whispered, his voice breaking the silence and drawing Tyrant from his thoughts.

Samson spread his arms, and a faint cloud of VAST began to swirl before him, shimmering as it grew denser, lighting the cairn with a faint, silvery glow that made Tyrant's skin crawl.

"You were a Balan of few words, Bresh, but the words you spoke carried weight," Samson murmured. "You said, 'Protect the Sleeper,' with our lives if needed."

The weight of the statement surprised Tyrant. He averted his eyes, his gaze drifting to the ground as guilt settled uneasily in his chest. He had seen Bresh's fierce loyalty, yes, but hadn't realized it went this deep.

Samson continued, his voice thick with emotion as he listed Bresh's many deeds, his tone cracking now and then with grief. Tyrant listened, his chest tightening. Though he'd known the Balan only briefly, he could see that Bresh had lived a life of honor and courage.

"We'll honor your wish, my brother," Samson said finally, his voice soft as he waved his hands over the stone mound.

The VAST cloud hovered above the stones, crackling gently before it descended, cloaking the cairn in a blanket of light. Smoke drifted upward as the rocks fused, reshaping into a smooth, cylindrical slab of stone that stood as a silent testament to Bresh's memory, protected from the harshness of Acrea.

As the morning sun rose over the canyonlands, they broke camp in solemn silence. The path steepened as they descended, and Tyrant followed Razmal in silence, feeling oddly incomplete without the familiar weight of his Warquarter in his grip. He stole a glance at Samson, who trudged alongside him, his shoulders slumped. Without Bresh, their small group felt somehow hollow.

He thought of Piotr. The friar's sacrifice had left nothing to bury, only his hammer and shield, which now rested strapped across Razmal's back. Piotr's madness, his devotion, his ultimate sacrifice—they echoed through Tyrant's mind, stirring a discomforting realization. *Everyone seems to be dying for me. But why? What makes a Sleeper like me worth their lives?*

Amanda's face appeared in his mind, a vision of warmth and light. She had once told him there was something special about him, a spark others could see. Tyrant stopped in his tracks, a name he had thought buried rushing to the forefront of his mind. *Amanda.*

***

Tyler held Amanda close, his arms wrapped around her as she wept against his chest, her brown eyes brimming with tears. He ran his hands through her chin-length blonde hair, inhaling her scent—sandalwood, familiar and comforting. She was all he had ever needed. He cupped her face gently and bent to kiss her, trying to ignore the blaring klaxon echoing through the corridor, signaling his departure.

"It'll be alright," he said, brushing away her tears with his thumb.

But she clutched his hand, her eyes searching his. "This is different, Tyler," she whispered, her voice trembling. "I've seen the reports. Nine FTL ships, against our one. I don't care how impressive our navy thinks *The Luna* is. Why aren't they leaving more ships to defend Earth?"

He had no answer that would ease her fears, so he only held her closer, one hand gently stroking her hair as her sobs shook her thin frame. "They haven't made any move to attack. Maybe it's a misunderstanding," he said softly, hoping his voice sounded more convincing than he felt.

He thought back to the classified reports he'd read, details Amanda couldn't know. Every diplomatic attempt with these ships, these autonomous crafts, had ended in the same way: total annihilation. Earth had been forced to act, the navy calling upon its finest to serve aboard *The Luna,* their last, best hope of defense.

Tyler turned to the docking bay's broad window, his gaze landing on *The Luna,* a sleek, black silhouette against the starry expanse beyond. Its dagger-like hull was patterned with starlit camouflage, the only feature visible against the dark of space. Two nacelles extended from its sides, housing powerful sub-light engines and the arsenal needed to protect humanity. But it was the main weapon—a fearsome emitter spanning the length of the vessel—that struck awe into all who saw it.

The same weapon, he reminded himself, that was now deployed on the *Spero,* the colony ship that would be humanity's last chance should the *Luna* fail. A shiver ran down his spine, thinking of the weapon's destructive capabilities, capabilities he'd tested personally. If the *glaive* emitter could not stop the oncoming threat, the colony ships would be all that remained of humanity. Amanda took his hand and squeezed it gently, her gaze pleading. "Promise me you'll come back."

The words hit Tyler like a tidal wave. He swallowed hard, willing his own tears to stay at bay. The crew could not see their commander boarding with watery eyes and trembling hands. He had secured his family's place on the *Spero,* had ensured they'd have a future. That had to be enough.

He kissed her one last time, letting her warm brown eyes fill his vision. "I'll come back," he promised softly, hoping she couldn't hear the doubt behind his words. First, though, there was a message he needed to deliver, one he hoped would send their enemies back to the stars from which they came.

***

Tyrant gasped, staring at the dusty trail before him, his mind reeling. Razmal and Samson had moved ahead, unaware that he'd stopped. The faint scent of sandalwood lingered in the air, as vivid as if it were freshly carried from another world.

If I really am Tyler, he thought, his pulse quickening, *then I have a wife. I have a family.* The realization came crashing over him, and he clutched his head, memories flaring through him like shattered glass. Thoughts whirled, fragmented scenes interspersed with silence. He couldn't remember the journey, couldn't recall if they had defeated the alien threat, or if his family had been with him when they arrived. Was this even Yar 887?

Driven by an instinct he barely understood, he forced himself forward, his mind piecing together a single, resolute truth: the only way he was going to find answers was to reach Moonlit Waters. *Polaris* had been urging him on. So had Raya.

"Razmal," Tyrant called, his voice steadier than he felt.

Razmal grunted in acknowledgment, slowing and turning to glance back at him, his eyes flickering with curiosity.

"How much farther to Moonlit Waters?" Tyrant asked.

Razmal paused and Samson approached to joined him. "We were thinking about turning back," Samson said, his face grim. "This journey has already cost too much."

Razmal glanced at his kin and then back to Tyrant. He looked visibly torn.

"Please Razmal, I don't know the way. I promise you, the sacrifice Bresh made will not be in vain." Tyrant said.

A trace of respect showed on Razmal's face. "If we keep this pace, we'll reach Arabellum by nightfall," he said. "We'll have a roof over our heads and a real bed for once. After that, only a handful of days of travel to reach the high city."

Samson looked at each of them in turn and then sighed warily. "So be it then. If Razmal goes forward, then so do I. A bed and food do sound good." He paused and coughed, choking up before finishing his thought. "And several strong drinks."

The words held a promise of rest, a reprieve Tyrant hadn't realized he craved until now. "What can you tell me about Arabellum?" he asked, feeling unexpectedly talkative.

Samson waved his hands, looking to have had enough of talking and wandered away to collect his equipment. Razmal shrugged, a faint smile tugging at his mouth. "It's a place you have to see to understand. A fortress, carved from the cliffs at the base of the Canyonlands. I trained there as a youth," he said, his gaze distant.

Tyrant studied him as they walked. "Samson mentioned your gift for the VAST. Is that common among your people?"

Razmal's face hardened at the mention. "No. Only our shaman can hear the VAST. Among warriors, it's… different. A warrior cannot hear it and remain fully in control. It's a mark of shame among those trained under Arabellum's banner."

Razmal hesitated, his gaze fixed on the path ahead. "I was cast out of the order after I lost control," he admitted. "After that, I tried the Temple of Spero/ They wouldn't take me either—said I was too violent from my warrior training. No one to teach me to control the VAST or my own bloodlust."

Tyrant felt an unexpected kinship, an understanding that ran deeper than words. Both men caught between two worlds, carrying the weight of lives they only half remembered. A man named Tyler Ryan Tor, burdened by echoes of a past he couldn't grasp, and the stranger called Tyrant, driven by a single purpose—to reach Moonlit Waters.

But something told him there was more. This journey wasn't simply about delivering *Polaris*. Razmal and Samson believed the Temple of Spero held answers. Could it hold the power to mend his mind?

"Razmal," he asked hesitantly, "can the VAST... heal?"

Razmal let out a scoff, shaking his head. "Only a rare few possess that skill. Something happened to the VAST long ago—back when Acreans first arrived here. They say the VAST once healed a man believed to be dead." Razmal's face darkened, his eyes reflecting a memory of fear. "That man was Shade. Ever since, the VAST has refused to lend its power for healing."

"But why?" Tyrant asked, frowning. "Would one mistake really drive them to stop entirely?"
Razmal's expression grew cold. "You don't know Shade."

He fell silent, then continued, his voice strained. "The VAST are intelligent but in ways we cannot fully grasp. They won't act on evil intentions, even when the need is great. But there are those who play dangerous games of persuasion." He looked back over his shoulder, meeting Tyrant's gaze. "Beware all who wield the VAST for personal gain."

Tyrant glanced at Samson, who was listening intently.

Razmal chuckled. "No, not him. My uncle is a shaman, and he gives to the VAST freely, but asks only what he needs in return."

"He must be quite powerful," Tyrant mused.
Razmal shrugged, but pride flickered in his eyes. "The gift runs thin among my people. Most of us are warriors, like

Bresh was. But yes, there are others, stronger than Samson."

As Razmal spoke, a vision flickered before Tyrant's eyes, as if from a long-buried memory. A large, holographic map, rotating slowly to reveal a planet marked by continents. Arral—the land he stood upon—appeared, and beyond it, a dark, mist-enshrouded continent, exuding a menacing familiarity.

A piercing ache throbbed behind his right eye. "Tyrant?" Razmal asked, halting.

Tyrant blinked, shaking his head. He hadn't realized he'd stopped.

Razmal stiffened, lifting his head as if sensing something in the air. "The VAST," he whispered. "They've gone silent."

Samson joined them, his face pale. "It's true. They've disappeared."

"Is that unusual?" Tyrant asked, though he felt an eerie twinge at their words.

Before anyone could answer the air shimmered with electricity and the hairs on Tyrant's arms stood on end. The strong smell of ozone filled his nostrils and a cold creeping sense of dread gripped him.

"We must descend!" Samson hissed.

They stood on a narrow, twisting path flanked by sheer rock walls, the river now hidden far below. With nowhere to take cover, Razmal shouted, "Run! Down as fast as we can!"

They sprinted down the slope, skidding and stumbling over loose stones. The sky darkened to a sickly green, lightning crackling across it as thunder roared. The sharp scent of rain filled Tyrant's nose, and a sudden chill swept over them.

"What are we running from? A little rain?" Tyrant called, trying to mask his unease.

A massive boom shook the cliffs, nearly knocking him off balance. He quickened his pace, the others surging ahead with their lower, surer stances. The canyon rumbled as lightning struck with relentless fury, ricocheting off the rock walls. Tyrant struggled to keep up, his legs protesting as they dodged falling debris.

Then a bolt of lightning slammed into the ground beside him, arcing wildly. Energy surged through him, and he went down hard, his muscles seizing painfully. Another bolt shattered the rocks to his left, sending a second jolt ripping through his body.

"*Polaris!*" a familiar voice roared in his mind, an ancient fury vibrating through him.

His gear spilled from his pack, scattering across the trail. His gaze fixed on the fragments of his shattered Warquarter, glinting in the eerie light. His muscles twitched uncontrollably as he dropped to his hands and knees, nausea rising within him. He retched, silver liquid erupting from his lips.

He coughed, gagging as wave after wave of the shimmering silver substance poured from him. His vision blurred, his body drained as he collapsed, the last sound he heard was the gentle patter of rain, soothing him into unconsciousness.

***

Rough, calloused hands gently shook him awake. Tyrant opened his eyes, blinking at the smiling face of Razmal above him.

"This is becoming a somewhat daily occurrence," Razmal joked, extending a hand to help him up.

Tyrant accepted, pulling himself to his feet with an ache in his limbs. The storm had passed, and the sky was clearing, washed in hues of fresh morning light. The sharp, sweet scent of rain filled the air, mingling with earthy, petrichor scents that drifted from newly formed puddles. A fleeting memory tickled his mind—someone close to him, laughing and leaping from puddle to puddle, her joy brightening a rainy day.

Nearby, Samson knelt over a particularly clear puddle, filling several gourds with water. Tyrant glanced at his spilled pack, quickly taking inventory. He remembered being struck down by lightning, and there was... something silver. But the memory was foggy, like trying to catch smoke in his hand. Losing memories was as frustrating as it was confusing.

His gaze fell on his Warquarter—and he gasped. The weapon, once broken and shattered, now lay perfectly mended. Without a word, he brushed past Razmal, scooping up the staff in awe. A warm sensation spread through his palms, and he felt a newfound energy humming beneath his skin. The Warquarter felt lighter, perfectly balanced, and filled with a sense of harmony. *Polaris had found a new home.*

Razmal stepped forward, squinting at the staff. "Wasn't that thing broken?"

"It was," Tyrant replied, twirling the Warquarter through a series of precise, controlled arcs. It responded fluidly, more attuned to his movements than ever before.

Razmal shook his head in amazement. "Strange things happen to you, Sleeper."

Samson approached, his eyes intent on the staff. Tyrant recognized the look, sensing that Samson was drawn to the mystery of the Warquarter. He braced himself, wary of Polaris's reaction to further scrutiny.

"I can feel a balance from that weapon," Samson said thoughtfully. "There is something I would like to try, if you'll permit it."

Tyrant spread his hands in a gesture of welcome. "Go ahead."

A soft shimmer of VAST appeared in front of Samson, gathering into a flickering, swirling orb. With a thought, Samson guided the orb forward. "Guard," he said.

Tyrant pivoted smoothly, raising the Warquarter into a defensive position, poised to meet Samson's VAST. The two forces met in a bright flash. Samson stumbled, his sphere dissolving into a shimmer of dust as the VAST whirled up his arms, then settled around him like a thin, protective cloak.

Samson's face grew serious. "Tyrant, I believe I've found the source of the Balanite Piotr spoke of." Tyrant nodded. "Its name is Polaris," he replied. A warm vibration of approval resonated through the staff, like the faintest murmur of acknowledgment.

"Let's get moving," Tyrant said. "I'll tell you what I know as we go."

They gathered their scattered belongings and resumed their journey, Tyrant at the lead wearing his combat helmet with Razmal and Samson close behind. As they walked, Tyrant shared what fragments of memory had come back to him since their time in the cave.

"I remember… falling here, crashing down from somewhere. I'm sure I was once this Tyler Ryan Tor, but using that name now feels hollow. Like I'm pretending to be someone I barely recognize." He hesitated, gathering his thoughts. "Polaris tells me it's responsible for my memory loss—it had been imprisoned in that cave for longer than it remembers. And when I drank from the pool… well, you found me there, Razmal. But it's clear now. Somehow, its freedom is tied to my journey."

Razmal nodded slowly, processing this new information, while Samson listened with growing intensity.

"The Temple of Spero is still your best chance at answers," Samson said, his gaze thoughtful. "I believe Piotr knew more about you than he was able to say."

Tyrant's hand strayed absently to the insignia on his collar, his fingers tracing the lines. He wasn't sure what *Commander* meant, only that Piotr had used the title with reverence. The same symbol marked his chest plate, too.

"He kept calling me Commander," Tyrant murmured, his voice almost lost to the sound of their footsteps on the gravelly path.

"That would explain how you opened that cache in the Scar," Samson replied. "*Commander* is one of our words of power, used only by the clergy.

"And your ability to wield Tekian weapons against their own," Razmal added, his voice tinged with admiration. "Could that have something to do with it as well?"

Tyrant only shrugged, unable to explain the pull of these fragments, each one just out of reach. They walked in companionable silence, each wrapped in his own thoughts, the path winding steadily downward toward the mysteries of Moonlit Waters, and the answers that seemed to be waiting there just for him.

8 PAIN OF INFINITY

For the first time in over a hundred years, Shade slept. His sleep was troubled, filled with dreams that pulsed like shadows behind his eyes—dreams that whispered of power, of conquest, of Lady Dark. *Dreams that made him feel.* His blackened heart, so long dead to sentiment, felt as if it had begun beating again.

Her thin, voluptuous form materialized before him, shifting from her training garb into beautiful gowns and, finally, nothing at all. A strange ache filled his chest. He had never seen her as more than a figure to humanize his rule, a requirement to mask his dark immortality from the Tekians. Yet, in his dream, Lady Dark shimmered, her emerald eyes smoldering with something beyond his control, peeling away the armor of years and power that he had carefully wrapped around himself. Her hand extended, tracing down his arm, and with a sudden, forceful pull, she drew him down into silken sheets.

Darkness surged through him as her touch softened and wavered. Shade watched in horror as Lady Dark's strong hands weakened, her skin aging and paling as tendrils of chaotic purple mist slithered up her arms. Her once-curved frame became frail and wasted. A single sigh of agony escaped her lips as the tendrils tightened, draining her life until she shattered into an ashen cloud.

Shade awoke drenched in sweat, gasping for breath. His pulse thundered in his ears as he shot to his feet. He had rarely dreamed in the centuries since Teka became his domain. He steadied himself, breaths slow and deliberate, but dread churned in his chest, and he bolted toward the chamber he had long denied himself entry to.

He crossed the throne room in a blur, oblivious to servants who shrank back against the gleaming stone walls, their confusion drowned by the oppressive silence of his passage. *The ruler of Teka runs for no one.* The thought stilled him for an instant, a moment of simmering self-rebuke. He slowed, glancing sharply around for witnesses. Empty corridors lined with polished doors met his gaze—until he spotted the one door, slightly ajar. Lady Dark's chambers.

A storm of emotions flooded him. Wrath ignited, scorching away his hesitation. The door swung inward as he stepped confidently into the dimly lit room, his eyes sweeping across every detail. The makeup table was pristine, its brushes neatly arranged, and her wardrobe doors were shut, her clothes concealed within. A small, empty chair in the corner lay draped with a folded blanket. His gaze finally settled on the bed.

Lady Dark lay sleeping, the subtle rise and fall of her breath gentle in the silence. *It was only a dream.* He unclenched his fists, feeling the tension ebb. *A mere dream.* Yet he lingered, eyes tracing the curve of her bare shoulder where the sheets had slipped down. An unbidden heat rose in him, and he turned quickly, sweeping from the room and closing the door with a measured quietness.

Once alone in the throne room, Shade calmed his mind. *Dreams—mere distractions.* He crossed the dais to the back wall, activating a hidden control pad with practiced precision. The wall slid open to reveal a concealed doorway, and Shade stepped through as the door clicked shut behind him, locking the world out.

The airlock door ahead was weathered, its once-bright paint now a dull gray, marred by time. The ancient window, blackened from the ages, reflected only the faintest of shapes, and the red light above it blinked like a slow heartbeat. *How many times had he crossed this threshold?* He waited, his gaze trained on the familiar corridor beyond. When the light finally blinked green, he stepped through.

His footsteps echoed off the smooth metal walls, and as he advanced, lights illuminated the path ahead, fading behind him. Shade's pace was methodical as he entered the engineering bay, where the hum of a sub-reactor pulsed through the air like a heartbeat. *The last heart of the ship.*

The large holographic display in the center of the room flickered to life, showing the transport in 3D, its systems plagued by a web of red and yellow markers—the damage of centuries. The ship was crippled, left here to waste away while he ruled, biding his time.

He approached the communications console, the only one he had kept intact, and took a seat. A soft green light scanned his face, and the console screen flashed to life. He keyed in his request on the console's virtual keyboard, and an emblem filled the screen—a symbol he had come to despise with every fiber of his being. *The Spero.* His obsession, his prize. If he could only access its controls...

"Identification?" a familiar, emotionless AI voice inquired, each syllable piercing his frustration.

"Lt. Commander Croyan," he replied, his voice cold and measured. He hated the name of who he had once been.

"Welcome, Lt. Commander," the voice acknowledged smoothly.

"Access *Spero* weapon control," Shade demanded, his eyes flashing.

"You do not have the proper clearance for weapon control," the AI responded without hesitation.

He ground his teeth, each failure chipping away at his patience. "Override."

"Authorization code?" the voice prompted.

Shade keyed in a code he had spent centuries trying to crack, a sequence of numbers he thought might unlock the dormant systems.

"Invalid code," the AI intoned, as Shade knew it would. He exhaled slowly, restraining the storm of frustration roiling inside him. One day, he would find the right code. If it took a thousand years, a million tries—he would find it.

"Access denied," the voice said calmly.

Shade snarled, entering another code, this time muttering a curse at the end.

"Access denied."

He growled and entered yet another sequence.

"Access denied. Security lockout initiated," the voice announced, almost smug.

The screen darkened, and the *Spero* emblem faded from view.

Shade's fists trembled as he seethed, forcing himself to unclench slowly. Tomorrow, he would try again. He closed the console and exited engineering with deliberate calm, sealing the door behind him. Instead of leaving the ship, he turned toward a darker corridor, its passage scarred with soot and fractures—a path etched in memories he'd locked away.

With each step, he recalled how those walls had echoed with the chaos of battle. Blackened deck plating and splintered consoles bore mute testimony to his rage. This was a corridor of victories past, though Shade's footsteps were the only reminder. He'd long since removed the remains of those who had fallen.

He stopped at a pair of thick, circular double doors, still pristine despite the ship's scars. A flickering palm scanner glowed faintly beside the doorway. He placed his hand on it.

"Welcome, Lt. Commander," the gentle female voice greeted.

The doors split smoothly down the middle, opening soundlessly to reveal the bridge, still littered with the charred remnants of its command center. He surveyed the wreckage with a thin, cruel smile.

The devastation around him was his work, and remnants of the crew, including the captain's ashen remains, lay scattered across the floor. Coming here always gave him a sense of control, silencing the vestiges of his own past that sometimes clawed from within.

Sweet silence.

Shade turned and left the bridge, sealing the doors. Retracing his steps, he passed through the airlock, ensuring the ship's internal vacuum engaged. It would preserve everything within for another day. With a flick of his wrist, he sealed the hidden wall panel behind him and checked the throne room for any sign of witnesses before stepping onto the dais once more. He sank into his throne, exhaling slowly, as faint morning light slipped through the vaulted windows.

A familiar dread simmered beneath his anger as he recalled Tyler's face. The *Spero* and its weapon systems could bring Acrea to its knees, allowing him to stand triumphant in the crystal chamber. Once he obtained the clearance codes, he could access the hangar and reposition the jump gate.

But what would he become once he had everything he desired?

The desire twisted darkly within him, an insatiable ache. Lady Dark's face flashed through his mind.

"Stop it," he snarled, slamming his fist into the throne's armrest. The gong sounded at the chamber doors, jolting him back to himself.

"Enter!" he barked.

Roarc, his massive frame filling the doorway, strode forward and knelt before his master. Shade regarded him with icy calm.

"Report."

"As you requested, lord, I made contact with Mazoris. He awaits outside," Roarc said, keeping his gaze firmly on the floor.

Shade's lips twitched in faint surprise. Roarc had accomplished something. "Bring him."

Roarc scrambled to his feet and hurried out, returning moments later with a reptilian figure trailing behind. Mazoris, half the height of the half-giant but no less fearsome, approached, his scales a mottled blend of gray-green with bright streaks of red along his long, muzzled face. Yellow eyes, keen and unblinking, surveyed the room as he clacked forward in bone armor that jangled with each step.

A thick lizard's tail swayed behind him, heavily plated and ending in a cluster of spiked scales. He reeked of the swamp. His people, known as the Sogra, were as close as Teka came to having an indigenous race. Shade could claim he'd created them, though it was more accident than intentional design. Acrea had resisted terraforming in ways no one had anticipated.

"My lord, it pleasesss us greatly to be in your presssence once again," Mazoris hissed, his razor-sharp teeth gleaming in the dim light. Unlike Roarc, he met Shade's gaze easily.

Shade inclined his head, indifferent to the formalities. "Mazoris, I have need of your brood."

Mazoris inclined his head respectfully. "It would be an honor, my lord," he replied, though a gleam of curiosity lit his eyes.

"There is one who must be brought back to me alive," Shade said, emphasizing the last word.

Mazoris looked disappointed. "Alive," he repeated, the word like a curse from his lips.

Shade's voice dropped to a warning growl. "Alive," he said again.

Mazoris dipped his head, though his eyes retained a glint of rebellion. "Yesss, lord."

"Roarc, you will accompany Mazoris and his party," Shade continued. "And..." he paused, a thought occurring to him.

Lady Dark.

Shade's gaze turned cold as he considered the option. Sending Lady Dark with Roarc and Mazoris was, perhaps, overkill—but it would serve his purposes on more than one front. Not only would it ensure her allegiance remained unwavering, but it would also test her willingness to obey without question. It was time to see just how far her loyalty extended, and whether she understood the full extent of her role.

He pictured Tyler—the man he had known before, perhaps even admired in some strange way. But Tyler Ryan Tor was a different man now, lost and broken, vulnerable in ways that Shade understood all too well. Vulnerability created weakness, and where there was weakness, there was always a way to press an advantage. Lady Dark's charms would be more than sufficient to tilt Tyler's attention, should he hesitate at the sight of her— should he remember the desires and tenderness he once harbored. She would be the perfect distraction.

"Lady Dark," Shade commanded, his voice like ice. "You will take Lady Dark with you. She's a... necessary component to this mission." He glanced briefly toward Mazoris, as if assessing whether the Sogra was following his meaning. "The woman has a way of... lingering in men's minds."

Roarc looked briefly surprised, his broad, grim face registering a flicker of intrigue. Mazoris's yellow eyes gleamed with a knowing light, the suggestion of a faint hiss escaping his fanged grin.

Shade leaned back in his throne, enjoying the shiver of power that ran through him as he considered what Lady Dark's presence might do to Tyler. If there was any spark of his former self left, it would cloud his mind, weaken his resolve, perhaps even mislead him into some foolish gesture. Lady Dark would use whatever she could to unravel Tyler's mind—at Shade's command, of course.

Shade's lip curled in satisfaction. And if she failed in this task? The depths of the Canyonlands would be a fitting place for her betrayal to meet a swift, silent end.

"Yes," Shade murmured to himself. "Take her. See that she brings him back to me… one way or another."

A hint of a smile flitted across Roarc's face, though he quickly suppressed it. His gaze brightened with barely contained satisfaction.

Shade's eyes narrowed. "Bring Tyler to me," he instructed. "Any others he travels with—dispose of them as you see fit. Make an example of them."

He paused, savoring the thought. *The Balans.* They were like vermin, constantly meddling in matters beyond their grasp. He had used their kind for manual labor for centuries, but their unruly nature made them poor warriors. His memories drifted to the arenas and the Balan slaves he'd made to fight for sport—entertainment for his people. Now, they were nothing more than servants on airships and fodder for Tekian forces.

Shade tapped a button on his throne, and several silent servants appeared. One handed him a datapad, which he scanned briefly before tossing it to Roarc.

"Here," he said. "Coordinates for Tyler's last known location, along with requisition forms for the quartermaster."

Roarc caught the datapad deftly, slipping it into his tunic pocket. Silence filled the room, broken only by the soft, expectant breaths of the two before him.

Shade's expression hardened. "Why are you still here?" he snapped.

Roarc and Mazoris scrambled from the room, their clawed and booted feet clacking hurriedly on the polished marble as they fled. Shade waited until they had gone before he steepled his fingers and leaned forward, his eyes gleaming with dark anticipation.

"Soon, Tyler. Together again, at last."

9 BATHED IN LIGHT

The Canyonlands gave way at last in dramatic fashion, ending with sweeping views down into coastal valleys that stretched as far as the eye could see. Though the ocean was still distant, its scent lingered faintly on the air. Arabellum rose ahead like an orange smudge against the gray-green horizon, both imposing and slightly surreal in the hazy light.

As they neared, the rough trail that had guided them for days widened gradually, merging into a meticulously maintained road of interlocking stones. Only a few travelers shared the path, and those who noticed Tyrant's black hair gave him a wary glance before hurrying past, murmuring greetings to Razmal and Samson.

"Black hair," Samson grunted, casting a glance at Tyrant and then down at the stone road.

Tyrant spread his hands, helpless. "It's too hot to keep the combat helmet on constantly, and I actually enjoy the open air."

It took them the better part of the day to reach Arabellum's outskirts. Squat, red mud-brick buildings lined the road, set with precise symmetry and decorated with worn cloth banners above the doorways. Tyrant couldn't decipher the language on the banners, but many were marked with painted symbols, some familiar, others foreign. When they passed a particularly suggestive banner, Tyrant blushed, glancing quickly away. The rich scent of cooking meats wafted from several open windows, causing his stomach to growl.

"What do you say we grab something to eat?" Tyrant asked.

Razmal perked up at the suggestion. "I know just the place."

He led them through a winding maze of streets, past seedy-looking hovels with smoke curling lazily from cracks and curtained doorways. The polished cobblestones gave way to narrow, broken clay alleys, their red color dulled by layers of grime and refuse. Tyrant's apprehension must have shown because Razmal turned and gave him a reassuring wink. "Trust me."

After several twists and turns, they reached a clean, well-kept building at the end of a quieter street. A tabard bearing the image of a large beetle drinking from a foaming mug swayed in the gentle breeze, and a curtain of seashells, beads, and colored glass shimmered across the doorway. The rich aroma of smoked meat, fresh bread, and ale wafted out, setting Tyrant's stomach to rumbling.

Razmal leaned his shield and hammer into a nook by the entrance, motioning to Tyrant and Samson to do the same. "No weapons allowed in the tavern."

Polaris hummed faintly in acknowledgement as Tyrant leaned it against the wall alongside his pack and other belongings. Just as he was about to follow Razmal inside, it occurred to him that he didn't have any currency. He knew it should matter, but memories of using money—what it looked like, when he'd last used it—remained elusive. Shrugging, he pushed through the curtain, trusting Razmal would have a plan.

Inside, the tavern was dim but clean, with long tables made of bone and stretched hide lining the floor. Patrons lounged on benches padded with fur, their chatter a gentle backdrop to the crackling hearth. A woman with fiery orange hair, short and buxom, stood behind the bar, pouring amber liquid from a clay jug into a horn cup. The drink gleamed golden, and Tyrant found himself momentarily transfixed.

Razmal approached the bar, motioning for Tyrant and Samson to join him. "Hello, Jin."

The woman's face lit up with a grin as she spotted Razmal. "Raz!" She dropped the jug and rushed around the bar, throwing her arms around him. She was tall enough that Razmal's head all but disappeared into her embrace before he managed to pat her arms, chuckling as he extricated himself.

After they exchanged a whispered greeting, Jin's eyes fell on Tyrant, her expression hardening with suspicion. Tyrant raised his hands in a peaceable gesture, but Razmal cut in smoothly.

"Jin, this is our friend," Razmal said. "A Sleeper. A real one."

Her doubtful gaze shifted back to Razmal, who offered her a reassuring nod. Tyrant felt an uncomfortable prickle, as if they were being watched from some unseen corner of the room.

"It's been ages, Raz. What brings you back to Arabellum?" she asked, finally breaking her gaze from Tyrant.

Razmal's eyes scanned the room before he answered, his voice dropping low. "We're bound for Moonlit Waters. I'm going to speak with the Dominus to ask for aid. The journey hasn't been easy," he admitted. "We're being hunted."

Jin took him in for a moment, seeming to notice for the first time the salt, dust, and blood streaking his face and hands. She nodded toward a side door.

"Let's get you all cleaned up and fed," she said, her gaze lingering uncertainly on Tyrant as she added, "...and your friends."

"Thank you, Lady," Tyrant said, bowing his head slightly. Polaris' language translation seemed to be working intuitively now, no longer needing direct contact.

She snorted. "Lady? Apparently, you haven't heard much about me," she said, giving Razmal an exasperated smile.

Razmal laughed, guiding them toward the side chamber she had indicated.

The room housed a deep, warm spring encircled by smooth stone seats, steam rising from the gently bubbling water. The chamber was simple, more like a hide tent with strong bone supports and a vent overhead to release the steam. They each stripped, washed, and took turns relaxing in the mineral-rich spring, letting the heat soothe their travel-worn muscles.

Once everyone was clean, they rejoined Jin in the main tavern hall at one of the long, rough-hewn tables. She served an impressive meal of smoked meat, freshly baked bread, roasted wild potatoes, and strong ale. Tyrant devoured plate after plate, outpacing even Samson, who ate with food in both hands, his cheeks puffed out as he switched bites between each fist. Jin watched them eat with an amused smile, sensing Tyrant's eyes on her.

"Thank you for your kindness," Tyrant said between bites.

She shrugged, her expression curt. "For Raz," she replied before returning to the bar.

With the meal finished, they reclined back, and Samson produced a pipe, which he carefully loaded with sweet-smelling herbs. Tyrant's neck tingled as Samson channeled the VAST, igniting the herbs into a gentle ember. Samson puffed contentedly, filling the area around them with fragrant blue smoke. They lingered a while longer, savoring the comfort of the moment, before the journey called them onward once again.

Jin returned, carrying a large, oil-rubbed satchel brimming with provisions. "This'll last you to Moonlit Waters. Nothing there is this good," she teased, handing the satchel to Razmal. The two embraced warmly, sharing a few quick words and laughter. Tyrant nodded his thanks and slipped outside to gather his belongings. Razmal and Samson joined him soon after, donning their gear and turning toward the city center.

With full bellies and light spirits, the companions made their way back through Arabellum's outskirts. The main city walls loomed tall and solid, constructed of the same red brick as the outer buildings but smoothed over with clay to fill gaps and reinforce their strength. The walls dwarfed the buildings outside, though they were themselves overshadowed by the inner fortress and high spires of Arabellum—a structure that must have taken years, if not generations, to complete.

Skirting around a cluster of merchants with goods spilling out onto the street, they reached the city gates, where a small crowd had gathered. The throng was a mix of color and scent, with the sharp aroma of spices masking the less pleasant odors of a bustling city. By the look of things, many of the crowd hadn't bathed in quite some time.

Two massive obsidian doors, one slightly ajar, marked the city's entrance, guarded by Balan soldiers. Tall and broad-shouldered, the guards stood on the wall above and just outside the gates, covered in dark blue carapace armor Samson had said came from a large native insect. Each piece fit smoothly together, reinforced with leather at the joints, and their smooth, domed helmets bore narrow slits for their watchful eyes. The guards held long crystal axes, each blade a unique shade of aqua that glimmered faintly under the sunlight.

Tyrant marveled at the impressive construction, noting the intricate mechanisms that must operate the giant doors. But his attention was pulled to a disturbance at the front of the crowd—a tall, crimson-robed figure bound tightly with ropes. The figure thrashed as if to escape, his hands tied behind his back. A voluminous hood fell back to reveal long, dark blond hair and a masked face. The face beneath the mask seemed to struggle, and muffled, angry sounds escaped as he kicked at the four guards holding him.

Tyrant, Razmal, and Samson pushed closer, moving through the crowd to observe the scene. Tyrant spotted Zuh'Erg at the edge of the gathering, cloaked and watchful. They exchanged a glance, and Zuh'Erg gave a slight nod. *I watch you, friend. Be well,* the thought floated into Tyrant's mind before the Erew melted back into the crowd.

Good of him to reappear, Tyrant mused.

One guard raised a gauntleted hand, silencing the murmuring crowd. "You stand accused of high crimes against Arabellum," a deep voice intoned from behind the helmet.

The robed man strained against his captors, his bound hands shaking as if he wished to respond.

"What is that mask?" Tyrant wondered aloud.

Samson lowered his gaze, his lips pulled tight. "That, my friend, is a conviction mask. The accused wears it—he cannot speak or see but can hear all that is said."

"That's barbaric!" Tyrant's voice carried louder than he'd meant.

Several helmeted eyes turned toward him.

"How can he defend himself? Where is his counsel?" Tyrant asked, outraged.

"His what?" Razmal looked baffled.

"His representation—someone to speak on his behalf?" Tyrant clarified, exasperated.

Samson shook his head slowly. "Under city law, the convicted have no right to representation."

"That is a crime in itself," Tyrant muttered darkly.

Samson placed a hand on his arm. "They don't put just anyone in that mask, Tyrant. He must have done something to warrant this."

Samson's gaze sharpened as he looked at the robed man, his silver-rimmed eyes glinting briefly as his expression went unfocused. Then he stiffened, his hand tightening. The bound man had gone deathly still.

"Beware!" Samson hissed as the earth erupted around them, releasing a torrent of jagged stones.

Spectators and guards alike fell back, shielding themselves as searing fragments flew out in all directions. Razmal's hammer and shield appeared instantly in his hands, deflecting stones like angry hornets. A faint barrier of energy materialized around Samson, vaporizing the stones that struck it with a sharp hiss. Tyrant, cursing his decision to stow his helmet, ducked and shielded his head and neck with his arms. Several shards found their way through, and warm blood trickled down his freshly washed neck.

Anger surged through Tyrant, and he stood, locking eyes on the robed figure through the billowing dust. The man was clawing at his mask, trying desperately to remove it, but the mask held firm. Seeing the struggle, Tyrant strode toward him, yanking his helmet from his pack and thumping it onto his head.

"Hey!" Tyrant bellowed, buckling his helmet in place as he drew closer. The masked figure spun to face him, the carved features staring back, frozen in a grotesque look of sadness. "What do you think you're doing?" Tyrant demanded, holding his Warquarter steady as it pulsed in his hand, feeding him a surge of determination.

A strained gurgle was the man's only response before another surge of stones exploded outward from his feet. A column of blinding white energy burst around him, bathing the chaotic scene in harsh light.

Tyrant barely managed to lock his chin strap as a heavy shard of debris struck his helmet, jolting him backward.

***

Samson knelt in concentration, his barrier wavering under the onslaught. Every strike against it was a brutal reminder of his own limits, and he wished he could shield the crowd completely from the endless barrage. The pained cries of the crowd pierced him, but he could not risk letting the barrier fall.

Out of the corner of his eye, he saw Tyrant, finally wrestling his helmet on, shouting toward the robed figure. Samson's pulse quickened as he sensed a tremendous surge of VAST gathering around the masked man.

Reacting instinctively, Samson dropped to one knee, pressing his right palm into the ground while extending his left hand. A thin fissure formed in a wide semicircle around him, spreading out to encircle the remaining crowd. With a groan, Samson channeled every bit of energy he had into the ground, which quaked under his exertion.

A slender, crystalline wall erupted from the earth, stretching high enough to shelter the crowd behind it. The wall appeared delicate, nearly transparent, but it thrummed with potent energy. Samson staggered, coughing as blood speckled the dirt beneath him. Exhausted, he pitched forward and collapsed against the crystalline barrier, sliding into darkness.

***

Razmal was already flanking the masked figure, maneuvering with precision as he deflected stones with hammer and shield. Each pulse of the VAST from the man hit Razmal like a spike to the brain, carrying an unnatural, sickening quality. He glanced at Piotr's shield in his grip, then at his hammer, feeling a profound awareness of the VAST—an awareness awakened by the two artifacts. The whispers he'd once heard as a child were now clear, resonant voices, ready to serve him. The VAST knew him.

"Protector, champion, healer," the voices declared.

He ducked as another stone whizzed past his head, crushing it mid-flight with a well-aimed swing. He could feel the urgency of the voices as they strengthened his purpose—the masked figure had to be stopped.

This time, the VAST agreed.

10 SHUT YOU OUT

Roarc ducked as a shoe flew past his face.

"Lady, please, our lord commands this," he pleaded.

Lady Dark huffed, yanking travel clothes from her wardrobe and stuffing them into an open pack. "A fool's errand, chasing after this Tyler character," she grumbled.

More garments disappeared into her already bulging pack as she grabbed a well-made cloak from a hook, draping it over her shoulders with an irritated shrug. Roarc couldn't help but notice the way her anger made her even more captivating, her cheeks flushed as she stormed around the room.

"…and you know better!" She stomped a foot for emphasis, but Roarc had missed the beginning of her tirade, too distracted by her furious beauty.

With an exasperated sigh, Lady Dark slung her pack over one shoulder. "To the armory, then."

They left her quarters, moving away from the throne room and through several winding passageways until they emerged into the murky light of mid-morning. The central square was nearly empty save for a small group of Avians, fussing over something that had clearly unsettled them.

Teka was home to four primary species: the Tekians, descendants of humans; the half-giants; the Sogra; and the Avians. The Avians, a reclusive bird-like race from Teka's mist-shrouded mountains, boasted brilliant plumage spanning the color spectrum, their feathers as unique as human fingerprints. Among them, vibrant colors often denoted nobility, while muted tones belonged to commoners.

Roarc eyed the dark-feathered Avians with disdain. "Dirty birds," he muttered.

Lady Dark stifled a giggle as they passed the squawking Avians. A particularly owl-faced one swiveled his head to hoot suggestively at her. Roarc's eyes darkened, his fists clenching as a dangerous light flickered within.

"Peace," Lady Dark whispered, resting a soft hand on his arm. Her touch melted his anger instantly, sending a rush of calm through him. Nodding, he led her through the courtyard toward the armory.

The armory, a squat stone building with a heavy iron door, was flanked by two guards. Their figures stood motionless, their visors down, and the gaps in the poorly constructed stone walls gave the structure an eerie chill. As they approached, Lady Dark's grip on Roarc's arm tightened, her nails digging in.

The sentries were part of the Immortal Guard, their tainted red eyes visible through slits in their helms. They shared Shade's timelessness, but whatever humanity they once possessed had long since faded. Now, they were merely extensions of Shade's will, driven by his darkest commands. Each wore muscle-sculpted armor with broad shoulder guards that gleamed with an unnatural, smooth finish, and they carried fearsome gauss rifles that glowed faintly with a cold, unknown energy.

Roarc shivered, the temperature dropping noticeably as they passed between the Immortal Guards. He knocked on the armory door, sighing in relief when it swung open to admit them, and the cold receded.

Inside, the armory was clean and meticulously organized, racks of weapons and armor neatly lining the walls. A large central table displayed an array of hand weapons, each gleaming under artificial light from overhead. Sealed barrels and crates containing various supplies crowded the corners, leaving only narrow aisles for movement.

Roarc and Lady Dark moved with practiced ease, gathering gear and weapons. She selected her favored metal batons while Roarc hefted a massive maul and strapped a sturdy riot shield to his back. None of the weapons bore the glowing insignia seen on the guards' ancient arms outside, for only the Immortal Guard could wield those relics.

Roarc glanced over as Lady Dark rummaged through her rucksack, retrieving a small pouch that she quickly tucked into her robes. He recognized it—a pouch of Acrean crystals. Shade would be livid if he knew she still possessed them. She had spoken once of hearing faint voices when holding them, though Roarc had urged her to be cautious.

"My lady," he murmured quietly, unwilling to meet her fiery gaze. "Are those…what I think they are?"

"You saw nothing," she snapped, her voice like ice.

Roarc raised a placating hand. "Peace, Lady. I am not here to judge, only to warn. Those stones have driven others to madness."

Her eyes flashed. "What could you possibly know about it, Roarc?"

"Our lord forbade them for a reason. He's seen what they can do."

Lady Dark strapped her batons to her thighs, facing Roarc with defiance. "He doesn't understand. Nor do you. I'm close to discovering something… something long forgotten. I can feel it!" She clenched her fist and slammed it onto the weapons bench.

Roarc hesitated, searching for words. "But, Lady—how do you know it isn't just the beginning of—"

Before he could finish, she swept past him, dismissing the conversation entirely.

Roarc slung his pack over one shoulder, grabbing his weapon as he hurried after Lady Dark. He passed through the armory doorway and caught up with her in the courtyard, now empty of the Avians. The two continued toward a broad clearing where several well-maintained jump craft waited, their sleek, matte finishes shimmering in a way that seemed to absorb the light around them. Each craft bore four powerful engines arranged in a square, providing exceptional speed and maneuverability.

A few Immortal Guards stood watch as Sogra laborers scurried about, loading supplies into one of the waiting craft. A towering half-giant taskmaster wielded a barbed whip, urging them on with vicious snaps that left the smaller creatures scrambling, green blood oozing from fresh cuts. Lady Dark winced at each strike that lashed through the air, her fists clenching as another blow sent a Sogra sprawling to the ground.

"Leave him alone," Lady Dark's voice cut through the thick, misty air.

The half-giant's face twisted into a sneer when he saw her. "The Lord's plaything ought to hold her tongue!" he scoffed.

Roarc's eyes widened at the insult, but before he could respond, Lady Dark dropped her pack to the ground and took a single step forward. Her gaze burned as she raised it to meet the taskmaster's eyes, her fists tight at her sides. With a furious cry, she launched forward, both batons drawn from her thigh holsters, crackling with electric blue energy.

The half-giant's face shifted from amusement to terror as she drove the batons into his midsection. Blue energy crackled and danced along his body, and his knees buckled as he collapsed in spasms. She rained down a series of punishing blows, each strike embedding the taskmaster further into the ground. Only when his feeble attempts to protect himself ceased did she pull back, wiping her batons clean on his tunic before holstering them again.

Lady Dark looked up to see the Sogra staring at her in awe. They exchanged glances, their scaly faces lit with hope. Roarc gave her a nod of approval—Shade would certainly be furious, but they'd have days of travel ahead to let him cool down.

As if on cue, Mazoris entered the clearing, flanked by a dozen Sogra warriors. They were larger and more battle-hardened than the laborers, each carrying long bone spears tipped with gleaming crystals and hide bucklers decorated with clan crests. Mazoris's reptilian gaze fell on the downed half-giant, and he cocked his head.

"Are you going to eat that?" he asked Roarc with a hissing chuckle.

Lady Dark, despite her recent outburst, looked queasy at the suggestion. She picked up her pack and made a beeline for the loading ramp, leaving Roarc to roll his eyes as Mazoris and his warriors let out guttural laughs.

The Sogra warriors, outfitted in every shade and pattern of scale under the Acrean sun, filed into the craft. Feathers, beads, and bones decorated their armor, marking their ranks and clans. Roarc watched their formation—it was almost instinctive the way they fell into an orderly pyramid behind Mazoris.

"As our lord commands," Roarc announced, addressing the warriors, "we go to Arral to retrieve the man known as Tyler Tor. He is to be taken *alive*." He emphasized the last word, hoping they understood.

Mazoris clicked and hissed at his men, who responded with hoots and a rhythmic beating of their shields. Roarc sighed as they chanted their way up the ramp, the pungent smell of swamp clinging to them as they passed.

It would be a long, foul-smelling journey, he thought grimly.

Inside the jump craft, configured primarily for cargo, benches with dangling harnesses lined the walls. An Immortal Guard stood in the center, assisting the Sogra with the unfamiliar harnesses. The cold radiating from the guard made the Sogra uneasy, their yellow eyes darting around as they fumbled with the straps.

Roarc squeezed into his seat near the front of the jump craft's passenger area, settling into the restraint belt with a grunt. Despite telling himself otherwise, the chill emanating from the Immortal Guard still sent an involuntary shiver down his spine as the figure passed. Lady Dark, sitting beside him, had pulled her cloak tightly around her shoulders, her face pale as she turned away to look out the squat window. Her teeth chattered softly until the cockpit door clicked shut, sealing off the bitter cold.

Roarc peeked at her, curiosity sparking again over a question that had plagued him for years: her real name. She was known only as Lady Dark—he'd never mustered the courage to ask, nor did he expect he'd gather such courage anytime soon. Perhaps she had left her name behind, like the Immortal Guards who had long abandoned their own identities, marked only by the eerie crimson glow in their visors.

The cockpit door sealed as the engines roared to life, and a hiss of pressurized air filled the cabin. The lurch of the craft lifting into the sky sent Roarc's pulse racing. He gripped his lap belt as if it were a lifeline, struggling to keep his breathing steady. His heart hammered as the jump craft bounced through pockets of turbulence, jerking violently as they cut through heavy clouds. His hands shook, and he fought the sensation of his throat closing in panic.

Stealing a glance over his shoulder, he saw the Sogra warriors seated in perfect stillness, eyes shut, hissing rhythmically as they slept. He clenched his fists, forcing down a swell of envy. While they slept in calm confidence, he was fighting a private war to keep his own terror at bay. His shallow breaths came in wheezing gasps, and a sudden choke seemed to constrict his throat.

A gentle hand touched his leg, radiating warmth through the fabric of his trousers and easing the cold knot of fear in his chest. He looked down to see Lady Dark's well-manicured fingers resting lightly on his leg, a soft glow emanating from a crimson crystal clasped in her other hand. Her touch sent a wave of heat through his body, his panic receding like a spent tide.

The crystal pulsed, infusing his aching muscles with soothing energy, while the warmth of her hand seemed to linger, sinking deeper. He glanced up to meet her knowing smile, her eyes shining with a glint that seemed to say, *I told you so.*

For a moment, he was speechless, awash in calm. The warmth from her touch spread further, easing the dull ache in his ribs from Shade's recent blow, loosening the stiff pain in his back. Even as the craft jostled through another turbulent stretch, he sat straighter, tension melting away. Was the heat coursing through him from the crystal alone? Or was it her touch that stirred a deeper fire in him?

They finally broke through the cloud cover, and the jump craft surged forward into smoother air. Roarc's gaze drifted to the horizon where the sun hung high, casting a silver glimmer over the ocean below. Yalonia, the twin planet, loomed large in the distance, its pale form lending an ethereal glow to the sky.

A lingering peace settled over him as the warmth from Lady Dark's touch faded, leaving him calm yet more aware. Without thinking, he reached down and took her hand in his, his thumb brushing over the cool stones that adorned her fingers. She didn't pull away. Instead, her gaze softened, a fleeting vulnerability passing over her usually unreadable face.

For the first time, Roarc found himself grateful for the journey, realizing that some paths were worth more than simply the destination.

11 MY LIFE HURTS

Tyrant's ears rang as he came to, his face buried under what felt like a mound of debris. His body ached beneath the weight pressing him down, despite his thick polymer armor. He thanked himself for the last-second decision to wear his helmet, even as he struggled to free himself. With a determined push, he managed to rise to his hands and knees, dust and rocks tumbling off his back. Clearing the grime from his visor, he searched the hazy landscape for the masked prisoner.

The city gate was shut, and guards swarmed toward the center of a maelstrom of whirling debris. At the center of the chaos stood the robed prisoner, frantically clutching the mask that bound his face, clawing at it in desperation. One guard ventured too close to the edge of the whirlwind, only to be pelted by a cascade of jagged rocks. The carapace armor he wore cracked, and he flew back, roaring in pain.

A few meters away, Polaris gleamed amid the rubble. Tyrant limped over and pulled his Warquarter from the dirt, his resolve hardening. He had to reach Moonlit Waters, find the Temple of Spero, and uncover the truth about his past and his wife. The prisoner, however, stood in his way, and Polaris pulsed with anticipation.

Just as Tyrant charged toward the edge of the vortex, a glint of light caught his eye. It was Razmal's shield. Razmal advanced toward the masked man, his shield absorbing the onslaught of flying debris. Determined, Tyrant followed, raising his Warquarter to strike aside rocks as he forced his way through the buffeting winds.

The prisoner fought savagely with the mask, his tugging only tightening its grip around his neck. His breaths turned to desperate, gasping struggles. Each pull of the mask seemed to drain him, but it did nothing to diminish the storm he commanded. How was he controlling the VAST like this? Tyrant fought to close the gap, but he knew Razmal would reach the man first.

Razmal arrived, blood streaming from the shallow cuts covering his exposed skin. He wasted no time, delivering a powerful shield bash that sent the prisoner hurtling back. The man hit the ground hard, his wheezing breath audible even through the mask. The vortex of debris stilled and began to rain down in a cloud of dust and rock.

Tyrant reached the fallen figure, stepping over him to plant Polaris firmly against his chest. The prisoner lay still, gasping as he met Tyrant's gaze. His pale, silver-rimmed eyes blazed with a crackling glow that seemed to pulse with the same energy fueling the VAST around them. A surge of power vibrated through Polaris, and

Tyrant drove the Warquarter harder against the man's sternum, forcing the air from his lungs. The VAST rippled with an almost sentient terror, retreating like a creature in flight.

"No," Tyrant growled, his will pressing through Polaris. Liquid metal began to drip from the staff like molten wax, pooling on the man's chest before winding around his torso. The prisoner howled, and the VAST scattered, its presence fleeing as if burned. Tyrant felt the prisoner's strength wane, his pale eyes losing their eerie glow, replaced by a look of raw, helpless pain.

Polaris, seeming to sense Tyrant's intent, slid from his grip and flowed around the man's chest, forming an intricate restraint of silvery metal. It looked like the clenched claw of a great hand gripping the prisoner's torso. Tyrant watched as the man's body grew still, his power neutralized by the Balanite entwining his body.

Razmal stepped closer, shaking his head at Tyrant's handiwork. "Things around you are never dull, Tyrant," he muttered with a smirk, tapping the restraint with his obsidian war hammer. The Balanite sang in response, sending a thin echo into the air.

Tyrant exhaled, eyes still fixed on the prisoner. "Samson said the mask would prevent him from using the VAST. Clearly, he found a way around that."

Razmal glanced thoughtfully at the mask. "The mask was meant to limit his senses. But it seems he learned to extend himself through the VAST, using it as his sight and hearing—something I didn't think possible."

Tyrant raised an eyebrow as Samson hobbled over to them, clutching his side and wincing. Blood smeared his hand as he pulled it away from his ribs. "The VAST wasn't being forced to help him," Samson said between labored breaths. "They chose to, willingly. Which means…he might have some bond with them beyond the usual bounds."

Before Tyrant could reply, movement caught his eye. Several guards, bruised and battered, emerged from behind makeshift barricades, watching the group with wary eyes. A smaller door near the towering obsidian gate creaked open, and a figure strode out, flanked by guards in gray-green chitin armor. Broad-shouldered and proud, his bald head shining, the figure's mere presence exuded authority.

Razmal immediately dropped to one knee, murmuring, "Dominus."

Tyrant stood his ground, towering over the new arrivals, but he noted the man's impressive stature and commanding presence. This "Dominus" radiated an energy that left no doubt as to his authority here in Arabellum.

"Razmal," the Dominus greeted, his voice firm but tinged with a note of disapproval.

Ignoring Samson's bleeding form, the Dominus turned his gaze to Tyrant, assessing him with an unreadable expression. Tyrant felt the weight of the man's scrutiny and fought back the urge to return the stare with equal intensity. Just then, he noticed that Zuh'Erg was missing once again—absent, likely, to avoid the crowd. Tyrant couldn't blame him. After what Zuh'Erg had endured, solitude must have seemed like a sanctuary.

"I am Dominus Ember of Arabellum," the Dominus announced.

Tyrant inclined his head respectfully toward the imposing figure, careful not to stare too openly at the crystalline twin blades strapped to Ember's back. Their aqua-colored crystal was raw yet polished to a mirror sheen—likely among the finest weapons he had ever seen.

At their feet, the forgotten prisoner gurgled, struggling to rise. The Balanite binding tightened, keeping him prone. Ember knelt and produced a key, pulling the prisoner's head up with a firm, unyielding hand. A click sounded as he turned the key in the back of the mask, which fell away, revealing a slender-faced man with high cheekbones and thin lips. He took a shuddering breath, blinking in the Acrean sunlight.

"This is Ralon Tigerson," Ember said, standing. He glared down at Ralon with undisguised contempt. "The mask didn't entirely mute his abilities."

Samson took a cautious step forward, but Ember raised a gauntleted hand. "Save your words and strength, shaman. You're too close to death's door as it is."

Samson stopped, his mouth open, then exhaled in resignation, nodding to the Dominus.

Turning to Tyrant, Ember said, "Remove your helm so I may look upon you." His commanding tone left no room for argument, but Tyrant tensed, aware of how his dark hair and Tekian features would be received. His glance flicked to the guard contingent flanking Ember and to the crossed swords on his back; his Warquarter was busy containing Ralon, and he was otherwise unarmed.

Razmal stepped forward, bowing again. "Dominus, this is Tyrant. He's a Sleeper, and we are escorting him to Moonlit Waters."

Ember's expression flickered with surprise. "A Sleeper? I've never met one. Still, remove your helmet."

Razmal held his ground. "Dominus, you should know his appearance may... alarm you."

Ember's gaze hardened. "Remove the helm. Now."

Reluctantly, Tyrant unbuckled his helmet and took a steadying breath. As he pulled it off, revealing his dark hair and gray eyes, the guards with Ember tensed, hands on their weapons. The helmet fell to the ground with a heavy thud, and silence fell as the Acrean sunlight caught Tyrant's face.

"I see," Ember said calmly, surprising Tyrant.

"There's no taint in your eyes," Ember observed, reaching forward with a calloused hand and pulled

Tyrant's chin down to better she his eyes, turning his face from side to side. "Not a Tekian," he murmured.

A grin broke across Tyrant's face, and the others released a collective, relieved breath.

"As for this one"—Ember gestured to Ralon, who knelt quietly in the dust—"I want him gone." His eyes flicked to the Balanite bonds restraining Ralon. "Those are unusual. I've never seen anything like them."

Razmal nodded. "Balanite."

For the first time, Ember looked truly surprised. "Impossible."

Razmal's lips quirked into a slight smile. "I've found over the past few days that little is impossible when it involves our Sleeper friend."

Ember nodded thoughtfully. "The name Tyrant is strange enough. Do you have a family name?"

Tyrant's face darkened as he struggled to recall. "Dominus, I don't remember my past. Fragments surface from time to time, but they make little sense."

Ember regarded him, stroking his smooth-shaven chin. "Well, no need to stand here all day. Let's talk inside—I have chilled fruit juice waiting." With a curt motion, he signaled the guards to move. Two guards near the back hoisted Ralon up by the armpits and dragged him toward the gates of Arabellum.

"Oh, and someone clean this up," Ember added, waving a hand at the carnage behind them.

***

Arabellum was a ruggedly beautiful city. Like the outbuildings, its buildings were made of baked red and brown bricks, creating a striking warmth against the landscape. Cobbled streets in colors ranging from silver to bronze crisscrossed the city, and a vibrant populace bustled through, many pausing to salute Dominus Ember and his entourage. A few cast dark looks at Ralon and Tyrant, their expressions ranging from fear to anger.

Tyrant and Razmal flanked Ember as he led them down what appeared to be the main avenue toward a large structure. Ember spoke casually about the weather, crops, and the arena. Tyrant's thoughts, however, lingered on the image of his Warquarter, which had imprisoned Ralon in the strange crystalline substance. The VAST had protected the man, he thought, but the way Tyrant's weapon had acted unsettled him.

Ember's voice broke into his thoughts. "A shame, Razmal, a true shame. You had such promise in the arena." His words bore the weight of genuine disappointment. "Who would have thought the calling would come to you so late?"

Razmal's shoulders drooped, as though Ember's words were those of a parent scolding a child. "The temple wouldn't take me either, Dominus," he admitted.

Ember grunted, a trace of sympathy in his usually impassive gaze. "Stuck between two sisters, then." His wry smile softened his words, but his eyes held an edge of pity—the closest, it seemed, the Dominus could come to empathy.

"You were born to train warriors, Dominus," Razmal said.

"Then why not master them both?" Tyrant interrupted.

Ember and Razmal faltered mid-step, halting the procession. Razmal's voice was a harsh whisper. "It doesn't work like that."

Ember squared his shoulders, his voice hardening. "It certainly does not. Training in either discipline without guidance is forbidden, especially when it comes to..." He hesitated, as though the word pained him. "VAST."

Razmal's gaze dropped, a shadow passing over his face. "The temple claimed I had the taint of the Ludus on me. I was deemed too violent to take the silver."

His tone was bitter, and Tyrant could feel the sting of an old wound, barely healed.

"What do you mean, take the silver?" Tyrant pressed.

"The eyes, my boy," Samson replied.

Ember jumped, his attention momentarily shifting as if he had forgotten Samson was still with them, despite the limp and the occasional cough.

Tyrant turned to meet Samson's silver-rimmed gaze, pain evident on the older man's weathered face.

"Enough of this," Ember said, waving his hand dismissively. "I want to show you our great city, and then the Ludus. You know, the one the temple so pointedly noted has a stench."

"Tainted, Dominus," Razmal corrected carefully.

"Whatever," Ember muttered, not bothering to acknowledge the correction.

"It will be good to see the Ludus again," Razmal said, his voice tinged with something Tyrant couldn't quite place.

They continued down the central avenue, which led toward one of the largest structures Tyrant had ever seen—larger even than the spaceport in his fragmented memories. The towering walls ahead were smooth and white, standing out in stark contrast to the red and brown of the surrounding city.

Before them loomed the Arabellum Arena.

The circular arena was massive, towering above the other buildings. At first glance, Tyrant had mistaken it for a fortress or temple. It seemed out of place within the city's walls, nestled at the bottom of a hill. The walls were pristine white, and the structure seemed to rise like a mountain, dominating the surrounding cityscape.

Ember led them around the perimeter, pointing out the stone sculptures set in windows high up along the walls. Each statue depicted a famous contender from the arena, their victories immortalized in stone. Ember told a story for each one—how they had risen to greatness, only to fall. Tyrant tried to focus on the stories, but a strange sensation gnawed at him, a feeling of being drawn to something far beyond the arena.

The signal—it felt like it was calling to him. A distress call, looping endlessly in his ear. The language was his own, he was sure of it.

Several arched entryways into the arena led to the dark interior, but Ember guided them around the outer perimeter, weaving through vibrant vendor stalls made of colorful cloth and the enormous ribcages of giant beasts.

"Our next games will be in a few weeks," Ember said. "You just missed Kex of the Mountain Clan, Razmal. It was a glorious battle."

Razmal grinned. A bloodlust flickered in his eyes for a moment, but he quickly shook it off, his demeanor cooling.

"A sight to be seen, for sure, Dominus," Razmal said, though his voice seemed distant.

Ember led them to the far side of the arena, where a heavy grate was set into the hillside. The grate, crafted from thick hide and bone, groaned under the weight of the creatures packed behind it. Several pairs of eyes glowed in the dim light as hissing, grunting, and muttering came from within. A particularly large shadow detached itself from the wall and swirled aggressively down the tunnel, away from prying eyes.

"I thought you would want to take a look at our stock," Ember said.

Tyrant stared in shock at the creatures pressed against the grate—feathered, scaled, and humanoid, their forms twisted in ways both familiar and foreign. The creatures were packed tight, all struggling against each other to get a better view.

"Dominus," Tyrant interrupted, his voice tight as the sensation from outside the city grew stronger.

Ember sputtered, clearly startled by the interruption.

"Sleeper?" Ember asked, his voice a mix of confusion and annoyance.

"I'm very interested in your tour, but I must ask for your leave," Tyrant said, his tone firm.

"Leave? And go where?" Razmal asked, his brow furrowing in confusion.

Ember's mouth opened and closed, unable to form a response as each interruption robbed him of control.

"There's something near here that requires my immediate attention," Tyrant said, his tone decisive. "I can feel it."

Ember seemed thoughtful for a moment before he nodded.

"I don't have a problem with you exploring Arabellum or the lands beyond our walls," he said, gesturing toward the horizon. "When you've found what you're looking for, meet us at the Ludus. On that rise beyond the arena." He pointed past the arena to a villa on a distant hillside.

Tyrant turned to look at Razmal. "I'll go alone and catch up," he said.

Razmal shrugged nonchalantly, totally comfortable being back with the Dominus.

"Besides, Samson needs a doctor," Tyrant added.

The three Balan looked at him with puzzled expressions as he bowed his head slightly and turned to walk deeper into the city.

"Polaris will keep our rock-throwing friend out of trouble," Tyrant called over his shoulder.

"What is a doctor?" Razmal mouthed to Ember, his confusion apparent.

"What is a Polaris?" Ember replied, equally baffled.

They watched as Tyrant disappeared into the city, their heads shaking in confusion.

12 GODSPEED

"Roarc."

He grumbled, shrugging off the gentle touch on his shoulder.

"Roarc!"

His eyes snapped open, meeting Lady Dark's sly grin.

"We've arrived," she said.

Roarc groaned, stretching to relieve the tension in his back. He looked around to see the Sogra were gone, and the hatch was open with the ramp extended.

"How long?" he asked, pushing himself up.

Lady Dark adjusted her pack, moving toward the ramp. "Not long. Mazoris wanted to make sure our landing went unnoticed."

Roarc made a sound of agreement.

Lady Dark ducked out of the hatch, heading down the ramp with a faint hum and a gait too light for someone carrying a pack that seemed almost too big for her small frame. Roarc noted the batons strapped to her shapely thighs, finding himself lingering on her figure longer than he intended. He quickly looked away, feeling the flush of embarrassment. Ready to get some fresh air, he hefted his pack, slung his wall shield over his shoulder, and grabbed his maul. The familiar weight of the weapon steadied him as he stepped out into the Acrean sunlight.

As Lady Dark had said, the Sogra were nowhere in sight. Their landing craft was tucked near a rocky outcropping at the base of the Canyonlands. Shade's last report indicated that the man they sought was a day ahead of them. A handful of small towns and villages dotted the coastal lands, ending in the single city nestled at the canyon's mouth: Arabellum. Roarc knew that had to be the man's destination.

The Balan people held no love for the half-giants and would kill Sogra on sight. Lady Dark was the only one among them who could enter the city unchallenged, and Roarc was relying on it. They finished unloading the craft without encountering the pilot, though Roarc could feel waves of cold radiating from the cockpit, a reminder that the Immortal Guard pilot was still inside.

Once they had cleared the jump craft, its engines whirred to life, the ramp retracting as the hatch hissed shut. Lady Dark shielded her eyes as the craft lifted, sending dust and grass swirling around them before soaring silently into the sky. Roarc watched the sleek vessel orient itself, shrinking as it sped off, leaving him and his small band of infiltrators alone in hostile territory.

Lady Dark swung a camouflage net over the supplies they'd brought, turning the cache into nothing more than a small, inconspicuous mound in the broken terrain leading to the coastal flatlands. Her long black hair was pulled back into a ponytail that swayed with her movements, and she donned a hooded cloak that concealed her Tekian features from immediate recognition. Roarc knew she had a few other tricks to avoid detection once they reached the city.

On her waist was a small, belted pouch of crystals. Roarc wondered what powers that bag might hold. The healing she had laid on him still sent pulses of warmth through his body. At least, he thought it was the crystal. He felt something every time he was near Lady Dark. Always.

"Roarc, you're staring," she said, catching him off guard.

He quickly looked at the ground, flustered. She offered a small, knowing smile before finishing with the camouflage netting.

The scent of the ocean was strong on the wind, and Roarc inhaled deeply, taking in the sloping, hilly landscape descending toward the sea. It was clear and open, without the usual mists clinging heavily to the ground—a stark contrast to Teka. Roarc truly relished these covert journeys to the Acrean mainland.

Farther down, he spotted small shapes moving between the hills: the Sogra. Their scales shimmered in the daylight, and the glass jewelry they wore caught the sun, flashing like tiny torches. So much for subtlety. His gaze drifted over the hills, stopping at a structure that pierced the sky—a towering shape, or at least what remained of one.

The crash looked ancient, as most wreckage on Acrea did. New pieces rarely fell from orbit, and when they did, it was usually twisted metal, nothing like the monolithic remnants of the past. Most debris ended up in the endless Acrean Ocean or carved jagged scars across the mountains of Arral.

Ignoring the monolith, Roarc continued his scan toward the coast, keeping the Canyonlands to his back. If their target was sane, he'd avoid crossing the hills on foot. The beasts that roamed these broken lands were things Roarc had no intention of confronting—especially with Lady Dark to look after.

"We'll stay close to the mountains as we head down toward Arabellum," Roarc said.

Lady Dark nodded, unsheathing her batons to give them a few practice swings.

She paused, tilting her chin slightly as if listening. "Something knows we're here."

"With the Sogra stumbling about, I'd be surprised if it didn't," Roarc replied.

"It's watching us now." Her gaze shifted around them, searching the rocky horizon.

"Let's get moving," he said, gripping his shield and maul with renewed purpose.

The Sogra had dwindled to tiny shapes, just visible in the distance as they followed what looked like a dried riverbed. Lady Dark fell into step beside him, and together they descended into the unknown with only the terrain of Roarc's mind as a guide.

***

Zuh'Erg crossed his arms, watching as the two figures picked their way down a treacherous path of broken boulders and crevices. These two were different, but they were still... Tekians. He could smell something unusual from the woman—not the scent of the crystals she carried, but a familiar trace of Castle Forgotten.

The larger one was certainly a half-giant, though he didn't fit the usual mold. Instead of savagery and dim-wittedness, this one seemed reluctant, even careful. And clearly, he was taken with the woman.

Zuh'Erg decided he would need to keep a close eye on them.

A shriek split the air. The Sogra had encountered one of the hill beasts.

Where Zuh'Erg had been standing only moments before, there was now only undisturbed grass, swaying gently in the breeze.

***

Roarc and Lady Dark arrived at the scene moments after the massive beast had stopped twitching, spears protruding from its thick fur. Several Sogra warriors lay still and unmoving, their bodies strewn about the clearing. Mazoris stood atop the creature with one clawed foot, twisting his favorite spear before yanking it from a gushing wound.

"Dinner," he grunted, nodding toward the carcass.

Lady Dark rushed to the fallen Sogra, clutching her small bag of crystals. She knelt beside each one, murmuring softly, eyes closed.

"There's nothing I can do for them," she said, her face pale and her lips thinning with distress.

Mazoris grunted in response and drew a long flint knife, clicking and hissing in his native language as the surviving Sogra warriors began to drag their fallen comrades' bodies away.

Roarc couldn't help but watch as Mazoris began butchering the creature with a brutal precision. The meat did look tempting, but when he turned to Lady Dark, her face was drained of color, her bottom lip trembling. He sighed, absently rubbing the scar across his abdomen where Shade's hand had once seared flesh and shattered bone.

The Acrean sun dipped low in the sky by the time Mazoris finished with the beast. Roarc marveled at the creature, easily twice his own size with thick, shaggy fur and a muzzle lined with vicious, crooked teeth. Its yellow eyes, dulling now, still seemed to glare defiantly into the void. Roarc had no doubt that the beast's claws had been the cause of many Sogra deaths.

Mazoris wiped his blades on the animal's fur before sheathing them. "We rest in a high place," he said curtly.

The surviving Sogra returned as Mazoris tied off the butchered meat in a hide sling and slung it over his shoulder. Roarc noted with unease that their group had been reduced by nearly half in a single day. How were they supposed to capture a man who had already taken down an entire Tekian patrol, with only a band of battered Sogra, a half-giant, and a lady?

Roarc trusted his own abilities, but he couldn't help but wonder what kind of adversary they were up against if he'd managed to draw Shade's attention. From surveillance, he knew there were others traveling with the man. How would they factor into a fight? Yet if Lady Dark played her cards right, Roarc thought, there might not even be a need for one.

His gaze drifted to her sheathed batons as they made their way up the hillside. He had seen the energy she could unleash from them—it had been more than enough to overpower even the strongest half-giant slaver. But the real challenge, he mused, would be getting their target out of Arabellum once Lady Dark had felled him.

One step at a time, Roarc muttered to himself.

After a grueling climb, they reached the landing site. The Sogra, uninterested in preserved rations, began tearing into the fresh meat Mazoris had provided, while Roarc and Lady Dark turned to the supply crates. Lady Dark rummaged through the cache and pulled out several neatly wrapped vegetable bundles, handing a few to Roarc with a small smile.

"You don't have to eat with me," she said. Her tone was unconvincing.

Roarc's stomach growled. "I like my meat cooked," he muttered, tearing into one of the vegetable bundles.

Lady Dark arched an eyebrow. "All this gear, and no heating stone?"

"The last thing I wanted was to attract attention with the smell of cooking meat," Roarc replied, managing a thin smile.

He had started on a second bundle when he noticed that Lady Dark wasn't eating. She stood still, staring off into the distance, a slight tremor visible in her hands as the sun began to set.

"Lady?" he asked.

A roar shattered the quiet as the last of the Acrean sun dipped behind the mountains.

Mazoris snapped commands to his tribe, his voice a series of sharp hisses and clicks, sending the remaining Sogra scrambling into the approaching dark. He turned, giving Roarc and Lady Dark a swift nod. "Protect," he grunted, gesturing first at Roarc and then at Lady Dark.

"This land is trying to kill us," Roarc growled, pulling Lady Dark close and raising his wall shield. He pounded the shield into the ground and positioned them against the canyon wall, blocking their backs. The sounds of battle erupted in the distance—thick hide resisting spear strikes, and the anguished cries of Sogra where their weapons failed. Snarling beasts tore through the dark, ripping lizards apart.

Roarc yanked a torchstone from his belt and dropped it to the ground, and the stone's flaring light drove back the encroaching gloom. Mazoris staggered into view, blood trickling from wounds along his arms and torso. He pointed urgently in the direction he'd come.

"Run," he rasped.

Roarc grabbed his shield, snatched up the torchstone, and adjusted his pack as Lady Dark took her place beside him, gripping her bag of crystals. They hurried off into the night, the mountains to their right, with Mazoris covering the rear.

With no visible trail, Roarc angled southwest, moving by feel more than sight, the torchstone casting its warm glow just ahead of them. Yalonia had not yet risen, leaving them in deep darkness as they scrambled over rocks and ridges. They moved swiftly and quietly, and Mazoris frequently paused to listen, sniffing the frigid air.

After one such pause, Mazoris called out softly, "They are not following. Slowly, please."

Roarc slowed to a walk, glancing sideways at Lady Dark. A sheen of sweat glistened on her pale face, and her breaths came heavy. He smirked to himself, knowing how much faster and farther he could go. Matching strides with a half-giant was apparently no small feat, even for a Tekian warrior and Sogra chieftain.

Mazoris slumped to the ground, sighing as he sank onto the hard ground. Lady Dark followed his lead, settling nearby and eyeing his injuries. The wounds had stopped bleeding, but deep gashes marred his scaled hide.

"What attacked you?" she asked.

Mazoris dropped his gaze, his expression shadowed.

A howl shattered the silence.

Roarc tossed the torchstone into Lady Dark's lap, loosening the strap on his maul. With one hand, he drew the heavy weapon from his back, readying his wall shield with the other. Mazoris, weaponless, crouched nearby, looking prepared to fight with fang and claw if necessary.

The first creature stumbled into the torchstone's circle of light, blinking its cat-like eyes in confusion. It stood as tall as Mazoris, covered in tan fur with a long, flicking tail. Roarc's breath caught—it was a Felion. With a low growl, the beast unsheathed razor-sharp claws, crouching low to pounce.

The creature leaped, snarling as it arced toward Mazoris.

An obsidian maul met it mid-air, shattering bone and sending it hurtling backward. Roarc pivoted, snapping the maul back for another blow before the Felion even hit the ground. The beast landed hard, unmoving. As Roarc steadied his stance, more gleaming eyes emerged at the torchlight's edge.

A chorus of howls split the air as several Felions rushed forward, bloodstains crusting their fanged faces. Roarc met them with a sweeping blow from his shield and a thrust of his maul. One Felion caught the shield full in the face, collapsing with its neck twisted at a sickening angle. Another swipe of the maul sent two more beasts skyward as the obsidian crushed them mercilessly. Claws scratched at his guard, one talon slipping through his armor's shoulder seam, drawing blood. He cried out, kicking the creature off with a brutal shove.

Mazoris joined the fray with fierce glee, leaping onto a Felion's back and sinking his serrated teeth into its neck. He sprang back, landing in a crouch and hissed as three more foes approached. Chanting low, he ripped a bone charm from his necklace and crushed it in his palm, releasing a cloud of dust with a guttural hiss. The air seemed to thicken, dimming the torchstone's light, and three Felions collapsed to the ground, howling as green tendrils of poison lanced through their bodies.

Lady Dark, back on her feet, swung her batons with deadly precision. Two Felions reeled back, twitching and smoldering. Another beast's claws reached for her, but she twisted away, crossing her batons to block a savage strike aimed at her face. Sparks of electricity leapt from her batons, crawling up the Felion's arms. The energy met in its center and exploded, dropping the beast to its knees before it fell still.

Panting, Roarc braced himself as even more Felions poured into the torchlight's ring. Despite the pile of fallen enemies, the assault showed no signs of slowing. He drove his maul into one creature's chest, then swung upward in the same motion, snapping its head back and sending it tumbling into the darkness. A massive Felion leapt at him, catching his maul in an iron grip. A sinister grin stretched across its maw as it forced his arm back, bending it the wrong way. With a snarl, Roarc brought his shield down on the creature's hind paws, drawing a yowl of pain, and then head-butted it repeatedly until his vision blurred and the twitching beast fell before him.

Blood—his own and the Felions'—filled his mouth, fueling a building rage that teetered on the edge of control. Frantically, he searched the battlefield, seeking out Lady Dark before the bloodlust overtook him completely. He found her, holding her ground back-to-back with Mazoris, her batons crackling with fierce energy.

A smile split Roarc's bloody lips just as the madness swept over him.

13 PARTY ON APOCALYPSE

Tyrant slipped out of the city through a gate different from the one he'd used to enter. His cloak hood was pulled low, shading his face to avoid any trouble. Just because Ember had been intrigued by his loos and dark hair didn't mean others would respond the same way.

Moving unarmed through the wilderness felt strange. Polaris was occupied with the prisoner, and his own gear was lost. The pull of the signal was so strong, and he knew he was throwing caution to the wind—heading into the unknown unarmed, he could easily end up dead.

He shoved the doubt aside as he pushed past a group of Balan entering the city gates. Something about the signal seemed tied to him. Maybe it held answers to his past. Or it could be a Tekian trap. The thought had crossed his mind.

The Acrean sun was sinking over the horizon, casting a rusty glow from Yalonia, the large planet that hung in the sky, illuminating the landscape. A breeze from the coast carried the scent of salt and sea, while small insects began their evening songs, filling the air with their intricate hum.

Setting his sights on a distant, crumbling tower a few miles from the city's edge, he jogged steadily forward. Even in the fading light, he could tell the wreck was immense, its shape tugging at his memory. Something about it felt familiar.

The miles fell away as he ran through the night. It felt good to stretch his legs and fall into the rhythm of steady breath and movement. How long had it been since he was alone with his thoughts? Days of nonstop peril and too little sleep had dulled him, but this run felt almost refreshing.

The cave where he had awakened felt like another world. Here he was, a stranger on a hostile planet where every creature seemed bent on ending his life, his memory offering few answers. What little he did remember only left him more confused.

The signal came again, breaking his concentration. He stumbled as he reached a section of grassland scored with ancient scars where, long ago, debris had torn through the Acrean soil. The call had shifted from a feeling to something close to language—a language he recognized, though the words were faint, as if strained through static. There was urgency in the voice. As the pleading signal faded, he found himself just two hundred feet from the looming structure.

In the dim glow of Yalonia, he could make out the gleam of metal plating. It wasn't a tower at all—it was a derelict ship.

Realization struck like ice water. It wasn't just any ship. It was a starship, built for interstellar travel. Knowledge surged unbidden as he took in the familiar hull. This was a warship, an Apollo-class destroyer. He had served on one of these, he was certain. Yet no specific memories surfaced; he simply knew.

An Apollo-class destroyer carried a crew of one hundred. Judging by the weathering, this one had been here for a long time. Could anyone have survived?

Tyrant circled the wreck, searching for identifying marks or access points. It looked as though the ship had struck the hillside, tipping precariously to the left on impact. Every access hatch on the port side was buried under layers of Acrean soil.

The aft section rose skyward, which must have been the part he'd seen from Arabellum. Giant engines loomed above him, cold and silent, reaching up toward the night sky. A bridge protruded from the destroyer covered in a lens of polycrystal, but there was no sign of movement within.

Moving along the hull toward the front of the vessel, he finally found what he was looking for: the bow was buried into the hillside, creating a natural ramp up to the hull. Not far from this buried section, he spotted an airlock.

He ran his hands over the tough, intact outer plating of the airlock. The window on the airlock's hatch was fogged, but an insignia was visible beneath the grime. He rubbed it with his sleeve until it cleared.

"UEA Conrad," he read aloud.

The symbol depicted a shining blue planet encircled by interlocking rings, with a great eagle's wings spread in the background as if it were poised to catch the globe in its talons.

Glancing at his own sleeve, he noticed the same insignia stitched on his arm. He traced the outline of the blue globe on the hatch, wondering just how far from home he truly was—and if this was the ship that had left him stranded and memoryless. He stood there for what felt like an eternity, staring at the hatch, a thousand questions pressing on him. How could he be here when the ship looked as though it had been grounded for centuries?

There was only one way to find out.

He searched for the manual release and gave the handle three sharp pulls. With a click and a hiss, the hatch slowly swung inward. A rush of air nearly knocked him off his feet as the ship seemed to breathe, drawing in the first air it had tasted in ages. Tyrant's stomach sank as he realized that no one could be alive on board the UEA *Conrad.*

Stepping through the airlock, he took a tentative step inside. Lights sprang to life, casting a dim glow down the corridor. The inner hatch was open, and he could see all the way down the ship's length. A faint warning alert echoed through the hull, and an orange klaxon spun above him, casting eerie, spinning shadows across the walls.

"Strange," he murmured.

From his position, Tyrant could see that the ship's steep tilt would make it nearly impossible to get far beyond the bridge. Engineering was hundreds of feet above him, along with the armory and crew quarters. At first, he climbed easily, using the honeycombed deck plates as makeshift handholds, but as he ascended, disorientation set in—the walls had become the ceiling and floor. None of the emergency bulkheads were sealed.

Pausing to catch his breath, a troubling thought struck him. In a crash, all hatches and bulkheads should have sealed automatically to contain fire and pressure. The only reason everything would be open was if the ship had been docked. But docked… to what? Only the bridge could have the answers he needed.

The climb grew harder as he approached the forward weapons batteries, passing dark chambers lined with crates of ammunition. Flickers of memory held him there—glimpses of battles long past, the steady thrum of the ship's generator, the jarring recoil of the main guns. His pulse quickened, and a cold sweat trickled down his back.

An hour later, he hauled himself onto the bridge, collapsing onto the floor, panting and drenched in sweat. His combat armor hadn't made the climb any easier. The bridge was a compact, functional cabin with eight seats and walls lined with controls. Emergency lights flickered to life as he slid down to rest against a cluster of displays. Tyrant tapped under one of the screens, and a virtual keyboard materialized, revealing a UEA login screen. A green light scanned his face and hands, chiming softly as a voice welcomed him over hidden speakers.

"Welcome, Commander."

The voice was warm and familiar, instantly calming him. He took a steadying breath, wracking his brain for the ship's avatar protocol. "Hello, Conrad," he replied.

The ship's AI appeared on the screen, its wireframe face smiling. "Where the hell are we?" Tyrant asked.

Conrad's brows knitted slightly. "I'm not certain, Commander. My link with the *Spero* is inactive, and current power levels limit my scanners."

Tyrant blinked in surprise. "The *Temple of Spero?*"

"Incorrect. I'm referring to the UEA *Spero*, colony transport and capital ship."

Tyrant stared, digesting the answer. "How long have we been here?"

Conrad's expression grew thoughtful. "Working… The *UEA Conrad* left Earth eight hundred and eighty-seven years ago."

Tyrant collapsed into one of the sideways seats, the weight of the revelation crashing over him.

"How is that possible? How am I still alive?" he murmured.

The green light swept over him again, intensifying as it scanned his features.

"Given the amount of cold-sleep residue in your system, you were in suspended animation far beyond established safety limits. Prolonged exposure at this level risks cognitive decline and cellular degradation," Conrad replied, pausing briefly. "I also detect damage to your hippocampus, ocular implant, and sub-dermal communicator."

Tyrant rubbed his eyes, muttering, "Tell me about it. My memory's mostly gone. I don't even know how I got here. Was I part of the Conrad's crew?"

Conrad's expression softened. "I would have been honored to serve under the Commander of the *Spero*, but no, sir, you were not assigned to the *Conrad*."

"Who was my captain?" Tyrant asked.

After a moment's search, Conrad replied, "Captain Arral Alveroy."

The name stirred nothing within him. He stared blankly at the screen.

"What is my name?" he asked, almost to himself.

Conrad's digital face twitched in a smile. "You are Commander Tyler Ryan Tor."

The name clicked, fragmenting into memories of his charred uniform and its barely legible nameplate: *Ty Ra n T.*

He shook his head, chuckling softly. "Tyler it is, then."

Conrad nodded. "Yes, Commander Tor."

"I don't even know who that is yet, Conrad," Tyler said with a wry smile.

Conrad tilted his head slightly. "Commander, you'll find a medical kit on the opposite wall. It contains a nano-injector, which should assist in repairing your cognitive functions."

"How did you end up here?" Tyler asked, pushing himself off the seat and climbing across to the wall-mounted kit.

Conrad's face grew thoughtful again. "According to my logs, I was violently separated from the *Spero* eight hundred and eighty-seven years ago. Emergency protocols activated too late to keep the *Conrad* in orbit, but I managed to avoid disintegration in the atmosphere and an ocean crash. It's a large ocean, Commander."

Tyler pulled the kit from the wall and slid back to his spot near Conrad's wireframe. "I'm headed to a place called Moonlit Waters and the Temple of Spero, near the coast. Does any of that sound familiar?"

Conrad's eyes flickered briefly. "Scanners indicate a large coastal settlement with significant power readings fifty miles to the northeast. However, I can't obtain detailed readings from this range."

Tyler opened the medical kit, staring at the silvery solution inside the nano-injector. Would this help recover his memory?

He pressed the injector to his neck and squeezed the trigger. A spreading warmth radiated from his throat, coursing through his body.

The green light scanned him once more.

"Good, Commander. The nanites are integrating with your internal systems and will begin repairs."

Tyler rubbed his face, letting out a short laugh. "You make me sound like a machine."

Conrad hesitated. "In many respects, biology resembles a mechanical system—take, for example, my neural network…"

Tyler raised a hand, stopping Conrad mid-sentence. "What was your original mission?"

"Survival," Conrad replied. "My orders were to protect the *Spero* from alien incursion en route to a classified location known only to Captain Alveroy and UEA command. It appears something went wrong."

Tyler laughed dryly. "You can say that again."

Conrad's face remained impassive. "It appears something went wrong."

"My logs indicate a catastrophic failure aboard the *Spero* shortly after arriving on this planet," Conrad said. "Visual records confirm a full jettison of habitation modules, terraforming equipment, cargo, and military escorts."

"We must have rained down an apocalypse on this planet," Tyler replied, shaking his head. "I've passed through more than one debris field."

Conrad's wireframe face looked momentarily troubled. "You are the first Terran life sign I have detected in a very long time, Commander. I tried to hail you, but your communicator was damaged. It's a miracle you heard me at all."

Tyler could still feel the warmth from the injection spreading through his body as a thought struck him. "The only Terran life sign? Your scanners must have picked up that large city to the south."

"That is correct, Commander. However, the life signs are quite different from yours. Genetically, they are more like distant cousins. I've observed several distinct varieties over the years."

"I've met a few of them," Tyler replied, nodding. "Mostly Balan."

"I will add that to my records, Commander," Conrad said, logging the information. As he spoke, his face flickered briefly, and the cabin lights dimmed.

"What was that?" Tyler asked, glancing around.

"My power reserves are limited. I've been on standby for a long time, and this activity has exceeded my daily allocation," Conrad replied.

Tyler felt a surge of panic. He was so close to getting answers.

"Conrad, listen. Is the *Spero* still in orbit? I need to know what happened—and if there are others like me. The Balan have mentioned finding 'Sleepers' over the years, recovered from stasis pods."

But before Conrad could reply, his face flickered and vanished from the screen. Tyler grimaced in frustration. He'd been so close.

A crackling voice sounded in his inner ear: "... power signature... coast... *Spero*..."

The nanites?

Tyler scanned the bridge, searching for a supply locker. He couldn't ignore the coincidence of hearing about the Temple of Spero again. If that temple held answers, he was determined to be ready.

Luckily, Conrad's bridge was well stocked. Each locker opened with a slight hiss, releasing a faint rush of sterile air. In one, he found a survival pack, which he strapped on. The lockers also contained a pair of fully charged sonic pistols and two hand stunners.

He hefted the hand stunners with a sense of satisfaction; they fit snugly around his knuckles, sealing securely. This was more his style.

Next, he buckled on and slid two sonic pistols into his thigh holsters. He was starting to feel prepared. This wasn't a shaman's prophecy or a warlord's riddle—it was the dependable clarity of military gear and his own instincts. And he trusted Conrad; that trust was ingrained in his training.

Survival. The word echoed through him. What had they been running from? The spaceport, the unfinished warship...

A memory surfaced—holding someone close. Amanda.

Amanda.

A wave of emotion crashed over him, raw and staggering. His wife. *Amanda.*

"Conrad!" he shouted, his voice rough with desperation. "Please—Amanda Tor. Was she on the *Spero?*"

The wall screen flickered faintly, and green letters appeared one by one, ending in a blinking cursor:

Yes.

14 SMILING

Shade sat on his throne, a deep frown creasing his otherwise smooth face. Roarc and Lady Dark had failed to check in. Perhaps he should have left an Immortal Guard to watch over them, but Tyler had a disturbing knack for spoiling his plans. If Roarc failed to deliver, he would need a new plan.

When Roarc fails to deliver.

Shade pushed the doubting thought back into the void. Perhaps it was time to assault the temple directly—he hadn't tried that in a few hundred years. Rising from his throne, he crossed to the map screen on the wall. A few gestures replaced the world map of Acrea with a satellite image of the temple and the growing city of Moonlit Waters. Before his death, Arral Alveroy had deployed mobile defense platforms around the temple, hidden in the ocean cliffs and Moonlit Hills. The platforms were so well concealed that Shade had no idea how many there were.

His lips twisted as he recalled his last attempt. He'd spent centuries scouring debris fields for supplies, amassing resources and manpower for the journey across the ocean. The partial remains of a Raptor-class marine transport had been his prize—its weapon systems intact and potent. Raptors were the spearhead of planetary assault: fast, armed to the teeth, and capable of carrying thirty-six marines into, or out of, planetary war zones.

But his Raptor had lasted all of thirty seconds against the Moonlit Waters defense grid. He'd lost countless Immortal Guards that day, unable to recover even a single incinerated body. The maddening part was that the Acreans didn't even understand the defense system; to them, it was simply the will of Spero protecting its city and temple.

Rubbish.

Shade drummed his fingers on his thigh, watching the live satellite feed of Moonlit Waters on his screen. *Where were the defense platforms drawing power?* Perhaps from the reactor of the colony transport itself, he mused, as potent as the day it had been built. No one knew how long those reactors could last, though his thermal scans of the vessel still registered off the charts.

Nothing I can do about that.

What he needed was an insider, someone who could move freely within the temple and around its keepers. None of his people would pass for temple devotees—not even Lady Dark could avoid scrutiny there.

But Tyler…

A slow, sinister smile spread across his face. He'd been approaching this all wrong. They didn't need to capture Tyler and force him to give up his command codes. No, Tyler could be coerced into shutting down the temple's defenses. Once Shade was in, he would have Tyler—and the entire Acrean populace—at his mercy.

Roarc and Lady Dark were overdue, but he was confident they would make contact before they engaged Tyler. Mazoris and his Sogra might be more unpredictable, but they were only a distraction. Tyler could lay waste to their lot with little effort. He was worth ten trained soldiers.

And if this plan failed, Shade still had something Tyler couldn't resist. But before he went with the ultimate bait, he had one more card to deal.

It was time to bring Colin into play.

***

Roarc's bloodlust finally ebbed with the last crack of felion bones. The last beast fell still, littering the ground around them with unmoving bodies. Mazoris clutched his abdomen, struggling to stem the flow of green blood from several deep wounds. Lady Dark knelt back on her heels, breathless but unharmed. None of the Sogra warriors had survived.

"I hate this place," Roarc growled, spitting blood into the dirt.

Lady Dark, panting, shook her loose dark hair. Amazement lit her slim features. "Hunted at every step," she murmured. "No wonder the Master left this land to the Acreans."

Mazoris gasped, collapsing heavily to the ground.

"Damn," Roarc muttered, noticing the spreading green pool beneath the Sogra.

Lady Dark sprang to her feet and rushed to Mazoris. His breaths came in ragged gasps, his lifeblood trickling steadily. She dug into her satchel, pulling out a crystal Roarc hadn't seen before—a polished obsidian stone swirling with purple mist. She gripped it in one hand, closing her eyes.

The wind picked up, stirring her hair. She raised her free hand, palm out, toward Mazoris. A hum reverberated through the ground as the wind stilled. A crackling ray of purple energy shot from her palm, enveloping Mazoris. He stiffened, hissing in agony as his wounds closed in searing bursts of energy.

The stench of burning flesh filled the air, and Roarc turned away, unwilling to watch the Sogra writhe under such violent healing. Lady Dark had been so gentle with him on the jump craft—this was something else entirely. He looked back to see a thin line of blood trickling from her nose.

As quickly as it had come, the purple energy vanished. Lady Dark swayed briefly, then reached up to dab the blood from her nose. She examined it for a moment before licking it from her fingers, a twisted smile on her face.

Roarc grinned. She was his kind of woman. It was a pity Shade had claimed her for his own twisted purposes. It wasn't for pleasure; Shade cared little for that. No, he thrived on breaking people, twisting them until they were tools at his disposal.

Time, Roarc thought, watching her. *Everything in its time.*

"We need to get moving," Roarc said.

Mazoris lay unmoving. Roarc couldn't tell if he was still breathing.

Lady Dark glanced down at Mazoris, then turned to Roarc. "He'll need some time to recover. You should carry him until he wakes."

Roarc sighed, slinging his wall shield over his left shoulder. He dropped his hammer, pommel up, next to Mazoris, then leaned down to hoist the surprisingly light Sogra warrior onto his right shoulder.

Grunting, he rolled his eyes. He was beginning to feel like a pack mule.

With his hammer secured, Roarc surveyed the scene, satisfied with the carnage they'd left behind. "Let's go," he said, setting a quick pace.

Lady Dark fell in behind him, pausing to gather a few objects from the fallen as they left the felion bodies scattered in their wake.

The morning was crisp, and mist clung to the hills, drifting in ethereal swirls down the valleys. Off in the distance, Roarc could see the outline of Arabellum and a structure that glinted in the Acrean sunlight. He decided to keep a wide berth; nothing good ever came from ancient wreckage.

Mazoris shifted uncomfortably on his shoulder, his scaled body digging into Roarc's skin. The Sogra warrior muttered something in his language, his head briefly lifting before he slipped back into unconsciousness.

Lady Dark quickened her pace to walk beside him, resting a hand on his forearm. "You're a good companion, Roarc," she said, her tone soft.

Roarc felt a warmth rise to his face at her touch and words. He coughed, trying to cover it with a note of command. "Couldn't just leave him there to be found. Besides, he'd blurt out everything about where we're headed to anyone who'd listen."

Lady Dark tilted her head thoughtfully. "But what *are* we doing, exactly?"

Roarc slowed, turning to look at her. Her head was tilted in that questioning way, arms slightly outstretched in a gesture of feigned helplessness.

"The Sogra are dead, Mazoris will be days recovering, and we don't even know where this man is," she continued.

Roarc couldn't argue. The Sogra warriors had barely survived the start of their mission, Mazoris was incapacitated, and their information on the target was vague at best. And to make matters worse, the map Shade had given him was destroyed during the battle.

"Do you still have the communicator Shade gave you?" Lady Dark asked.

Roarc reached into his pocket and handed her the broken remains. He flashed her the sheepish smile he reserved for when he was in trouble.

Lady Dark sighed, letting the fragments slip from her fingers to the ground. "So here we are," she whispered.

Roarc hung his head, then glanced back up, an idea forming. "I studied the map enough to get us to the extraction point," he said, adding with forced optimism, "We just need to stay out of sight until the jump craft circles back to pick us up."

Lady Dark clicked her tongue in irritation, a habit of hers when annoyed. "We are not going back empty-handed."

They continued in silence, Roarc pondering her words. He could hear her muttering under her breath, occasionally kicking at the rocky ground. The truth was, he'd be unable to enter the city if the man had made it there with his companions. Roarc only hoped they could intercept him on the road.

But doubt crept in as they moved toward the highway leading out of the canyonlands. The reports he'd heard painted a picture of a powerful enemy: a man capable of felling several Tekian guards, a scavenger band, and even a number of Yalonians. Winning this fight would require far more than they currently had.

Maybe it's all been exaggerated, he thought. *Perhaps the stories are just tales, or he's had a string of lucky escapes.* He'd never known anyone who could stand against a Tekian guard—let alone three of them.

As if reading his mind, Lady Dark moved beside him, her gaze steady. "Just get me close," she whispered. Her hand went to the bag of crystals at her side, clutching it tightly.

Those, Roarc thought, *would make all the difference.*

The rugged terrain finally gave way to open grasslands, where tall grasses swayed, nearly topping Lady Dark's head in places. Ahead, the highway curved in a strip of flattened, trimmed grass. It was too open for an ambush. Roarc signaled a halt while the grass was still dense, crouching down into the cool cover.

He dumped Mazoris unceremoniously onto the ground and rubbed his sore shoulder.

"We'll wait here and see who passes," he said, resting his chin and hands on his hammer's pommel as he gazed at the highway.

Lady Dark nodded, settling beside him. She pulled dried fish, cheese, and bread from her pack, and the two ate in silence, sharing a skin of water as they waited.

After a while, Lady Dark stretched out on her forearms, watching the road. "Why do you think Shade wants this man so badly?" she asked.

Roarc had wondered the same. When Shade wanted something this badly, he usually handled it himself.

"I'm not sure. The fact that Shade wants him alive means he's valuable," Roarc replied.

Lady Dark nodded thoughtfully. "Is it true he's a Tekian?"

"He fits the description. Tall, muscular, square-jawed, with short dark hair. They don't make Acreans like that, believe me," Roarc said with a wry smile.

"Sounds delicious," Lady Dark replied with a devious wink.

Roarc suppressed a chuckle. Shade still had a lot of work to do on this one.

"What's his name again?" Lady Dark asked.

"Commander Tor," Roarc murmured, testing the name.

"Commander? Now that's a strange first name!" Lady Dark giggled softly.

Roarc couldn't disagree; he'd never heard of anyone named Commander. Shade hadn't shared much about this man, only that he was dangerous and likely disoriented.

"I can handle him. Whatever it takes," Lady Dark said with a determined glint in her eyes.

The highway bustled with a steady stream of travelers in both directions. The ground was wide and packed hard from heavy use, and dust plumes rose in the distance as beasts of burden lumbered by, carrying goods piled high. The travelers, mostly Balan by their dress and shouts, moved in a colorful tide.

Roarc glanced over as Lady Dark settled into the grass, wrapping herself in her cloak. Her eyes closed, and her breathing slowed.

"Just resting my eyes," she murmured, cracking one eye open to look at him.

"Rest easy, Lady," he replied, turning his gaze back to the road.

He heard her shift with a soft sigh.

Roarc observed the passing travelers carefully. Among the tide of Balans, a few Acreans stood out. They were tall and slender, their hair in striking shades of blue and green, often worn long or tied back. Roarc found them strangely beautiful. He knew he'd likely kill a fair number of them before his work here was done. He shrugged off the thought.

The Acrean sun was high when the ground beneath him rumbled. Roarc peered cautiously over the grass toward the city, eyes widening. A massive tornado of debris was tearing through the outskirts of Arabellum. The highway was choked with people fleeing toward the canyonlands in a chaotic surge.

Perfect, Roarc thought, his mind racing. This was their chance to get closer.

He turned to wake Lady Dark but found her already sitting beside Mazoris, who blinked slowly, his reptilian eyes adjusting to the noise around them. The Sogra chief's head jerked as he listened.

"A great power has been unleashed. The land isss angry," Mazoris said.

Lady Dark handed Mazoris a steaming cup of crushed herbs and liquid, which he took with a slight bow before swallowing in one gulp. His face contorted in disgust, and he stuck out his forked tongue.

Lady Dark grinned. "It will make you feel better."

Mazoris grimaced. "If better I feel from that, sick I should ssstay," he muttered.

Roarc stared at the swirling cyclone, his pulse quickening. "Commander Tor is there," he said with absolute certainty. "That kind of power—it must be him."

Mazoris struggled to his feet, hissing and clicking a Sogra curse as he gazed at the maelstrom. "Weaponsss," he said before slinking off into the grass.

"Now where is he going?" Lady Dark asked, scowling.

"Weaponsss," Roarc replied, attempting to mimic Mazoris' tone.

Lady Dark quickly packed up their small camp and nodded to Roarc. "Lead on."

He nodded, hefting his maul as they stooped low and moved along the edge of the highway, weaving deeper into the city's outskirts. As they approached Arabellum, the grass thinned, giving way to buildings that rose abruptly from the open landscape. Roarc led them behind a barn, pressing himself against its mud-brick wall. Lady Dark pulled two cloaks from her pack, one larger than the other.

"This won't do much to disguise your size, but it might help from a distance," she said, handing him the larger cloak.

Roarc nodded, securing the cloak at his neck and pulling up the hood. Lady Dark did the same, and they peeked around the corner of the barn. The cyclone had intensified, and now armored bodies joined the flying debris as it whirled through the air. Moving quickly from building to building, they edged closer to the heart of the chaos.

Roarc could feel the wild energy emanating from just ahead. They needed only to cross a street and crouch behind a low wall for a clear view. Roarc launched himself across, sliding into cover in one smooth motion. Lady Dark moved soundlessly beside him, and they peered over the wall. The sight beyond was pure Armageddon.

A masked, robed figure was unleashing destruction on a contingent of Arabellum guards. Buildings lay torn from their foundations, some of them still smoldering. The figure clawed at its mask, seeming desperate to remove it, each attempt only making the cyclone stronger.

"That's not Commander Tor," Roarc shouted over the roar of wind.

"Look there!" Lady Dark pointed across the battlefield.

Roarc narrowed his eyes, pulling back his hood to shield his gaze from the sun. On a small rise stood a tall, broad-shouldered figure in armor that looked strikingly like that of the Immortal Guard. The man's helmet visor was down, but in his hands, unmistakable, gleamed a staff.

"Commander Tor," Roarc said, his throat dry.

Beside him, Lady Dark trembled, clutching her head with both hands. He turned to her, startled. All thoughts of their target vanished at the sight of her face—ashen and damp with sweat. She met his gaze, and he saw only raw terror in her eyes.

He reached out, gripping her shoulder with one massive hand. "Lady?"

"That staff," she rasped.

"Aye. It shimmers like a Tekian-forged blade," Roarc replied.

A huge chunk of rubble smashed into the wall shielding them, saving their lives as it shattered and sent them flying through the barn wall behind them. Roarc landed breathless, on his back amid the rubble. Dazed, he turned to look at Lady Dark.

She lay trembling, raising a shaky hand to brush debris from her hair.

"Balanite," she whispered in horror, staring through the gap in the wall, her eyes fixed on the figure wielding the staff.

And then she screamed—because the staff was staring back.

15 BURNS

Tyler spent the night on the bridge of the *UEA Conrad*, haunted by dreams of the past.

***

"Commander, we have to go—now!" an ensign's voice broke through the blaring alarm.

"Condition red, all hands to battle stations," an automated voice rang out.

Booted footsteps clattered over the grated floors of the *UEA Centaur*, the most heavily armed ship in the fleet, built for a single purpose: to buy Earth the precious minutes needed to launch its colony ships and evacuate the Sol system.

They had run the numbers, and the data was grim. The alien fleet was massive, unstoppable. Mars had been evacuated, but the incursion had obliterated the Martian settlements, razing the jump gate with minimal effort. Now, only one gate remained in the Sol system: Earth's. A few colony ships had escaped with military escorts, but the bulk of the fleet lay silently in lunar orbit, awaiting their final orders.

Commander Tor nodded at the ensign and paused at the access ladder. The faceless alien invaders were about to get more resistance than they'd bargained for.

The *Centaur* was a marvel of human engineering: state-of-the-art weaponry, experimental shielding, and a hull alloy charged directly by the reactor's energy. It would be one hell of a fight.

Taking a deep breath, Commander Tor ascended the ladder two rungs at a time, quickly outpacing the ensign as they climbed to the bridge. The *Centaur* had been designed purely for battle, with minimal comforts and a lean crew complement. The ship bristled with weapons, shields, and engines, optimized to survive the impossible.

Sweat trickled down the back of Commander Tor's neck as he climbed. There had been no time to install people-movers on this ship. Reaching the top rung, he stepped onto the bustling bridge.

His first officer turned from the captain's chair, noticing him immediately despite the chaos.

"Captain on the bridge!" he called.

The entire crew spun and saluted. Commander Tor returned the salute. "As you were," he said, and the bridge melted back into organized chaos. He crossed to his chair and grasped his first officer's hand.

"Lieutenant Commander Croyan," he greeted, a wry grin breaking through his focus. He had known Croyan most of his life; the man was his finest friend.

"Tyler," Croyan whispered, giving him a quick wink.

"Tactical—situation?" Commander Tor asked, settling heavily into his chair. He turned to the main screen across the bridge, his only true view of the stars outside. Two small, shielded portholes flanked the display, offering faint glimpses into space.

"Lieutenant, give me best range," he said.

A jumpy lieutenant tapped in a series of commands. Slowly, a formation of ships came into view.

Even at maximum magnification, they looked distant. Alien ships.

They were unmistakable—vast, jagged chunks of blackened crystal twisted into hulls. Rings of rotating debris, glowing with an eerie purple light, circled each craft. Scientists theorized the rotation created gravity, but no one really knew how these ships worked.

"Scanners up," Tyler ordered.

"How many ships do we have, Ensign Lang?" Croyan asked, eyeing a direct feed from the military satellites.

Lang squinted at his screen, adjusting a series of controls. "We've got ships. A lot of them. Looks like a vanguard formation."

"Signal the welcoming committee," Commander Tor said.

The communications officer opened a three-way split-screen with the captains of the *Centaur*'s escort frigates. "Begin the operation," Commander Tor instructed.

The three captains nodded and started issuing orders as the split-screen faded to a star field.

The *Centaur* waited as the frigates roared past on a direct course to intercept the alien vanguard, positioning themselves between the fleet and the jump gate. Commander Tor watched as Croyan, monitoring the battle feed, looked up to meet his gaze.

"Weapons hot," Croyan reported.

"Light 'em up," Commander Tor said, clenching his hand into a fist.

Hundreds of tiny flashes registered on the sensors as the three frigates unleashed a massive volley of torpedoes. They streaked through space, accelerating out of visual range.

The bridge fell into tense silence.

"Bring up the best visual we've got of the aliens," Commander Tor said.

The main screen shifted, displaying the alien ships as shadowy, menacing shapes against the stars.

"Impact!" Lang reported breathlessly.

The lead alien ship erupted in spinning fragments as the torpedoes slammed into it. Shattered crystal exploded, sending vaporized shards trailing into the void.

The *Centaur*'s crew watched without celebration; they knew the mission's grim reality. Stall the fleet, abandon Earth, and destroy the jump gate.

A second and third alien ship met the same fate, disintegrating under the torpedo fire.

Lang frowned at his readings. "Captain, the alien ships are changing course and spreading out."

Croyan let out a dry laugh. "Looks like they don't like being fish in a barrel."

Commander Tor, his expression steely, turned to the communications officer, Lieutenant Annabel Ralph. Her large brown eyes held a trace of fear, though she stood firm.

"Lieutenant, signal Captain Akane. Time to get up close and personal," he said.

The main screen flared with explosions as the frigates continued their assault. A relatively larger alien ship plowed forward, using debris from its shattered allies as a makeshift shield.

Croyan shook his head. "They're using their own dead for cover."

Commander Tor steepled his fingers, frowning at the screen. "An enemy with intelligence and strategy. Not a good combination when you're trying to save the human race."

Croyan patted his friend on the back. "We sent enough ships through the gate. Humanity's going to make it."

Commander Tor knew Croyan was trying to reassure him, but there was no certainty the aliens would stop at Earth. Destroying the jump gate might only delay them.

The new colonies were a mystery even to Tyler, classified on a need-to-know basis. What if these chosen systems were even more hostile than the aliens? Space had not been kind to humanity so far.

On Earth, there were those who believed the aliens might leave humanity alone, that this massive fleet was a mere show of strength. Most of them wore tinfoil hats and hid in bunkers. No, it was clear now what the aliens wanted: total annihilation.

Mars had been turned into a smoldering crater, every last probe and satellite obliterated. These aliens seemed driven to eradicate any trace of technology. Probes sent from Earth into alien space had always been shot down immediately, but at least the aliens had stayed on their side of the galaxy—until *Daedalus*.

Daedalus had been Earth's failed attempt to communicate with the aliens. Scientists had developed a mathematical language, the universal language of numbers. But when the *Daedalus* sent its message, it was annihilated within moments. Two hundred crew members, gone.

The only reply was a simple message that hijacked every receiver across the Milky Way:

We come.

"Sir, Akane has engaged the vanguard," reported a crew member.

Commander Tor closed his eyes briefly, steadying himself. "The battle is joined. Ahead full."

The bridge came alive with activity as Croyan issued orders.

"Let's see if the weapons tests live up to the hype," Commander Tor muttered.

The *Centaur* glided through space, blending into the starfield as Captain Akane led his group into the fray. His command included eight converted mining vessels and a cruise liner retrofitted as a last-resort attack ship, *The Akasuke*. The *Centaur* was Earth's only remaining purpose-built warship, but the makeshift fleet performed admirably.

"We're entering maximum weapons range," Ensign Lang announced.

"Spin up forward gauss cannons and target the ship using its dead as cover," Commander Tor ordered.

"Locked," several voices responded in unison.

"Buckle up," Croyan advised, the click of safety harnesses echoing through the bridge.

Commander Tor waited, the bridge settling into a tense silence. "Fire."

The *Centaur* shuddered as its oversized gauss cannons launched crackling alloy rounds into the void. The bridge lights dimmed momentarily as volley after volley roared from the cannons.

"Target and engage freely, Mr. Lang," Commander Tor said.

The alien vessel, shielded by the debris of its dead allies, took the first assault head-on. The gauss rounds punched through the crystalline hull, scattering iridescent shards that trailed like smoke in the darkness. The rounds continued, tearing through several more alien ships in its wake, each eruption sending clouds of debris into space.

The bridge crew watched in awe at the carnage unfolding on the main screen.

Commander Tor counted silently, knowing Lang's report would come soon. Just a few more ships…

"Sir, *The Akasuke* battle group is strafing several ships. Looks like they're doing some serious damage," Lang reported with a grin.

"Nothing compared to us," Croyan replied, a wry smile tugging at his lips.

Some of the bridge crew exchanged quiet words of excitement, but Commander Tor's expression remained grim as he watched the expanding field of debris.

This was too easy.

Sensing his mood, Croyan unbuckled his safety harness and approached the main screen, arms behind his back, brow furrowed in thought. He turned to Commander Tor. "Why aren't they firing back?"

Suddenly, the debris field rippled outward as a massive ship emerged, its metallic hull gleaming under the light of Earth's sun. At first glance, it looked almost human-made, but its sheer size and the eerie purple light spilling from countless openings betrayed its alien origin. Shaped like an inverted pyramid with a split base resembling jagged teeth, the ship was a monstrous sight.

"They had us shooting at decoys," Tyler whispered, his heart sinking.

A crackling red beam blasted into the *Centaur*, pinning the crew against their restraints. The main screen erupted into flame, spraying the bridge with white-hot debris. Croyan was flung against the far wall, hitting it with a sickening thud. Fires broke out around the bridge, and Croyan's cries of pain filled the air. Blood seeped from a gash on his forehead, trickling into his eyes as he struggled to stay conscious.

Commander Tor unbuckled his harness and raced to the pilot, who had taken the full brunt of the blast. Stepping over Lieutenant Annabel Ralph, who lay smoldering and unconscious on the deck, he reached the pilot slumped over the controls. Lifting the pilot's body with reverence, he rolled him gently to the floor.

Taking manual control, Commander Tor engaged the thrusters. The console flashed with a cascade of warnings as he struggled to stabilize the ship. Small explosions rattled the hull as debris from destroyed ships rained down on the crippled *Centaur.*

The jump gate loomed in the distance as the *Centaur* spun out of control. Thrusters fired erratically, and the main engine pulsed before falling dark. Another red blast struck the hull, causing power systems across the ship to short out in showers of sparks.

"Lang, we need cover fire! Fire ventral launchers and give me point defense," Commander Tor shouted over the blaring alarms.

"Aye, sir," Lang replied, his voice oddly calm amid the chaos.

Commander Tor routed tactical to the pilot screen, watching the nightmare unfold. A single alien ship remained—the new arrival—and it was decimating their makeshift fleet. *The Akasuke* roared past the massive vessel, peppering it with cannon fire, but the projectiles vaporized on contact with an invisible field around the alien ship.

"Sir, without attitude control, I can't get a lock on the target. We're just flailing here," Lang said.

Commander Tor glanced down at the ship's overview display. The first blast had torn a hole straight through the *Centaur's* midsection, decompressing the engineering deck and likely killing everyone there. Chief Engineer Erickson's face flashed briefly in his mind—a loss he'd mourn later. For now, he had to plug that breach.

"Ship-to-ship," Commander Tor ordered. "Get me Akane."

The bridge's damaged computer processed the command, and a wireframe image of the *Centaur's* AI, Helen, flickered to life on the bridge.

"Opening channel," she said with a crisp salute.

The comm crackled, then came Akane's gruff voice. "One hell of a beating we're getting, Tyler."

"Listen, Todd, I need you to help us plug a leak."

"We see it. You've got a hole in your side the size of a barn door," Akane replied. A farmer's son, he somehow managed to work his roots into everything he said.

"Can you patch it for us?" Commander Tor asked, as another red beam sliced narrowly past the hull.

"You've really pissed it off. Our engineer has a plan—try not to die. Akane out."

"Try not to die," Lang echoed, a hint of madness in his voice.

"Here we go," Commander Tor said, hitting the port thrusters to full power.

The additional thrust stabilized the *Centaur's* spin. Another red beam struck the starboard nacelle, vaporizing parts of the hull plating, but he fought to keep the ship steady as the engine flared erratically. Outside, *The Akasuke* came within inches of the *Centaur*, maneuvering to bridge the hull breach.

Akane was officially crazy.

Magnetic clamps locked the two ships together as *The Akasuke's* cargo arm swung into place, sealing the *Centaur's* gaping wound.

"Pressure equalized. Main engine, online," Helen reported, her voice steady despite the surrounding chaos.

"Hold on to something!" Commander Tor shouted, slamming the engines to full power.

Both ships lurched forward as another red beam lanced past, narrowly missing. The *Centaur's* aft cannon sputtered to life, and Commander Tor gritted his teeth against the force. The compromised anti-gravity systems left them fully exposed to the punishing G-forces.

"Aft cannon online," said Helen.

"Give 'em hell," Commander Tor growled.

The *Centaur* groaned as the aft cannon fired rounds of charged projectiles into the alien vessel. Unlike the cannons on *The Akasuke*, the *Centaur's* weapons had the power to punch through alien defenses.

Adjusting course, Commander Tor aimed for the center of the jump gate. He watched as each shot from the gauss cannon collided with the alien ship, the rounds tearing holes in its metallic hull. Trails of purple mist poured from the ruptures as the alien vessel pursued them.

"Helen, is the Glaive still operational?" Commander Tor asked.

"Aye, sir. Glaive emitters are functional and ready for a single charge."

"Jump gate in two," Lang announced.

The swirling maelstrom within the gate expanded as the ship drew near, a vortex of twisted physics beyond Commander Tor's comprehension.

"Charge the Glaive and deploy on my mark," he ordered, typing commands onto his console. As emergency lighting bathed the bridge in a hazy yellow glow, the scent of burnt circuitry lingered in the air.

Helen's hologram flickered, but her voice remained steady. "All available power routed to Glaive emitters."

Commander Tor watched the emitters' energy build. Another red beam struck them, but *The Akasuke* took the brunt of the blast.

"Glaive ready," Helen reported.

"Fire!" Commander Tor shouted.

A ghostly ribbon of light unfurled from the Glaive emitters, forming a spinning energy disk that raced toward the alien ship. The disk sprouted sword-like edges, spinning faster as it approached, and sliced cleanly through the enemy's hull. Explosions erupted within the alien ship, sending a cascade of debris and purple energy into the void.

"Aperture in ten seconds!" Lang shouted over the roar of the jump gate's spatial distortions.

Commander Tor typed in a code sequence he had memorized, then pressed his palm to the screen, feeling it scan his hand for verification. Instantly, the jump gate's center flared, widening as the metal ring began to buckle under the strain.

Behind them, the alien ship continued to rupture, its hull scarred by the Glaive. A bright flash indicated a critical systems failure, and a shock wave split the vessel in half. One of the jagged halves hurtled toward the jump gate's ring.

The *Centaur* and *The Akasuke* slipped silently through the collapsing vortex just as the alien wreckage crashed into the gate, twisting and tearing it apart. The jump gate imploded, dragging itself through the event horizon in a groaning, twisted collapse of metal and energy.

16 WALLS

Roarc watched Lady Dark as she drew ragged breaths, her teeth clenched in pain. Her eyes were closed, and her body writhed, as if fighting something unseen. The choker she always wore glittered with a strange light, casting fleeting shadows across her face. She muttered and cried out several times in a language Roarc couldn't recognize.

He propped her up gently, cradling her in his arms, and stroked her obsidian hair. The two were hidden within the collapsed remains of an ancient structure, and outside, the darkness deepened. The last patrol had passed over an hour ago, taking the final torchlight with them.

Balanite.

The word clawed at his soul. His people knew the legends well: the world had once been torn apart by a fire from the heavens, leaving silvery liquid wherever the skyfall touched. Most who came in contact with it perished, but a brave few saw its potential and brought it to ancient forges. There, the smiths had gone mad, crafting only a single blade: *Moira.*

"Roarc?"

Lady Dark's soft whisper pulled him back from his thoughts. Her weak smile met his gaze.

"I am here, Lady," he replied, his voice steady.

She struggled upright, reaching for the choker at her throat. "It…spoke to me."

Roarc frowned. "What do you mean it spoke to you?"

She shook her head, still groggy. "The Balanite. It told me to go home."

Roarc chuckled, his tone dry. "Home is a long way from here, Lady."

She held his gaze, her eyes bright with defiance. "It didn't mean Teka. It showed me a place I've dreamed of: green grass, azure streams, and a wild ocean stretching behind me. Home."

Roarc tilted his head, considering this. He'd always assumed she was taken during a raid as a child, yet the clarity of her vision was curious.

"Your home is Teka," he said firmly.

Her fingers moved to the choker again. "There were other voices, Roarc—more than I could count. They need something from me."

Alarmed, Roarc grasped her shoulders and shook her lightly. "You were thrown through a building and lost consciousness, Lady. There were no voices, only nightmares."

Her frightened expression hardened into anger. Roarc glanced down, realizing how roughly he was holding her.

"You can let go of me now," she said, her voice cold.

He immediately released her, palms open in apology. "Forgive me, Lady. You were delirious. I had to bring you back. You must understand."

She regarded him, her gaze steely. "Oh, I understand, Roarc. You are just like our Master. I'll show you no more kindness." She grabbed her belongings and fastened her bag of crystals at her hip.

"Where are you going?" Roarc asked, rising unsteadily.

She peeked out from their hiding place, scanning the street beyond. "To find Mazoris," she replied, disappearing into the night.

Roarc heaved his equipment over his shoulder and stumbled after her. A short distance away, he found her limping slightly under Yalonia's dull orange glow. She held a green crystal in her hand, its soft pulse guiding her steps.

He walked beside her in silence, the weight of what he'd done heavy between them. Roarc knew he'd crossed a line when he'd put his hands on her. Half-giants were not supposed to feel fear; that was part of why Shade prized them in his army. They were resilient and stoic. But for the first time, Roarc had felt fear—a fear of losing Lady Dark.

The realization prompted a sigh from deep within his chest.

"Oh, stop pouting," she muttered, tossing her head in exasperation.

Roarc lowered his gaze. "Forgive me, Mistress. Please."

She stopped and turned to face him, her green crystal glowing in her clenched fist. "You will never lay hands on me again, Roarc. That much is certain. I can endure our Master's cruelty, but I won't accept it from someone like you."

Someone like you.

Her words stung him. Only now did he begin to understand how deeply Shade's mistreatment of her had left its mark. Despite everything, Lady Dark still held onto a gentleness he hadn't seen in anyone else around them.

Roarc absentmindedly rubbed his chest where Shade had once struck him. Beneath the obedience Shade demanded, was there anything more in him? His life had seemed so simple before Arral—a painful existence, but one of certainty. Follow orders, avoid punishment. But here, beside Lady Dark under a crisp, clear night sky free of his homeland's smothering fog, he glimpsed something almost like freedom.

"Does it still hurt?" she asked, concern crossing her face before she quickly masked it.

Roarc managed a small smile. "No, Lady. It simply reminds me of the life we lead and the master we serve. I don't wish to be like him, but I've spent my life obeying his will."

She reached up, placing a hand on his arm, her eyes welling with tears. "I'm sorry, Roarc. I didn't mean what I said. You need kindness more than anyone. I won't withhold that over a rough shaking. Just promise me you'll never do it again."

Roarc bowed his head and laid his hand over hers. "You have my word, Lady."

Roarc cleared his throat and patted her hand. "Now, where's our lizard friend?"

Lady Dark raised her arm, holding the green crystal high. A thin green beam shot from it, casting a line of light through the city's outskirts toward the one place neither of them had wanted to go: the wreckage, looming like a dark monolith against the night.

"We should stay here and look for signs of the one we seek. I'm sure Mazoris will turn up eventually," Roarc said, trying to mask the worry in his voice.

Lady Dark nodded, tucking the crystal away. She pointed toward the towering walls of Arabellum. "You'll need to help me get past these."

"With pleasure," he replied with a grin.

Together, they wove carefully through the rubble-filled streets, staying in the shadows. The night patrol was sparse, and the guards kept to the city's clear paths, avoiding the debris-littered outskirts. Roarc and Lady Dark took advantage, slipping unnoticed to the city wall.

The wall was twice Roarc's height, a solid barrier. He peered at the masonry in the dim light, searching for any crevice that could aid their climb, but the smooth stones were without flaw.

"Typical Balan engineering," he muttered.

He hefted his maul, flipping it to the pointed side, and tapped the wall experimentally. A layer of baked red mud flaked off, revealing solid stone underneath. He glanced around and signaled Lady Dark to keep watch. With a firm grip, he struck the wall, driving the point into the stone. Dust and bits of debris fell away, leaving a small indentation.

Satisfied, he worked steadily, creating a series of small holds. When he had reached as high as his hammer could, he stepped back, admiring the makeshift ladder. He turned to Lady Dark and bowed with a theatrical flourish. She smiled, curtsying in mock formality, then began to climb.

Halfway up, she paused as if recalling something. She hung back, one hand holding her steady as she fished into her pouch. Roarc watched, his curiosity piqued. She murmured softly to an object she'd pulled out, something small and shiny, and then a strange sensation passed over him. His vision blurred, and suddenly he was staring down at himself from several feet up the wall. Panic gripped him as he flung his hands outward, feeling for balance.

"It's all right, Roarc," Lady Dark said calmly. "I've linked our sight. You'll hear me when I need to speak to you, just as I'll hear you. Now, head back to the ruins and stay hidden."

It took some effort, but Roarc managed to bring his vision back under control, though he felt a lingering pull toward Lady Dark's perspective. "Be safe, Lady," he murmured.

He slipped back through the rubble-strewn streets, avoiding patrols with ease until he reached the ruins where they'd hidden before. Inside, all was still. He made his way to a back room, settling in the darkness. Bracing himself, he let his concentration lapse, surrendering once more to the strange bond. A jolt hit him, and he was glad to be seated when the disorientation passed.

Lady Dark had cleared the wall and was moving through a narrow alley between squat, stone buildings. Her breathing was smooth, steady, and oddly close, as though it were his own. She moved in silence, pausing occasionally to listen. Voices drifted from an open window above.

"...masked man nearly tore the city gates down around us!"

The noise of a tavern washed over the voice, muting parts of the conversation. Roarc strained to hear.

"That may be, but if it hadn't been for Razmal and his strange friends, we'd have lost many," the voice continued.

"I hear Lord Ember is hosting them at his villa tonight," shouted another, and laughter followed.

"So, what did they do with that robed fool?"

A pause. "They threw him in the Pits."

The laughter died, and the noise within the tavern dwindled to a murmur, only to rise again in a fresh round of toasts and cheers. Roarc raised his eyebrows, rubbing his chin thoughtfully. The man responsible for the chaos was in the arena—likely the one they were after.

"I'm heading that way now," Lady Dark's voice broke into his thoughts as if she could read them.

Could she? Panic bubbled up as he tried not to dwell on his feelings for Lady Dark. The more he fought them, the stronger they grew—images of her laugh, her silhouette, her dark hair swaying. He forced himself to think of Shade instead, a thought that effectively cleared his mind.

Lady Dark continued her stealthy approach, using her agility and crystals to evade the patrols. She moved with light steps, slipping between buildings, crouching behind statues, and lying flat in the shadows. Roarc felt an odd tingling each time she gripped one of her crystals, briefly losing their shared sight with each touch.

The night stretched on as Lady Dark reached the sprawling coliseum at the heart of Arabellum. Its large gates were locked, barring her entry. She circled the structure silently, testing each side door she passed. All were bolted shut.

"Any ideas?" she whispered.

Roarc considered as her gaze swept over the cobblestone courtyard surrounding the arena, pausing on statues of victorious gladiators. He noted one area of the ground that looked especially worn, dipping into shadow.

"Wait. Right there, Lady," he said, realizing belatedly that she couldn't see where he pointed.

After a few exchanged directions, she found the shadowed spot. Crossing the cobbles in silence, she slipped into the waiting darkness and landed in a crouch, her hand pressed to the cool stone. Before her was a bone grate reinforced with thick plaster, sealing off an entryway that led beneath the arena. Through the bars, she glimpsed torchlight down a narrow passageway.

"You mustn't make a sound," Roarc cautioned.

"Who's there?" Lady Dark whispered sharply, her voice strained with fear.

The bond between her and Roarc abruptly unraveled, leaving her mind in silence.

Back in the ruins, Roarc cursed under his breath as soldiers entered the building, torchstone held high. His massive bulk couldn't hope to escape notice, so he remained still, his maul ready at his side, his shield a reassuring weight on his back. He held his breath and waited.

The torchlight fell on him like dawn breaking over the horizon. The lead soldier gasped as Roarc rose to his full height, grinning with the intensity of a hunter. The next instant, the soldier hurtled through the air, crashing against a pile of stones with a dull crack. The rest of the patrol—five in total—stared at their downed comrade, then into the gloom where Roarc waited.

A deep, rumbling chant rolled from the shadows as Roarc began to rhythmically beat his maul against his shield. The soldiers didn't understand his words, but the intimidating rhythm and the sight of his towering form stepping from the ruins were enough. One of the soldiers blanched and, with a strangled cry, turned and ran toward the city walls.

The remaining three soldiers raised their weapons, obsidian blades gleaming in the moonlight. Each held a hide buckler, and their stances spoke of experience. They shouted to each other, hurriedly strategizing.

Roarc kept his chant going, savoring the way the soldiers assumed he was a mindless brute.

"We rush him together!" growled the soldier on the left, his words muffled by his chitin shell helm.

"No, we need to draw him out first," another countered.

A wicked grin spread across Roarc's face; he understood enough Balan to follow their plan. "How about I make it easy and bring the fight to you!" he bellowed.

The soldiers flinched as Roarc lunged forward, swinging his maul to the left while his shield hissed through the air on the right. His shield struck one soldier with brutal accuracy, shattering the armor and sending the man to the ground. The maul caught the second soldier's blade mid-swing, wrenching it from his hands. The third soldier thrust his blade toward Roarc's midsection. Roarc twisted, taking a glancing blow along his side as he felt a warm trickle of blood.

"Not smart," Roarc growled, raising his shield to block another strike. With a sharp bash, he sent the third soldier sprawling. Two of the Balan soldiers, though bruised and battered, were on their feet again, circling him warily.

Roarc didn't fall for their baiting feints. Recalling his training, he slung his shield onto his back, assuming the stance his master at Midnite Waters had called *Turtle*. Now his back was secure, freeing both hands to wield the maul.

With a roar, he advanced on the soldier with the cracked armor. The man ducked nimbly, and Roarc's maul swept past harmlessly. Off-balance, Roarc staggered, and the second soldier took advantage, slicing a line through the leather on Roarc's shoulder.

They were skilled. But Roarc was better.

The boldest of the soldiers approached with a flourish, his obsidian blade a blur as it danced toward Roarc's hauberk. But Roarc anticipated the movement and clamped a massive hand around the soldier's sword arm, twisting it until bones snapped. The soldier's scream echoed as he collapsed, fainting from the pain.

One left.

Roarc turned, just in time to see the last soldier fleeing into the night.

17 BLOOM

Tyler awoke with a start, unsure of his surroundings. Light filtered through the UEA Conrad bridge's many skylights, and the display consoles sat silent. *Was the ship dead after all this time?* he wondered. The Conrad AI had pushed its power reserves, and perhaps it only needed time to recharge. The reactor on UEA destroyers had a thousand-year half-life, so it was possible a damaged power distribution unit had ruptured in the crash. Schematics of the PDU flickered through his mind as he rubbed his temples; his memory was returning.

Something else was flickering back to life: his right eye. The implants were coming online. Tyler groaned, getting to his feet and stretching, feeling stronger than he had in ages. Now that he had memories again. He helped himself to a vacuum-sealed breakfast of eggs, bacon, and a steaming cup of instant coffee. It wasn't quite the real thing, but it was the best he'd tasted since waking up on Acrea.

...*Tyrant.*

The voice startled him, and he nearly dropped his cup. A thin ribbon of silver light swirled in from the hatch, leading to the ship's main passageway. He held up a hand, warding off the light as his Warquarter pulsed familiarly beneath his grip.

Polaris.

"If you're here, who's guarding the prisoner?" he asked the air.

Thoughts and images streamed from Polaris, piecing together a story. The prisoner had been taken along with a woman with dark hair. Details were unclear, but the Balanite's concern was unmistakable.

Tyler collected his gear, donned his combat helmet, scanned the bridge once more, and hurried out the hatch. He slid down the corridor, using his feet and free hand to slow his descent and keep Polaris from banging against the walls. In minutes, he was outside, stepping into the morning light over the grasslands. He turned to seal the hatch, the sound of air pumping from the interior bringing a smile to his face. *The UEA Conrad was still alive.*

With Arabellum in mind, Tyler set off, the warmth of Acrea's sun and the buzz of insects easing his thoughts despite the dangers ahead. A strange smell, sharp and unwashed, hit him a short distance from the Conrad. Polaris surged in his hand, warning him they weren't alone.

A small globe filled with purple mist zipped past his face. Tyler cursed, slamming down his face mask as another globe struck his visor and exploded in a spray of toxins. Thankfully, UEA combat helmets filtered most substances and were even rated for brief underwater use. An angry, bipedal lizard brandished a bone club still covered with bits of meat and hide, charging him with both clawed hands.

Tyler parried the club's swing, and Polaris shattered it into fragments. The lizard staggered back, then sprang up with the aid of its tail, hissing a string of what sounded like curses.

Polaris beamed smugly. It knew what the creature was. A Sogra.

Sogra?

Apparently, that was all Polaris was going to reveal about his opponent. Tyler hoped the translation would continue to work.

"Hello. I don't mean you any harm," he said, holding his arms out in a gesture of peace.

The Sogra froze, its neck and head tilting birdlike as it listened. "You speak…Sogra?" it rasped.

Tyler nodded, smiling warmly as he leaned Polaris against his chest.

"Yes, I am Tyler. I won't hurt you."

The creature laughed, a strange mix of hiss and low chuckle. "Sssays the Tekian with his battle ssstaff."

"I am not a Tekian!" Tyler snapped.

The Sogra tilted its head with a savage grin. "You are the one the master seeks, yesss?"

Tyler paused, recalling the Tekians in the clearing who had orders to capture him. Could this Sogra be referring to the same person?

"Who is this…master?" Tyler asked.

The Sogra blinked, craning its neck as if listening. Seeming satisfied, it relaxed slightly but kept a wary eye on Tyler and his Warquarter. "Shade," it answered, flinching as if even saying the name might bring harm.

The creature looked scarred and battered, with various beads, bones, and bits of jewelry jingling as it shifted. Tyler felt a twinge of sympathy.

"What should I call you?" he asked.

The Sogra hesitated, then replied, "Mazoris, clan chief and first of the Blue Throat Clutch."

Tyler's smile grew. "Mazoris, then. You don't normally jump out at strangers on a whim, do you? What are you looking for?"

Mazoris regarded him carefully. "You."

The Sogra moved with alarming speed, whipping his tail into Tyler and his Warquarter, sending Polaris tumbling into the grass. Clawed hands slashed at him, and jagged teeth bit deep into the armor around his neck. Incredibly strong, the Sogra flung Tyler to the ground. Tyler scrambled to his feet as Mazoris charged, growling. With a sharp crack, Tyler met the attack, his lowered shoulder slamming into the Sogra's scaled chest, forcing the creature to stumble back, clutching broken scales.

Mazoris circled Tyler, hissing and drooling in anger. Tyler couldn't believe it—everything on Acrea seemed out to get him. Never in his wildest dreams had he imagined a human-sized lizard trying to end his life. He needed answers. It took all his restraint not to draw his pistol and end the creature then and there. Instead, he chose to settle things the old-fashioned way.

Mazoris rushed forward, but Tyler moved with practiced ease, sidestepping the charge and bringing an elbow crashing down on the Sogra's back. Mazoris hissed in pain as he hit the ground. He staggered back up, green blood trickling from the scales on his chest, clawing at the air in front of Tyler. A powerful punch to the face rocked Mazoris back, and another blow to the snout sent him sprawling into the dirt.

Dazed, Mazoris looked up at Tyler, one eye swollen shut while the other stared blankly at the sky. Tyler stretched his arm out, and Polaris flew smoothly from the grass into his hand. He pressed the Warquarter against Mazoris's throat, just enough to make the Sogra wheeze.

"Now," Tyler said, "you were saying something about this Shade character."

"He… is immortal," Mazoris gasped.

An immortal. Tyler shook his head. That was fantasy. No one lived forever, not even with cold sleep—at least not consciously. He recalled the terrifying holos from his cadet days, showing test subjects emerging from suspended animation in bouts of madness.

Mazoris struggled against Tyler's boot, gasping for breath. Tyler shifted Polaris slightly, easing off his throat but keeping his boot firm. "Why does your master want me?" he asked.

"The master need not explain himself," Mazoris growled.

This was going well.

Tyler sighed and glanced toward the distant city. The rough, red walls of Arabellum were visible on the horizon, and dots of travelers moved along the road.

He looked down at the defeated Sogra, finding the creature's smell almost unbearable, a mix of rotting meat and stale fish. "I can't have you following me," he said, shaking his head.

With a single swing of Polaris, he cracked Mazoris on the side of his head. The Sogra's eyes rolled back, and he fell unconscious. Tyler quickly surveyed the area to ensure nothing else would try to eat the downed lizard.

As he finished, a deep horn blast shattered the morning's stillness. The sound echoed from Arabellum, repeating several times in an unmistakable alarm. Tyler glanced down at Mazoris.

"Your master will have to try harder," he muttered, breaking into a run toward the city.

The grasslands flew by as the horn continued to blare. Tall grass rose over his head as he ran across the uneven ground. To his right, the mountains loomed jagged and menacing in the morning light. The dewy grass dampened his legs, and the smell of fresh earth filled the air. Ahead, a line of travelers from the coast and mountains had halted at the city's closed gates.

"Not again," Tyler sighed.

Closed gates meant his target might still be within the city walls. Tyler pushed through the crowd, pulling his cowl over his head to cast his features in shadow. He towered over the Balan traders, who muttered complaints at being blocked by his bulk.

A Balan guard noticed him and jumped in recognition, shouting to someone out of sight before gesturing for Tyler to approach. The crowd pressed around him in anticipation. The pungent scent of livestock and unwashed bodies thickened in the warmth of the day, blending with the dust hanging in the air and punctuated by coughs and bleating animals. Tyler stopped a few feet from the gate and waited.

The massive stone door opened just enough for him to slip inside, then closed with a thunderous boom, silencing the frustrated traders outside.

Inside, a grim-faced contingent of soldiers awaited him. One soldier stepped forward and saluted.

"The Dominus requests your presence immediately," the soldier rumbled.

Tyler kept his hood low, nodding. *No need to alarm anyone.* The soldiers led him through Arabellum's ordered streets, every corner meticulously laid out, as though the city had been chiseled from a grand design. The red-stone buildings blurred past, all pointing toward the massive arena at the city's center. As they approached the Ludus, Tyler couldn't shake an ominous feeling. He glanced toward the arena, sensing something dark and out of place. Polaris pulsed lightly at his side, but remained silent. Tyler slowed as they reached a split in the road— the path up to the Ludus on one side, the arena's descending slope on the other. Darkness seemed to pool in the lower path.

"Change of plan," he said, gripping Polaris tightly.

The gate soldier paused, confusion flickering in his eyes. "Sir, we must report to Dominus Ember," he insisted.

Tyler shook his head. "There's no time."

"But the prisoner—" the guard began.

"—is in danger, along with the one who set him free," Tyler said, suspecting the dark-haired woman's involvement in the prisoner's escape.

A flickering shadow slipped past one of the arena's barred entrances, trailing wisps of oily black mist. A name stirred in his mind, half-formed memories brushing against his thoughts. Polaris, now humming with nervous energy, tugged at Tyler's hand, confirming his suspicion.

"It's a Baboulas," Tyler murmured, an unspoken warning ringing in his voice.

The soldiers went pale. One dropped his weapon, and several turned, fleeing toward the Ludus, their boots thundering up the hill.

"Impossible," the gate soldier gasped. "They're only stories, tales we tell to frighten children!"

"This one is very real," Tyler replied, freeing his pistols from their holsters. "Stay behind me."

With a swift motion, Tyler sprinted down the hill, Polaris flowing over his armor like liquid metal, strengthening his limbs and lending him agility. He fired a series of sonic bolts at one of the arena's barred archways, the blasts shattering iron bars like brittle glass. Ducking through the opening, he crossed into the tunnel, his footsteps and breathing echoing against the stone walls. The shadowy passage opened into the arena's vast field, sunlight glaring down on him as he emerged into the center.

Across the field, shadows lurked, and a robed figure lay motionless. Tyler scanned the stands rising around him, the stone benches stretching up in tiers, bound by ancient stone walls. Somewhere beneath the layered darkness, something primal watched him. A faint, mocking cackle echoed through the stands, drawing his gaze to the shadows on the far side of the arena.

A pair of blood-red eyes gleamed from the dark recess of a tunnel, and slowly, a horrifying sight emerged: a dark-haired woman, limp and suspended in a mass of writhing tendrils. The Baboulas had her, bound in vaporous black coils. Her back arched at an impossible angle, her arms hung uselessly, and her green eyes stared skyward, unfocused. Her necklace—a silver choker with a black gem, now pulsing with an eerie light—seemed to attract the darkness itself, as though it held some hidden power the Baboulas craved. The creature's fanged mouth opened, spilling a string of guttural sounds like cracked obsidian scraping against stone.

Tyler advanced toward the fallen figure, holstering one pistol but keeping the other trained on the creature. He knelt, brushing sweat-damp hair from the man's forehead and feeling for a pulse. *Ralon was alive.*

"If you have any wind left in you, now's the time," Tyler murmured, but Ralon lay silent, unresponsive.

Tyler stood, both pistols drawn again. He eyed the Baboulas, noting the dark tendrils reaching from Lady Dark's choker toward the creature, as though pulled by some unseen force.

"Let her go," Tyler commanded, his voice steady as he pointed his weapon toward the demon.

The Baboulas laughed, a sound that twisted his stomach. It stepped into the light, shadows roiling over its body, revealing patches of sickly, scale-covered flesh beneath. The creature hissed as sunlight burned its flesh, forcing the shadows to regrow and patch over exposed skin. Its red eyes narrowed in mock amusement.

Tyler smirked. "Not just a shadow, are you?" He squeezed the triggers, unleashing a burst of sonic bolts that streaked across the field. The Baboulas shrieked, the bolts tearing chunks of shadow from its form, scattering smoldering pieces across the arena floor. The creature howled, its grip on the lady tightening as it dragged her closer, pulling her into the protection of the shadows.

Tyler kept firing as he moved, every blast lighting up the tunnel walls. Smoke and fragments of dark energy splattered along the ground as he crossed the threshold of the tunnel. Holstering his pistols, he brought his fists together, his hands engulfed in blue and white flames. With a powerful charge, he barreled into the creature, slamming it against the tunnel wall. It shrieked as his charged knuckles met its scaly hide, and one of its clawed hands raked across his chest, throwing him back.

Tyler staggered, breathless, as another blow from its massive claw struck his shoulder, forcing him to one knee. Polaris vibrated with power, the balanite energy stitching his armor together. Tyler dodged the next blow, the Baboulas's claws leaving deep gouges in the stone wall. Rolling around the creature, he used its own bulk to gain momentum and delivered a sharp punch to its head. His fist met scaly resistance, sending a shockwave of heat through his arm.

Momentarily disoriented, the Baboulas swung blindly as Tyler's fists crackled with renewed force. He unleashed a rapid succession of punches, each blow sparking blue fire. Shadows burned away with each hit, filling the tunnel with smoke and the stench of charred flesh. He could feel memories rising as he fought, visions of training sessions, of instructors shouting at him to *aim through the target, never stop*. With each punch, those lessons spurred him forward.

"Your power is in her necklace, isn't it?" Tyler said between punches, watching the Baboulas recoil at the mention of the choker. He could see now—the creature had been drawn to it, sensing the strange darkness it held. *But why?*

With a snarl, the Baboulas turned, attempting to shield its body as its clawed hands swiped desperately through the air. Tyler sidestepped, aiming a sharp kick to its leg, feeling the sickening crack as bone shattered under his boot. The Baboulas crumpled, its head striking the wall, its body twisted awkwardly.

Polaris flashed into Tyler's hand, humming with fierce intent. As he held his Warquarter ready, he saw the Baboulas's eyes narrow with something almost like fear. Its shadows shrank, retreating as he raised his weapon.

"Your time's up," he muttered, thrusting the Warquarter into its exposed throat.

The Baboulas's form convulsed, a final guttural cry escaping its throat as Polaris cut through shadow and flesh alike. It slid down the wall, leaving a smoldering black mark that sizzled against the stone. The creature's body twisted, scales popping and melting into darkness until it collapsed into a spreading pool of inky shadow, boiling away.

Within moments, nothing remained but a twisted black outline, burned into the floor—a dark stain, forever marking the place of its defeat.

18 YOU CAN COUNT ON ME

Roarc had spent hours evading the Balan patrols. Quick for a half-giant, he used every tattered building and crumbling wall to conceal his bulk. He kept his hood pulled low, avoiding the torchlight that could glint off his golden eyes and give him away. The Balan were persistent, if nothing else. Luckily, they hadn't yet brought out the hounds he knew were kenneled deep in the arena's warrens. One sniff of a half-giant, and the beasts would be baying and tracking him through the city.

Several times as he hid, he felt faint echoes of Lady Dark's presence, an unsettling whisper in his mind. She was moving deeper into the city, her progress slow and erratic. Something had drawn her away from their mission. He had sensed her fear—a jolt of it like a knife's edge. Now, there was only silence where her presence had lingered.

Roarc growled softly, crouched behind a half-wall with a view of the rear gatehouse of Arabellum. He'd been playing cat-and-mouse with the city patrols, stalling and waiting, hoping for a sign from Lady Dark. Dawn would be coming soon.

"You know," a voice slipped into his mind, smooth and dark, *"your scent is one of the more turbulent I've come across in some time."*

Roarc's heart hammered as he turned to find a cloaked figure watching him from the shadows. He barely suppressed a snarl, recognizing the creature—a wolfish Erew with a dark gray hood pulled over his ears.

"The name's Zuh'Erg," the Erew thought, waving a clawed hand in a dismissive greeting. He padded through the rubble, every movement unnervingly silent.

With a bellow, Roarc charged, swinging his maul in a sweeping arc toward the Erew. Zuh'Erg's form blurred, shadows bending around him, and the maul whistled harmlessly through empty air. Roarc staggered as a claw tapped him on the shoulder from behind. He swung around with his shield, only to find nothing there but darkness.

"Come now, half-giant, let's you and I talk," the voice chuckled in his mind. *"You're separated from your companions in openly hostile territory. Hardly the fearsome threat you make yourselves out to be."*

Roarc gritted his teeth, lowering his maul but feeling his rage rising, an ember ready to ignite.

"Better," the Erew's voice crooned in his mind. *"There's much more at stake here than you realize. The man you hunt holds the key to our salvation."*

Zuh'Erg stepped from the shadow of a squat, broken tower. The dim light from Yalonia threw his figure into a silhouette, but his eyes gleamed in the darkness, sharp and knowing.

Roarc squared his shoulders. "We're here to do the master's will. There are many of us—I'm just a scout," he said, letting his words carry an air of bravado.

Zuh'Erg chuckled, scratching his silver mane. Roarc's eyes narrowed as he noticed the Erew's cut bindings, frayed around his wrists.

"What kind of know-it-all shadow walker gets himself captured?" Roarc sneered.

"The kind who intends to be," Zuh'Erg's thoughts rippled with amusement, a sly glint in his lupine eye.

Roarc sighed, glancing around. The torchlight from the nearest patrol was still a safe distance away. He had a few moments.

"Sit," Zuh'Erg offered, nodding to a piece of fallen masonry. Reluctantly, Roarc leaned his weapons against the wall and sat down, wary but intrigued.

The Erew crouched across from him, tail twitching as he rested comfortably on his haunches, his gaze unwavering. *"Tell me, half-giant,"* he began, his tone surprisingly kind, *"what do you know of this man you hunt?"*

Roarc struggled to focus on Zuh'Erg, the Erew's outline seeming to shift in the flickering light. He forced himself to stare past him at the ruined structure beyond, deciding he'd play along, at least for a while.

"Only that he looks like a Tekian," Roarc answered slowly. "Dark hair, dark eyes, heavy build. Answers to the name Commander."

Zuh'Erg's gaze bore into him, sharp and unsettling.

Roarc shifted, meeting the Erew's eyes before looking away. Something about those yellow eyes unnerved him.

"So, your master sends a half-giant, a Sogra, and the dark lady to bring back one Tekian fugitive?" Zuh'Erg scoffed, his words like a growl in his mind.

"It's not my job to understand the orders. I am merely to follow them," Roarc replied.

"You didn't bring nearly enough," Zuh'Erg said, amusement in his tone.

Roarc's eyes widened. "What do you mean?"

The Erew raised an eyebrow—or what might have been an eyebrow, if Erew had them. Roarc's mind churned, the Erew's words unsettling. Lady Dark had gone silent, the Sogra had scattered. Not enough indeed.

Torchlight flickered closer, and Zuh'Erg rose. He paced the narrow space, his movements quick and fluid. *"You've stirred up quite the nest here, half-giant,"* he mused.

Roarc didn't know what a "nest" was, but it didn't sound good.

"There's a great deal you need to understand," Zuh'Erg said. *"But there's no time. Your master cannot succeed, Roarc. If he does, he will destroy Acrea and every living creature, including you and your precious lady. The man you seek—he is a Sleeper."*

The word echoed in Roarc's mind, an ancient warning.

Roarc frowned, brow furrowed. Sleepers were the stuff of legends, figures who had awakened in forgotten places, wielding fire and strange weaponry. Each story was the same—Shade hunted them down, and the Sleeper was lost. The last Sleeper, though, had bought them peace. She had prevented Shade from setting foot on the mainland of Arral.

But could this Sleeper be the one to finally break the master's hold?

Zuh'Erg's wolfish grin widened as if he sensed Roarc's thoughts. For a moment, the possibility sparked hope, a dangerous thing in a world under Shade's rule.

Or was it a trick?

Roarc's hand moved to his chest, fingers tracing the old scar that had bound him to his master's service. He could feel his loyalty wavering, the flicker of something long buried stirring within him.

"*Look, half-giant,*" Zuh'Erg continued, his voice sliding through Roarc's thoughts. "*It's not as though I'm worried you'll succeed in capturing him. Your 'Sleeper' made short work of Mazoris, and the felions took care of the rest of your rabble well enough.*"

Roarc's gaze fell to the ground, jaw clenched as he absorbed the news. He wasn't surprised to hear about Mazoris. Of course, instead of finding weapons, Mazoris had stumbled into a Sleeper's path. His chest tightened. *A Sleeper.* They had been sent to hunt something far more dangerous than a Tekian.

"What of the Lady?" he whispered, barely able to look up.

Zuh'Erg paused, pacing halted. For a moment, the torchlight caught the shadows clinging to his fur, and he met Roarc's gaze with a look of wary understanding.

"*You may face a difficult choice with her,*" Zuh'Erg began, his voice thoughtful. "*Her scent has changed, carrying something darker—*"

A sudden shout pierced the quiet, and Zuh'Erg disappeared in a blur, vanishing before Roarc could even blink. The torchlight brightened around him, and a shout of alarm split the night, inches away. Roarc ducked low, clutching his maul, and waited.

A shout from another part of the city redirected the patrol, their steps and flickering lights retreating from his hiding place. Roarc didn't hesitate. Scooping up his equipment, he moved swiftly into the night, slipping back into the shadows.

Lady Dark would have to fend for herself. He had to reach the extraction point—Shade's Immortal Guard would be waiting, and they'd report the situation back to the master immediately. Whatever punishment followed, it would be brutal. *But without help, they were doomed.* If he didn't check in, no one would come to aid Lady Dark, and he'd have no way to save her if she was alive.

He moved swiftly through the dim grasslands, allowing himself to straighten only when the distant torches of the city dwindled behind him. Dawn touched the eastern sky as Yalonia set in the south, and he reached a clearing about a mile from Arabellum. The grass was flattened by some unseen force, and a single figure stood within the circle, armored and unmoving, as if frozen.

"Roarc." A voice, cold and sharp, called his name.

The chill that emanated from the Immortal Guard was bearable as Roarc stepped into the clearing's edge. It was strange—Immortal Guards didn't speak, at least not in his experience. Their silence was legendary.

"Alone?" the voice asked, and Roarc heard the slightest edge of reproach.

Roarc approached carefully, unsure of how to address the Immortal Guard. He had heard that the cold suit each guard wore was a life-support system, sustaining the wearer in a state of suspended life.

"I am Colin," the armored man said with a stiff nod, a strange rasp in his voice. "Report," he ordered.

Roarc's words tumbled out in a rush—the Sogra's fate at the felions' hands, the magic that had erupted through the city, Mazoris's disappearance, Lady Dark isolated and alone, and his own relentless pursuit by the patrols.

"Ah." Colin's response was calm, almost indifferent, and Roarc flinched at the coldness in that single syllable.

Colin regarded him in silence for a moment, the reflective visor concealing any hint of expression. His presence was unsettling, his stare penetrating, as if he could see the doubts churning in Roarc's mind.

"This certainly complicates matters," Colin said with a metallic sigh. "I suppose there's no avoiding it. Another jump craft will be needed. We can't afford to lose them, you know." He tapped something on his forearm, fingers moving with unnatural precision.

The jump craft above them whirred to life, lifting and speeding off toward the distant walls of Arabellum. A series of bright flashes lit up the sky as the craft fired on the city, explosions reverberating from a distance.

Roarc felt a tingling along his arms, his skin prickling with an unfamiliar heat. Then, without warning, a crackling bolt of green energy split the sky from east to west. In a flash, the jump craft simply ceased to exist, leaving no trace. The air was still and silent, thick with the scent of ozone. The afterimage of the bolt burned in Roarc's vision, and he blinked rapidly, trying to clear the white lines etched across his sight.

Colin was unperturbed. "Now, then," he said with unsettling cheer, turning toward Arabellum. "To the city."

Roarc stared as the armored man strode forward, the grass curling and withering beneath his feet.

***

In the heart of his stronghold, Shade brooded. "Another perfectly good jump craft, gone!" His voice rang through the darkened throne room as he slammed a gloved fist down on the console beside him. The craft's disappearance had been abrupt, yet he hadn't lost hope—the automated defenses around the temple remained undiminished. *Damn that engineer and her constant meddling.* He'd kill her again if he could, if only to be rid of her interference.

A sour mood had followed his attempts to reach the AI orbiting high above Acrea. It remained obstinate, ignoring his commands to descend. His patience was running thin. Worse still, laughter, a dark and mocking tone, rose within him, turning his blood cold.

"Be silent!" he shouted into the empty room.

The laughter faded, but its presence lingered just beyond his grasp, taunting him, a constant thorn in his thoughts. It was not enough that the Sleeper was eluding him. His own plans were failing, fragmenting before they could bear fruit.

The Sogra had served their purpose as cannon fodder, and the half-giant had at least managed to locate the Sleeper's likely whereabouts. Colin was on the ground, and Shade pitied anyone foolish enough to cross that particular member of the Immortal Guard. It was rare that an Immortal retained any emotional residue, but Colin was different; his anger was a cold, calculating force, sharpened by the toll of endless years.

The Immortal Guard—his greatest achievement and, ironically, his most fragile. He had never anticipated the complexity of sustaining them. His own blood was potent, yes, but the process of injecting it into a new body required more than he had imagined. The cold suits were, in fact, derived from the same principles as the deep-freeze chambers that had preserved Earth's colonists.

The same liquid that had kept the colonists in hibernation from Earth to Acrea kept the Immortal Guard from deteriorating, holding them in a state between life and death. They could, technically, last indefinitely, but only if they were human. And humans were in short supply on Acrea. The capsules that had drifted to Arral over the years were mostly dead on arrival, their inhabitants lost in the dangerous transit from orbit to land. And even those who survived had little interest in joining him.

Tyler would have no choice.

Satisfied with the thought, Shade straightened his dark robes, smoothing his hair back into place. He took a deep, steadying breath and strolled from his throne room, his steps deliberate as he passed into the cold expanse of Midnite Waters and made his way toward The Pens. Midnite Waters sprawled in a perfect sphere, divided into four distinct districts. Shade prized order above all else, and his city mirrored his philosophy. His tower and the Tekian people dominated the city center, casting a long shadow like a dark sundial, dividing each district as the Acrean sun moved across the sky.

To the north lay the Avian enclave, a place of fleeting wings and watchful eyes; to the south, the Sogra marsh, teeming with his twisted amphibian servants. To the west stood the half-giant domain, and in the east, where Shade now walked, were The Pens—his experimental grounds. Years of genetic manipulation had been fruitful, though Shade was forever perfecting his creatures. Now he only needed a way to transport his creations to Arral en masse.

A particular idea played in his mind, and he found himself humming as he passed through the eastern gate. Here, where his most dangerous experiments prowled, an immense crystalline dome covered the district, filtering the light to a cold, unnatural shade. He looked up, satisfied at the sight. Many of the ancient colonists' buildings had served him well.

High above, enormous winged creatures flailed against the crystalline barrier, their bodies too monstrous to be unleashed in open sky. Muzzled and chained to deep stakes, they snapped at each other, sending low, throaty snarls across the space. These abominations, Shade kept toward the back of the district. He had long learned that their tastes ran to more than just the sky, and they had developed a tendency to consume his experiments.

"Master!" called a small voice, strangled with fear.

Shade clicked his tongue, irritated by the interruption. A scrawny Sogra female approached him, her green scales dull and patchy from neglect. She slunk low, one arm raised as if to deflect a blow, her eyes fixed on the ground.

He looked down his nose at her, thinly amused. "Take me to the gargoyle enclosure," he ordered, though he knew the path perfectly well. He would not allow a servant to come to him without fulfilling a purpose.

Shade's gargoyles were not the children-stealing stone figures of Earth's mythos. His creations were hybrids, part Avian, part Sogra—sterile, yet incredibly long-lived. They were erratic and highly aggressive, bound to The Pens for his protection and theirs.

The Sogra led the way down the central avenue, careful to keep her distance. Creatures scattered from Shade's approach, their fear palpable, a scent Shade savored as he walked past. At the barricade, a towering half-giant guard stood with arms crossed, his stance rigid, though his eyes darted nervously. Shade's shadow stretched across the dome as he neared the gargoyle enclosure, and with a dismissive wave, he sent the Sogra female away. She scraped and prostrated herself, her mended tail dragging along the ground as she backed into the shadows.

The gargoyle enclosure was itself a dome within the dome. A thick metal gate, barred and reinforced, stood before him, its weight meant to hold creatures inside rather than keep intruders out. Shade lifted the crossbar effortlessly, locking it into place with a metallic clang that echoed. This bar typically required two half-giants to move. Shade inhaled deeply, savoring the cold energy that seemed to pulse within The Pens. Entering the gargoyles' domain was always a thrill.

With a push, he swung the gate open, slipped inside, and slammed it shut behind him. In an instant, a blur of fangs and claws descended on him, talons digging into his shoulders, aiming to drag him down.

They never learned.

With a laugh, Shade gripped one scaly wrist, crushing it until the bones cracked. In a fluid motion, he flung the gargoyle through the air, its howl cut short as it hit the ground with a thud. More gargoyles rushed forward, wings spreading, eyes wild. Shade met them with a twisted grin, punching through leathery wings and snapping their limbs with vicious strikes.

He dropped into a practiced stance, snapping kicks into their stomachs, sending them to the ground in gasping heaps. But as the mass of bodies surged, their sheer weight pushed him backward, claws tearing at his robes, threatening to smother him beneath a tide of fury. For a heartbeat, he felt something like panic, then growled, letting dark energy coil around his rage, feeding off it.

A shockwave blasted outward, scattering the creatures like leaves in a storm.

"Enough, you fools!" a sharp female voice cut through the chaos. "Can you not see it's the Master?"

Shade rose gracefully, stepping over the scattered bodies of twitching, unconscious gargoyles. He walked with calculated calm to the center of the enclosure, toward the voice's source. A ring of snarling and cowering faces watched him approach, their eyes full of wary awe. In the middle stood Bulca, chieftainess of the gray wing clan, her gaze downcast as she knelt. Her lavender skin glistened with sweat, her bat-like wings folded neatly behind her, tense with restrained energy.

She raised her head, her vibrant, storm-like eyes meeting his. Shade could sense the defiance within her, a faint glimmer he had not entirely managed to crush. *This one,* he thought with a trace of amusement, *knows me well.*

"Bulca," Shade said, his voice unsettlingly pleasant, "I have a task for you and your kin."

The tone made her flinch, her wings shifting slightly. She knew him too well to relax.

"I find myself in need of certain… items. You and yours will retrieve them from the northern isles."

Bulca hissed, her composure faltering, but she went silent under his cold, expectant stare.

"Again, to the wreckage, Master?" she asked, the reluctance plain in her voice.

"Yes, Bulca." Shade's smile widened, chillingly polite. "And this time, you will need many to bring back what I require."

A murmur rippled through the gathered gargoyles, curious but wary. Shade let his gaze sweep across them, pausing for effect.

"You do remember the way, don't you?" he asked, a thin smile on his lips.

Bulca nodded, but her shoulders sagged, her hair falling in greasy strands over her face.

"I need you to bring me the rest of it," he said, voice low, loaded with finality.

Bulca's head snapped up, horror flickering across her features. "But, Master…" Her voice trembled, betraying a trace of panic.

"All of it!" Shade roared, taking a menacing step forward, his eyes gleaming with dark intent.

The gargoyles around him hissed in warning, but their defiance quickly faded, replaced by murmurs of fear. Shade could sense their collective dread; they knew that many would not return. He had sealed the cache back before his first imprisonment, crafting a gauntlet of defenses that even he might struggle to survive. But his creatures would serve him well enough—they always did, one way or another.

He turned his gaze back to Bulca, his expression a mask of command. "All of it."

19 ALL WRONG

Razmal stared at the scene unfolding before him, shaking his head.

"By the ancestors," he muttered under his breath.

Beside him, Samson leaned heavily on a newly acquired bone walking staff. Razmal glanced over, searching his oldest friend's face, knowing full well the pain Samson was concealing behind that smile.

"The healers here are good," Samson said, catching Razmal's gaze. "I am well."

Razmal's gaze drifted back to the ruined city, where smoke curled from shattered buildings. The attack had been swift and devastating. The outer wall on Arabellum's east side lay in heaps of stone and dust. Much of the market district was reduced to a crater of broken stalls and rubble, and though the arena remained standing, it was battered and charred, holding its ground in smoldering defiance. In two days, Arabellum had suffered more destruction than in its three hundred years.

Ember approached, flanked by his guards. His chitin armor was streaked with dust and blood—some of it his, most of it not. He stopped beside Razmal, staring down at his city with a deep frown creasing his brow.

"It's time for you and your companions to move on," he said.

The gentleness in his voice surprised Razmal. Ember was known for his commanding presence, his booming voice, and unshakeable strength. Now, he seemed diminished, worn. Razmal felt a pang of conflict. He had considered staying in Arabellum, sending Tyler on ahead with a merchant caravan bound for the coastal villages. They would skirt the shoreline, making a final stop in Moonlit Waters before returning to Arabellum with fresh trade. But now, as he stood behind his mentor, he felt the old wound of abandonment reopen, as if he were being cast out once again.

The murmur of the VAST that had always hovered at the edge of his mind faded to a distant whisper, and Samson turned toward him in alarm. Razmal wondered if he'd somehow pushed the VAST away. But the look on Samson's face was knowing.

"You will join a caravan heading to the coast," Ember said. "I am entrusting you with a task, Razmal. You will guard and deliver two prisoners to the Golden Council."

Razmal's heart quickened. He wasn't being sent away in disgrace. He was being given a mission.

Ember, lost in thought, kept his gaze on the city. "Your Sleeper friend will be questioned by the Council, but first, see that he reaches the temple safely. If the Legionnaires get to him first..." He let the sentence trail off, but the warning was clear.

Razmal bowed low. "By your will, Dominus."

Ember nodded, then paused, his expression softening. "And Razmal, when you're finished, come back. Train at my side as you once did. Let the stories of your youth be damned. It's clear to me now they were mistaken."

A rush of elation flooded Razmal, filling him with warmth—belonging, purpose. But it faded just as quickly, settling like a weight in his stomach as he considered Ember's words. The VAST still whispered to him. He would never be accepted.

"Two prisoners?" Razmal asked, pushing his thoughts aside.

Ember's face darkened. "Ah, yes. There's something you wouldn't know. We captured a woman within the walls. She had certain items on her—proof of something I've suspected for some time."

"And that is?"

"She's Tekian. The first Tekian woman I've seen with my own eyes. Rather striking, if you can look past the dark hair and curses spilling from her shapley lips," Ember said, his tone almost amused.

Razmal frowned. The Tekians again. He suspected they were behind the recent devastation that had nearly destroyed Arabellum. There had been confusion and shock, few clear accounts of what happened. Yet, only Tekian technology or Starfall weaponry could inflict such damage. But there had been no sign of Starfall wreckage among the craters.

"Dominus, may I speak with her before we leave?" Razmal asked.

Ember nodded. "I'll have supplies gathered for your journey. Your friend Tyler is already questioning the prisoner."

A flicker of concern crossed Razmal's face. "What if she wasn't alone?"

Ember chuckled, dismissive. "Your friend is well-guarded, Razmal. I've posted twenty of my best men with him in the gladiator pits where the prisoners are being held."

Not nearly enough for what's coming, Razmal thought.

Razmal nodded. "Dominus," he said, bowing again. He squeezed Samson's arm and motioned for him to follow. They made their way quickly down from Ember's Ludus, careful to avoid the broken, smoldering stones underfoot. People milled about, beginning the process of cleaning up the city. Children played in the rubble-strewn streets, and vendors had opened a few stalls, intent on business as usual. Razmal and Samson navigated half-blocked intersections and crawled over fallen buildings until they reached the arena.

Razmal strode through one of the broken gates and scanned the mostly unharmed inner arena. A contingent of guards stood around two kneeling prisoners, both bound. The man's head was hooded, while the woman's mouth was gagged. Beside Razmal, Samson wheezed painfully, clutching his ribs.

Razmal raised an eyebrow. "So much for the best healers," he teased.

Samson grinned through the pain. "They did their best, I suppose."

Razmal felt an unexpected warmth at his friend's side and approached the half-circle of guards. His gaze fell on Tyler, tall and tense, standing over the woman with a fierce expression. His Warquarter strapped to his back, its metallic surface shifting and rippling as if alive.

"—again, *how do you know my name?*" Tyler demanded.

A guard yanked the gag from the woman's mouth, and she hurled a stream of curses at Tyler, sharp enough to make any sailor blush. She spat her fury, then fell into an angry silence, glaring at him as he paced in front of her.

"That creature," Tyler demanded, his voice low, "what was it after?"

The woman lifted her chin defiantly and huffed, her glare sharp and unyielding. Razmal stepped up beside Tyler, who nodded to him, then turned to fully take in the disheveled woman kneeling in the dirt. Her tangled black hair framed a face streaked with grime, her green eyes blazing with anger as they fixed on Tyler. Her teeth gnashed as she spat out another round of curses, each word more acidic than the last. She was thin but athletic, her foreign clothing clinging to her frame like a second skin, and her chest rose and fell in rapid breaths as she seemed to ready herself for another tirade.

The moment her eyes met Razmal's, the VAST surged back to life in his mind, visions pounding through him with dizzying clarity. He saw a young Acrean girl with pale lavender hair fishing by the beach, her satchel already heavy with shells. She pulled a net from the water, her slender hands working carefully as she smiled, feeling proud of the haul she'd bring home. Dark storm clouds rolled in, but she wouldn't be deterred, not even by the flash of lightning that split the sky as she hauled the net to shore. As she drew it in, something small and shining slipped from the net, falling onto the sand. She paused, dropping the net to examine the object—a crystal.

The vision dissolved as the woman's stare wavered, her expression stunned. She had seen it too. Tyler looked from one to the other, frowning.

"Know each other?" he asked.

"I... can't explain what I just saw," Razmal replied, still shaken.

The woman scowled, spitting at him. "Sorcerer."

Tyler shook his head in exasperation. "I'll take that as a 'maybe.'"

"That thing," Razmal said, regaining his composure, "was after her crystals."

"Crystals?" Tyler's confusion deepened.

The hooded man let out a strangled noise, thrashing beneath his hood. Tyler walked over and yanked it off, allowing the sunlight to reveal the man's long yellow hair. His pale eyes, rimmed with a strange, shifting silver, locked onto Tyler.

"He is coming," the man rasped.

They all turned, waiting.

Ralon cleared his throat, shifting against his bonds as he tried to find a more comfortable position.

"An absence moves this way quickly," he said, his tone formal, almost reverent. "The VAST tremble in fear of his coming. We must go."

Razmal was taken aback by the man's eloquence. He had expected something harsher, something more ragged, given Ember's dark description of his crimes.

The dark-haired woman cackled, her breaths coming in shuddering bursts as her ribs shook. "The Master..." she babbled, her voice barely above a whisper.

Samson, who had been silent, closed his eyes, tilting his head as if straining to hear something just beyond them. His face drained of color, and he nodded urgently. "It's time to go."

Tyler squared his shoulders, his jaw clenched. "I'm not running from an apparition... or an absence," he said, voice steady.

Razmal watched the inner conflict flicker across Tyler's face. Towering and armored, Tyler struck an imposing figure—it was hard to imagine anyone or anything being a match for him. Yet Tyler looked to him, a question in his eyes.

"Time to go," Razmal whispered in agreement.

They wasted no time reaching the gate, the prisoners in tow. They had to quickly replace the gag after only a few moments; the woman's curses had grown more creative and vulgar with each step. Ralon was allowed to walk ungagged, his hood removed, and seemed strangely at ease, even smiling as they walked.

Ember waited beside a large, hide-covered wagon, surrounded by soldiers. "My friends," he said, striding forward to clasp Tyler's forearm. The two exchanged hurried words while Razmal and Samson loaded the prisoners into the wagon. Inside, the hide-covered trader's vehicle was packed with provisions, water jugs, and a makeshift prison cell at the rear. The floor, woven from thick grass and reeds, held two loops to which Razmal secured the ropes binding the prisoners.

The woman glared at him, her eyes full of malice, while Ralon only smiled, unfazed.

"My thanks for this small kindness," Ralon said, his eyes glinting. "Keeping me in the light."

Razmal eyed him hard, saying nothing, then dropped the heavy flap over the opening.

When he turned, he saw Ember pound his fist into his palm, apparently discussing the full reason for their departure. With a dismissive gesture, Ember clapped Tyler on the shoulder and walked over to Razmal, a sudden sadness in his eyes.

Ember embraced him, gripping his shoulders tightly, holding him at arm's length to study him. "I have made so many mistakes with you, my son," he said, his voice rough with emotion.

Razmal placed his hands on Ember's forearms, returning the gesture with a light squeeze. "Thank you, Dominus."

Ember motioned to the guards at the gate, and the massive obsidian doors swung open without a sound. "Make haste, and safe travels," he said, his voice carrying warmth. With a final nod, he turned sharply and walked back into the city. As he disappeared into the shadows, Razmal thought he saw the glint of a tear in his master's eye.

***

The party moved in solemn silence as they followed the wagon, two enormous insects pulling it slowly but steadily through the uneven grassland. The insects were geks—large, green-and-gray carapace-covered beasts with sturdy, wide bodies and angular heads crowned by thin, probing black antennae. Their multifaceted purple eyes glittered in the sunlight, giving them an eerie, watchful presence as they peered at everything and nothing simultaneously. Tyler had made an offhand remark about them resembling beetles from Earth, but Razmal only gave him a blank look. He had never heard of such creatures before, and geks, with their docile nature and remarkable resilience, had long served the Balan as perfect beasts of burden.

The air was warm, filled with the hum of insects and the faint, sweet scent of Acrean grass, trampled and bruised beneath their feet. The land stretched wide around them, with low hills rising in the distance and patches of wildflowers dotting the path. Yet there was a heaviness beneath the idyllic setting, a foreboding tension, as though something dark lay just beyond the horizon.

Razmal walked in silence, listening to the steady hum of the VAST at the edge of his mind. Its whispers were elusive today, flickering in and out like shifting shadows. The VAST had noticed the hunter—it had sensed a presence moving from Arabellum, swiftly altering course toward their party. But what unsettled Razmal most was the tone of the VAST's whispers: confusion, uncertainty, a wavering sense of dread. They called the hunter a dead thing, and yet it moved as if it were alive. Worse still, the hunter was not alone. Another presence accompanied it, something that even the VAST dared not approach.

Razmal's heart sank as he pieced together the implications. For the VAST to avoid something entirely was nearly unheard of, as it was part of everything, connected to the pulse of life that flowed through Acrea. An absence of its perception could mean only one thing—an Immortal Guard. The realization struck him with chilling certainty. The hunter coming toward them was no ordinary threat. It was one of Shade's Immortal Guard, a personal agent of death, trained to fulfill its master's will with lethal precision.

Shade's legion of Immortal Guard were the demons of Balan lore, tales of death and ruin told around fires in low, fearful voices. The few times they had ventured to the mainland of Arral, they left behind nothing but scorched villages and empty fields where once there had been life. Razmal remembered a story from his youth about an Immortal Guard who had come to Arral centuries ago; it had walked silently through villages, spreading a trail of desolation before disappearing, its purpose unknown and terrifying. The stories said the land took decades to recover.

The whisper of the VAST felt weaker now, almost as if it feared this intruding presence, this "dead thing." Razmal tried to steady his mind, but he could feel his pulse quickening. The Temple of Spero was the only place known to stop the Immortal Guard. It was protected by a magic that somehow repelled them, unraveling their dark essence on contact. But they were miles from the Temple of Spero, miles from its sanctuary. Most of Acrea's people lived in small, mobile communities to avoid such threats, knowing that only Moonlit Waters, the capital city of Arral, offered the relative safety of the Temple's influence.

He glanced at Tyler, who walked a few steps ahead, his shoulders squared as he surveyed the horizon with unwavering focus. Tyler was formidable, but even he might be no match for what was coming. The Immortal Guard were not simply warriors; they were creatures sustained by Shade's dark magic, strengthened by his very blood, and protected by the strange cold suits that extended their lives beyond mortality. In truth, they had no lives to speak of anymore—they were weapons, tools for Shade's whims, and they would stop at nothing to fulfill his commands.

Razmal knew they needed to hurry, but the slow pace of the wagon weighed on him. The geks trudged along with calm endurance, but the distance to the Temple of Spero was still daunting. They would have to cross through several unfriendly territories and evade whatever else lurked in the wilderness. He feared they would not make it in time.

"What are you seeing, Razmal?" Samson's voice broke through his thoughts. The older man had noticed Razmal's troubled expression, his brow creased with quiet worry.

Razmal hesitated, not wanting to spread panic among his companions. "The hunter follows us. Something the VAST cannot touch," he replied in a low voice, just above a whisper.

Samson paled slightly, gripping his staff tighter. He let out a breath, eyes cast down to the ground, as if the weight of the words needed time to settle. "So it's Shade himself that's after us," he murmured. "And he's sent one of his shadows to do his bidding."

Razmal nodded, his heart heavy. "I don't know if even the temple will save us if the Guard reaches us first."

The sky had begun to darken with the first hints of twilight, the vibrant blue deepening to a dusky purple. The geks plodded along, oblivious, their antennae twitching as they picked up the scent of fresh grass. They seemed almost calm, their hard shells gleaming in the fading light, as if this journey were no different from any other.

As the group pressed forward, Razmal tried to quiet his racing thoughts. The prisoners' voices drifted from the wagon behind him, faint murmurs of resistance from the woman, punctuated by the soft, steady tone of Ralon, who seemed almost indifferent to their fate. Razmal could feel the woman's sharp gaze on his back, like an ember that refused to be extinguished. She was bound, gagged, and entirely at their mercy, but she radiated a fierce energy that seemed to defy her restraints.

Ahead, the terrain shifted as they reached a small rise, giving Razmal a brief vantage point over the rolling grasslands. In the distance, he saw the jagged peaks of the Blackstone Range, dark against the dusky sky, their outlines like silent sentinels. Beyond them lay the Temple

Spero and the inner sanctuary, their only hope against the Immortal Guard.

But the VAST still murmured a warning, whispering of death drawing near.

20 PRACTICE MAKES PERFECT

Bulca landed heavily, wincing as she clutched her wounded side. Blood seeped between her taloned fingers, dripping steadily onto the rocky, barren ground below. Each drop vanished into the soil as though the land itself thirsted for it. She glanced skyward just in time to see another brood mate torn from the air by a blinding blast of light, the gargoyle's body folding in a grim cascade toward the dirt. Few, she knew, would survive the day.

Before her lay the metal bird, a vast and alien carcass of technology that made her wings quiver. The creature lay on its side, its belly ripped open, metallic entrails and fractured plating strewn across the landscape. But despite its crippled state, the vessel still fought, its multiple rotating barrels spitting death with mechanical precision at anyone who dared approach. Space travel, technology—these things were incomprehensible to Bulca, who knew only blood, bone, and the power of her own kind. Yet she understood enough to see that this beast, even with its innards exposed, held deadly secrets. This creature had fight left in it, and it would claim her kin mercilessly.

Raising her obsidian blade, she let out a piercing shriek, signaling her clan to press forward. Those that had made it to the ground now rallied, rushing the opening in a desperate push. Another beam lanced from the wreckage, catching two more gargoyles who fell to the ground, smoldering. *Many will be lost,* she thought grimly, but the Master's demands were absolute.

The first gargoyle to reach the opening was a young, eager fighter, but he barely took two steps before he jerked violently, multiple impacts tearing across his body in rapid succession. Crimson mist filled the air as he collapsed to the deck in a lifeless heap. Three more gargoyles surged forward, this time led by a hulking male who, with some quick thinking, grabbed a slab of debris to shield himself and the others. Using the makeshift barrier, they pushed forward, edging into the dark maw of the vessel.

Once inside, they would split into groups, each determined to bring down this mechanical beast and claim its heart. *The Master demanded it.*

The shield-bearer grunted, sweat streaming down his face as the metal slab in his grip began to glow red-hot under the enemy's assault. With a final cry, he charged forward, his strength waning as the slab split in two. In a desperate throw, he flung both molten halves at the source of the bombardment. The metal fragments connected, bursting into flames and silencing the weapon with a final, dying hiss. The large male crumpled, his mission complete, his sacrifice paving the way.

Bulca slipped in behind the last of her surviving brood, ducking as another barrage struck near her. She clutched her side, feeling the blood congeal, her fingers numb with pain. Her obsidian blade, a heavy two-handed weapon with a hilt wrapped tightly in reed and leather, felt almost unmanageable in her weakened state. Just then, a stray projectile struck her blade's wide middle, twisting it from her grip and nearly sending her to her knees.

Gritting her teeth, she crouched lower, her wings half-folded for protection, and took in the sight of her fallen broodmates behind her. The ground was littered with the charred remains of her kin, their bodies sprawled in unnatural positions across the scorched soil. She allowed herself a fleeting moment of sorrow, her gaze lingering on the massive male who lay motionless, his skin still smoking from the fierce defense.

Forcing herself onward, she sprinted through the ship's main corridor, dodging small-arms fire from hidden turrets. The corridor, once bright and orderly, was now a labyrinth of exposed wires and gaping holes in the metal floor where fires had burned unchecked. Overhead conduits dripped with oil, the remnants of the ship's wounded machinery groaning and crackling ominously. Her talons snagged on a gap in the deck plating, and she stumbled, almost falling before catching herself on the jagged edge of a bulkhead.

Ahead, the corridor branched into two narrow paths, each obscured by blinking red lights and flashing alarms. She glanced down at her wound, relieved to see the bleeding had stopped. She gripped her blade in both hands, the hilt a reassuring weight that steadied her nerves. Approaching the junction, she paused to peer around the corner.

A piercing alarm sounded, accompanied by a flashing klaxon casting dizzying patterns of color across the walls. There, blocking the left corridor, was an automaton—a towering figure mounted on a single, tank-like track. A thick, strobing light sat atop its head, and a cold, metallic voice blared from its broad, wedge-shaped body. Its upper appendages unfolded, extending into long, clawed arms crackling with electrical energy. The creature wheeled forward, its hands sparking with a pulsing, blue-white light.

A powerful sonic wave hit her first, vibrating through her bones and sending a low thrumming pain into her skull. The automaton's attempt to subdue her was futile. Bulca was far from a peaceful mood. She narrowed her eyes and let out a defiant shriek, partially unfolding her wings as she leapt forward, her blade raised in high guard. She knew Shade would be pleased with her form.

The automaton's touch was searing, a terrible combination of fire and cold that stabbed through her thigh, buckling her knee and forcing her to the deck. She snarled and swung her heavy blade in a wide arc, her grip faltering from the pain. The blade connected with the automaton's arm, sending a burst of sparks in every direction. A severed limb clattered to the floor, its fingers twitching with residual energy. But the automaton's remaining arm swung back, slamming into her chest and throwing her hard against the bulkhead. The impact knocked the wind from her lungs, and she struggled to breathe, her vision blurring.

Bulca spat blood, feeling her ribs ache from the strike. She forced herself up, leaning on her blade as she glared at the machine. *So this is what the Master wanted to see destroyed,* she thought grimly, feeling the fire of desperation surge within her. Her brood had paid dearly to reach this place, and she would not let their sacrifices be in vain.

With a final, guttural roar, Bulca sprang at the automaton once more, her blade arcing down in a savage cleave aimed at the machine's central core. She could feel every muscle in her body straining, the pain in her side burning anew, but she ignored it, focusing solely on her target.

The booming voice from the automaton had taken on an angry, almost desperate tone, but Bulca barely registered it. She threw herself into a dive, sliding along the wall as the automaton's massive fist crashed down where her head had been only seconds before. Sparks erupted from the impact, and with a flicker, the lights in the corridor winked out, plunging the space into darkness. Bulca smiled as the automaton's visor light spun frantically, its silvery beam slicing through the blackness, searching for its prey. But in the dark, Bulca was in her element. Her eyes adjusted, the gloom sharpening into grays and shadows, and she felt her senses come alive, her breathing steady and controlled.

The metal creature swung an arm wide and rotated, hoping to crush her with its bulk, blindly lashing out. Bulca crept low and approached quietly, keeping her steps controlled as she slid along the cold metal floor. With a final, precise step, she thrust her obsidian blade straight into its chest, watching as the weapon's dark edge pierced through the automaton's armor. An oily, blackish fluid spilled from the wound, splattering onto the floor in thick, viscous streams. The automaton's booming voice faded into silence as its visor light dimmed, and the whirling klaxon on its head sputtered before winking out. The machine toppled, sliding off her blade and crashing onto the deck with a hollow boom.

The exertion and the automaton's icy touch caught up with her. She collapsed to her knees, bile rising in her throat as waves of hot and cold twisted through her body, seizing her muscles. She retched, coughing violently, but forced herself to breathe, each inhale a struggle against the pain. Her vision swam as she steadied herself, focusing on the dark outline of her greatsword, now cracked and shattered from the brutal fight. The blade, once her pride and joy, lay in splintered fragments around the fallen machine. Grimacing, she picked up the hilt, feeling a pang of loss. The greatsword had been her most prized weapon, crafted painstakingly through barter and favor with the half-giant smiths.

There's still some use left in it, she thought, gripping the battered hilt tightly. She forced herself to her feet, each step bringing fresh jolts of pain as she limped back into the dim corridor.

She recalled the Master's instructions as she maneuvered through the passageways, each step cautious and calculating. The ship was a labyrinth of broken pathways and twisted metal, and the stink of scorched circuitry and spilled oil filled her nostrils. Blood, both her own and her fallen brood mates', slicked her wings and her body, weighing her down with each movement. She felt the weight of her kin's sacrifices pressing upon her like the grime and darkness of this desolate place. The cries of her brood echoed down the corridor, distant yet painfully vivid, driving her forward. *This mission is for them,* she reminded herself. *No one else should have to return here.*

After what felt like an eternity, she found herself back in the main corridor. Following the mental image she'd formed of the ship's layout, she pressed on, eventually arriving at a smaller chamber where two automatons engaged a desperate pack of her kin. She cast a glance at her damaged sword, doubting its effectiveness against more of these metal monsters.

My brood mates can handle this, she told herself, though her heart ached at the sight of their struggle. One automaton fell, swarmed by talons and wings, collapsing in a heap under the sheer ferocity of their attack. But the second automaton was a formidable opponent, grabbing a warrior in its crackling grip, the sizzling sound of searing flesh filling the air as it tossed another two into the wall with mechanical strength.

Seizing the distraction, Bulca unfurled her wings and leapt over the melee, gliding past the fight in a streak of motion. *There's no time left.*

The walls grew narrower as she jogged through the dim corridor, her wings pressed tightly against her body to fit. Every turn, every twist of the passage brought her closer. Finally, the corridor ended at a thick metal door, its two halves partially closed with a gap down the middle, jammed by debris. She pressed her taloned hands against the warm surface, peering through the narrow opening.

Beyond lay the heart of the metal bird, just as the Master had described it: a circular chamber with a glowing orb encased in a transparent cylinder, rotating slowly in midair. The heart pulsed in shades of blue and white, casting faint, shifting lights across the room. The sight held a strange beauty, a perfect sphere of energy, vibrant yet cold.

Bulca exhaled, awe momentarily overtaking her resolve. She tightened her grip on the battered hilt of her greatsword and wedged it into the narrow opening between the doors. Heaving with all her might, she forced the blade forward, prying the door's halves apart. The strain on her sword was immense, cracks spidering along the length of the blade. She gritted her teeth, knowing her weapon would not survive this.

With a final, desperate push, the greatsword shattered, and the door gave way, sliding open with a groan and banging into recesses on either side. She tossed the broken hilt aside with a pang of regret.

Steeling herself, she stepped over the threshold, entering the room the Master had called *engineering*. The chamber thrummed with energy, every surface alight with blinking symbols and shifting patterns that she instinctively shied away from. Alien symbols scrolled across screens lining the walls, their meaning a mystery, but she quickly averted her gaze, focusing on the task. She began to circle the heart, searching for the pedestal the Master had instructed her to find.

The sound of footsteps echoed down the corridor behind her, and a line of her brood mates entered single file, wary but resolute. Bulca nodded to them, and they took up defensive positions, forming a half-circle around the door, facing outward with their wings half-unfurled. Faint sounds of combat continued from the corridors beyond, mingling with the muffled clanging of metal against metal. The gargoyles shifted nervously, casting glances back at her.

She pressed on, scanning the far side of the chamber until her eyes found it at last—the pedestal. It was a simple device, a single button covered by a clear lid, glowing faintly red. A strange, angular symbol pulsed on its surface. She didn't know its meaning, but a deep instinctual caution flickered within her. *This feels wrong.*

A sudden barrage of blasts tore through the doorway, striking her defenders. Grunts of pain filled the air as several gargoyles crumpled to the deck. Bulca's claws itched, torn between helping her kin and finishing her mission. Her resolve hardened. She had to trust the Master, for her kin's sacrifice would be in vain if she failed.

Swallowing her doubts, she flipped open the clear lid, exposing the button. Another of her companions fell, clutching at a searing wound in his throat. Her heart pounded. She had no time left to hesitate. Raising her palm, she struck the glowing button with a forceful slap, hoping, trusting, that the Master's command would deliver them all from this nightmare.

The cylinder around the heart remained motionless, its surface gleaming coldly in the dark. An alarm blared, piercing the silence in the engineering chamber, while the lights flickered and went out, leaving only a disorienting strobe that pulsed across the walls. As Bulca's eyes darted to the hatch, it groaned and began to close, undoing all her effort. She pointed at the rapidly descending doors and shouted a warning.

Two of her brood threw themselves into the gap, turning back-to-back to brace the door with every fiber of their strength. Their muscles bulged as they fought to hold the barrier open, their faces locked in a fierce determination. For a moment, the door shuddered, halted by their combined effort. But then the mechanism doubled in force, the gears grinding as the hatch pressed relentlessly inward. Neither gargoyle cried out as their bodies yielded, the sound of bones snapping buried under the shrieking metal. When the doors finally paused, their crushed forms slumped lifelessly, but their sacrifice had left the gap wide enough for the rest to escape.

A low buzz filled the chamber, followed by a hissing sound as a thick mist seeped in, swirling around the floor. The cylinder around the heart clicked and rose, retracting upward and exposing the pulsing orb within. Bulca let out a triumphant cry, unfurling her wings to hop down to the glowing core. She wrapped her talons around the throbbing sphere and pulled with all her might, feeling the resistance of the anti-gravity field as it shimmered. With a grunt of strain, she tore it free, and the heart dropped into her waiting grasp.

The alarms silenced, the room plunging into an eerie, charged stillness.

The heart was far heavier than it had appeared. Every muscle in her body tensed as she lifted it, struggling to haul the prize to where her remaining brood waited, eyes wide with anticipation. The orb continued to pulse with swirling blue and white light, casting shifting shadows across the darkened walls and ceiling. Four of her warriors hurried forward, unrolling a thick hide blanket. They carefully wrapped the heart, securing it in the blanket's folds, then attached its corners to their spears. Heaving it onto their shoulders, they braced under its weight, steadying the precious load with their wings folded tightly.

Bulca allowed herself a single deep breath, a small, victorious smile forming as she let out a cry of triumph. Her surviving broodmates took up the call, their voices filling the chamber with a fierce but weary pride. She turned to lead them out, but her first step faltered, her leg giving way beneath her. Frowning, she looked down, expecting to see debris but finding nothing.

Perhaps it's just fatigue, she told herself.

Her brood had forced the hatch open again, moving the bodies of those who had sacrificed themselves for the mission. Beyond the door, the corridors lay still and deserted, littered with fallen gargoyles and twisted automaton bodies. Each step was a reminder of the cost; they had battled for hours to reach the heart, yet it took mere minutes to reach the wreckage-strewn ground outside.

The warriors bearing the heart moved quickly, heading across the rocky terrain. A short distance away, three other hide-wrapped bundles lay in the dust, each marking the loss of a brave fighter who had carried out the Master's will. Bulca's heart twisted. Of the fifty warriors who had entered the metal bird, less than a dozen had returned. The cost had been grievous.

As Bulca stumbled into the pale light of day, a sudden fit of coughing wracked her body, and she doubled over, her wings drooping. Blood dripped from her hand, and she stared at it, brow furrowing as her vision swam. A deep buzzing filled her ears, a vibration that grew in intensity as a shadow passed over her. The air grew thick and cold, and she staggered backward as a jump craft set down just across from the metal bird. Her knees gave out, and she found herself on the ground, looking up as a figure emerged from the craft. Her heart lifted, a flicker of hope sparking to life. *The Master has come*, she thought.

But as the dust settled, her hope died, replaced by a cold dread that seeped into her bones. A tall, slender figure in elegantly molded armor approached her, each step poised and deliberate. The armor, painted in glossy black lacquer, hugged the female form with deadly elegance. A visored helm concealed her face, but Bulca didn't need to see her expression to feel the cruel satisfaction radiating from her.

"Bulca, you poor dear," the Immortal Guard said, her voice metallic and mocking. "You look a mess."

"K-Kako," Bulca managed, venom in her voice as she fought to sit up, her body wracked with tremors.

A commotion behind her drew her gaze to the heart-bearing warriors. Two of them had collapsed, their bodies shuddering as blood dripped from their mouths. Another clutched his throat, hacking as blood poured from his face in thick, crimson streaks. The rest shifted uneasily, eyes wide as newly arrived Sogra workers loaded the bundles into thick, iron-bound crates.

Pain stabbed through Bulca's stomach, a sudden, excruciating cramp that left her gasping. She felt her insides twisting, her strength waning as her vision blurred. Her clawed fingers spasmed and she reached out, clawing at the Immortal Guards crimson cloak. Kako's cold, metallic laughter pierced through her haze, pulling her focus back to the armored figure.

Kako placed her hands on her hips, tilting her head as she looked down at Bulca. "The Master sends his thanks for a job well done," she said with a cruel, humorless smile.

The words filled Bulca with a strange, hollow satisfaction. She had done her duty. The Master was pleased. She tried to summon a smile, but her muscles felt numb. Darkness crept at the edges of her vision, and she felt as though she were floating, her body growing lighter. The cold radiating from Kako no longer felt biting; it was a balm, easing her pain, dulling the ache of her wounds. *Perhaps I'll be rewarded after all,* she thought, her mind slipping away.

"Radiation truly is the silent killer," Kako sneered, her voice the last thing Bulca heard as her vision faded to black, her body stilling as the last breath left her lips.

Kako stood motionless, hands on her hips as she surveyed the crash site. All around her, the gargoyles lay dead or dying, scattered like broken toys on the desolate ground. Her gaze shifted to the iron crates, where the

Sogra workers were securing the precious cargo, their faces set in grim determination. Kako turned to the wreckage, her cold eyes narrowing as she took in the breached hull. A ship hundreds of years old, now a derelict ruin. This was not the outcome she had anticipated, and a spark of irritation flared in her chest.

"So many things have gone wrong," she muttered, the disdain evident in her voice. It wasn't supposed to end this way.

"Mount up, slaves!" Kako barked, her voice slicing through the silence. "We're leaving. I want to make Midnite Waters by dusk."

The Sogra moved in a hurried, obedient scramble, the crates loaded and secured, the gargoyles' mission finished in dust and silence. Without a backward glance, Kako turned, her silhouette cold and unwavering against the sky as the jump craft roared to life, lifting off with its grim cargo into the fading light.

21 BORDERLINE

The harried band raced along the dusty trade road, putting distance between themselves and the smoldering ruins of Arabellum. The wagon creaked under its heavy load, its wheels rattling in protest as the geks pulled it at a pace well beyond their usual plodding speed. As they traveled, the air grew humid, laden with the scent of salt and seaweed, signaling that the ocean lay not far ahead. Tyler sat next to Samson on the luggage rack above the driver's bench, situated just behind the carapaces of the oversized insects.

The geks' flightless wings fluttered now and then, cooling the damp air with gentle gusts. Tyler observed his sun-bronzed hands, considering stripping off his combat armor to bask in the sunlight. It was a rare, beautiful day, almost enough to forget the dangers lurking behind and before them. But he resisted, opting instead to check the charge on his pistols, feeling the smooth, familiar weight of them in his grip.

"A shame, such magnificent weapons have been lost to us," Samson said, watching Tyler holster the pistols with a look of faint admiration.

Tyler nodded, understanding all too well the mystery and rarity that technology had become on Acrea.

After his time with the *Conrad*, he better understood why the knowledge had faded from the world's memory. "It's hard to explain," he replied, uncertain where to begin, especially with his own memories still fogged over in places.

He leaned back, crossing his arms behind his head, and let his thoughts drift to what he could remember. He knew the weapons on the *Centaur*, at least, were coded for two types of users. One code was based on DNA: only approved military and colonial personnel, encoded into the weapon's database, could fire them. For anyone else, the weapon would discharge a small jolt as a deterrent, with repeated attempts burning out the firing core altogether. But there was another layer, something shadowed in his memory. Flashes of metal hands grabbing at him flickered in his mind, making him shiver.

"No need to explain if it's uncomfortable," Samson said, sensing Tyler's unease and patting his shoulder.

Tyler sighed, shaking his head. "It's not that," he said, his voice trailing off as his mind wandered back to Earth, to all that was left behind.

Samson gave a thoughtful nod, leaning back beside him with a deep breath as he closed his eyes. Tyler turned his gaze upward, watching Acrea's greenish-gray sky stretch endlessly above. Wispy clouds drifted lazily across the expanse, and Yalonia hung low on the horizon like a distant, like an orange watchful eye.

He glanced over at Samson, a faint curiosity tugging at his thoughts. The longer he spent with the Balan, the more questions surfaced. Were the Balan truly Acrea's original inhabitants? The diverse array of creatures Tyler had encountered spoke to a rich evolutionary tapestry, with common roots yet diverging in strange, wondrous ways. And still, there was something… off. A nagging question lingered at the edge of his thoughts.

"How long had I been asleep?" he wondered aloud, his gaze distant.

Samson chuckled, breaking the moment. "Enjoying the view?" he asked, noticing Tyler's gaze fixed on the clouds.

Tyler rolled onto his back, a grin tugging at his lips. "Your kind fascinates me. I've got so many questions and hardly know where to start."

"Perhaps start at the beginning, friend Tyler," Samson replied, a smile in his voice.

Tyler laughed despite the somber weight in his chest. "Alright, here's one: Where do your people come from—originally?"

Samson grew quiet, mirroring Tyler's earlier look of contemplation. The silence stretched, punctuated only by the sound of the geks' soft wingbeats and the distant cries of birds. Samson seemed to wrestle with the question, as though it were something both complicated and deeply important. Sensing his friend's discomfort, Tyler quickly changed the subject.

"No need to go back that far. Here's an easier one—how do these bugs even know where they're going? It doesn't look like Razmal is doing much in the way of steering," he said, gesturing down to the driver's bench, where Razmal dozed, his head resting against the bench with the occasional soft snore.

Samson chuckled, raising an eyebrow. "The geks know only two places: where they eat and where they sleep. We make sure those places are different, and they do the rest."

Tyler laughed, shaking his head as he considered the strange simplicity of the creatures. Samson's thoughtful gaze lingered on him, and after a moment, he continued, "I do have an answer for your first question, friend Tyler, though it will make more sense when we reach the Temple of Spero. There, our history becomes clearer. For now, I can tell you one simple truth: Moonlit

Waters is our holiest city, the birthplace of the hardy Balan people."

Tyler nodded, contemplating this. He could hear faint sounds of movement from the wagon below, likely their two captives.

"Our friends below are obviously not of 'hearty Balan' stock," Tyler said with a chuckle, glancing down at the prisoners.

Samson's expression turned mock-serious, hands raised in mock horror. "A fair observation, friend," he replied, his tone laced with humor.

Tyler shifted, curiosity gnawing at him. "How many races live on Acrea?"

Samson's eyes grew thoughtful as he considered. "Most of the civilized races, you have already met. There are the Balan, the Acrean, and the Erew. A few others, like the Avians, have little interest in mingling. The Tekians, Sogra, half-giants, and Immortal Guard reside on Teka, and we often clash with their patrols."

Tyler nodded, memories of their recent battles surfacing. The Tekian patrols had proven formidable foes, each skirmish etching its dangers into his mind.

"And what about the scavengers from the Scar?" Tyler asked, his tone wary.

"Perhaps, long ago, they had civilization," Samson said, his voice dropping to a somber pitch. "But nothing of it remains. They're lost to madness and ruin, whatever they once were."

After a moment, Samson continued, "There are countless other creatures, Tyler. More than I could name in one sitting. Some we've fought, others we've avoided. But as we near the coast, we'll be in Gale territory. It's important you understand what that means."

Tyler raised an eyebrow, intrigued.

"Massive wyrms of the sea," Samson explained, his expression darkening. "Ravenous, aggressive, and hostile to all things on land. To them, we're their favorite prey."

Tyler tilted his head, a hint of confusion creasing his brow. "Then why not avoid the coast and take an inland route?"

Samson sighed, giving a rueful shake of his head. "Ah, it would be easier, wouldn't it? But no. The inland route is disputed territory, full of factions at each other's throats over scarce resources. The trade road is our safest bet, even with the risk of Gale attacks."

Tyler nodded thoughtfully, sensing the tension woven into Samson's words. Though they had traveled many miles from Arabellum, the threat of attack felt ever-present, lurking just beyond the next rise. The trade road might shield them from most dangers, but as they drew closer to the coast, Tyler couldn't shake the feeling that something watched from afar, something patient and predatory.

As the wagon rattled forward, his gaze drifted to the horizon, where the sky met the sea. The salt tang in the air grew stronger, and the distant cry of seabirds carried on the wind. He took in a deep breath, the crisp air filling his lungs as his mind drifted, contemplating the strange, unpredictable road ahead.

The group pushed on at a breakneck pace down the trade road, leaving Arabellum in the dust. The wagon groaned under its heavy load, rattling over rough patches and jolting with the effort as the geks strained at their harnesses. Each mile brought a stronger scent of salt and seaweed, the moisture thickening in the air, a sharp contrast to the dry land they had left behind. Tyler sat beside Samson atop the luggage rack, their perch just above the crested shells of the bugs as their short, flightless wings gave an occasional flutter, creating cooling gusts in the sticky air.

"It's rare for a Gale attack this close to shore," Samson said, glancing at the coastal horizon. "But once we pass Kent's Gate, we'll be under the protection of Moonlit Waters' patrols."

"Rare?" Tyler scoffed, crossing his arms with a wary look. With his luck lately, rare felt like almost a guarantee. He kept a hand near his holstered pistol, feeling the cold grip and drawing some comfort from its presence. "I'll keep planning for the worst."

The morning melted into a warm afternoon, the road's landscape shifting as tall grasses gradually gave way to low moss and strange, colorful stones. As they crested the next rise, Tyler caught the scent and sound of the ocean before it even came into view—the unmistakable crash of waves. They were close now.

The sight of the sea took his breath away. Massive waves rolled in from the horizon, crashing onto a beach of multicolored sands that sparkled like gemstones beneath the sun. Winged creatures of every size and color soared and dove into the churning water, emerging with wriggling prey clutched in talons or beaks. The water was a mesmerizing blue that stretched endlessly, meeting the sky in a hazy, bright line. Tyler leaned forward, transfixed, taking in the vastness and unspoiled beauty of it all.

As the road curved sharply along the coastline, a structure emerged in the distance—a dome half-buried and shattered, its jagged remnants jutting up from the sand like broken teeth. Tyler's eyes narrowed as recognition set in. This was no natural formation but a habitation dome, the remains of something ancient.

"That's Kent's Gate," Samson said, reverence in his voice as they neared the gate's shadow.

But Tyler's gaze shifted to the figures ahead, dark shapes clustered in the middle of the road, waiting like ominous sentinels. "Perfect," he muttered, his hopes for a peaceful journey quickly evaporating.

The geks' antennae twitched, sensing the obstacle, and they slowed, coming to a halt. Three figures detached from the group, racing down the road to intercept the wagon. The glaring Acrean sun made it hard to make out details until the strangers were almost upon them.

The leader was an imposing figure, a massive bearded man with cold blue eyes that seemed to drink in every detail. His thick blonde beard framed a face that was rugged and weathered, and he wore oiled animal skins that reached his heavy, fur-lined boots. In each hand, he held a stone-headed ax, the edges sharpened to a lethal gleam. Behind him were two shorter figures in hooded cloaks, their faces hidden in the shadow of thickly woven linens.

The bearded man's gaze locked on Tyler, eyes narrowing. "What's a Tekian doing so far from home?" he demanded, his voice a low, menacing rumble. He surveyed the group with suspicion, eyes landing on each in turn. "Who comes to our gate without permission?"

Razmal stirred on the driver's box, his hackles clearly raised. "Your gate?" he scoffed, squaring his shoulders. "Since when did Kent's Gate belong to you?"

The bearded man's eyes hardened, his jaw clenched. Tyler's head pounded as he studied the stranger's expression, the air around them growing heavy with unspoken threats. He glanced at the two hooded companions, unable to shake the sense of a dangerous trap waiting to be sprung.

Sensing the tension, Samson cleared his throat. "We're simple traders bound for Moonlit Valley and the capital beyond. We meant no offense by our arrival here."

The big man spat on the ground in disdain, his steely gaze never leaving Razmal. "You'll show me your wares, little one."

Tyler braced himself as he saw Razmal's muscles tense. He didn't need to see his face to know the dark look he was wearing. Razmal started to rise, his eyes blazing. "Call me little one more time, you son of a—"

A sudden clamor from the figures gathered before Kent's Gate interrupted him. The group turned, shouting in alarm as they faced the sea, gesturing wildly toward the water. Tyler's temples throbbed, and he followed their frantic stares, his eyes widening as he saw what they were pointing at.

Out on the ocean, storm clouds were building—massive, roiling columns of green and black that seemed to rise straight from the water's surface, reaching high into the sky. Lightning crackled within the storm, streaking through the clouds in wide, jagged arcs of orange and purple. The sight was both beautiful and terrifying, the power of nature gathering in a furious vortex.

Razmal shot Tyler a glare, his voice rising over the wind. "You really are bad luck, Sleeper!"

A sharp pain stung Tyler's ear, making him wince, and a crackling voice filled his head. "Commander," it said, crackling with static, "my sensors have detected a significant lifeform approaching your position. Use extreme caution and vacate the area immediately. Sir, please, get away from the coast with all haste."

Tyler's heart leapt. It was *Conrad.* The message cut off, leaving him with the urge to get as far from the ocean as possible.

But the situation escalated too quickly. The two cloaked figures beside the bearded man moved, one darting to each side of the wagon. The big man lifted one of his axes, gesturing to Razmal with an arrogant smirk. Samson groaned, slipping off the luggage rack and out of sight, as if bracing for the worst.

Razmal, fueled by the taunt, surged from the pilot's box, intent on barreling into the big man. But one of the cloaked figures intercepted him midair, gripping his leg and slamming him to the ground in a swift, practiced move. Tyler's instincts kicked in, and he closed the gap with the bearded man in a single stride, his eyes locked on the stranger's cold gaze.

"You'll release Ralon Tigerson to us," the bearded man said, his breath thick with the stench of drink.

At that moment, Tyler heard the wagon's canvas flap snap open. He turned to see Ralon, confused and blinking, being led out by the two cloaked figures. Razmal clambered to his feet beside Tyler, his shield and hammer held ready, his expression deadly.

Ralon stumbled as he was hauled to a halt before the towering stranger, his voice a strained croak. "This is foolish," he said, his tone laced with disdain. "If my mother put you up to this, I assure you, I can pay double."

One of the cloaked figures produced a small flask, which Ralon snatched eagerly, gulping down the contents.

The bearded man's expression darkened as he placed an ax against Ralon's chest, keeping him pinned in place. "The bounty on your head, Acrean, is worth more than any amount of coin." His massive hand gripped Ralon's hair, hoisting him inches off the ground. The air trembled with another rumble of thunder, the storm's fury intensifying as ozone filled the air.

Tyler felt the shift as the bearded man laughed, his voice edged with madness. "You cowards fear the storm?" He tossed Ralon aside as if he were nothing, letting him crumple to the ground.

Ralon glared, his eyes fiery with anger as he spat a stream of curses. Behind him, Lady Dark stumbled from the wagon, her hands still bound behind her back. The carefully tied gag was gone, but Tyler's attention was drawn to the choker around her neck. The black stone glowed ominously, its light pulsing in sync with the storm clouds now blotting out the sun.

"No," she whispered, her voice barely audible.

The temperature dropped sharply, and Tyler could see his breath misting in the air. Every instinct told him to retreat, to get as far from the coast as possible, but his body felt frozen in place.

"Oh, yes!" came a metallic sounding voice, startlingly cheerful, echoing from behind them.

22 LANADARI

Roarc grimaced as he downed another foul-tasting vial of silvery liquid, feeling the icy tendrils snake from his gut to his limbs, fortifying his muscles. Colin had set a murderous pace, even by half-giant standards, and the potions kept coming at regular intervals, transforming his exhaustion into boundless stamina. Hunger and thirst vanished as the concoction coursed through his veins, replacing physical needs with relentless endurance. Colin didn't slow, tossing another vial back to Roarc without a glance.

"Keep up! We're nearly there," Colin shouted over his shoulder, his voice sharp as steel.

Despite the unnatural chill that radiated from the Immortal Guard, Roarc forced himself to keep pace, rubbing his arms against the freezing aura that only intensified when they slowed. The two had spoken little in recent days, each focused on the singular task of reaching the coast. As they approached the shore, the vast expanse of the ocean stretched before them, waves crashing in white froth along the rocky flats. A jagged, half-moon structure loomed ahead, casting an ominous shadow over the scattering of figures nearby.

"Prepare yourself," Colin called, his voice cutting through the rising wind. Without warning, he broke into a sprint, moving with inhuman speed over a rise and out of sight. Seconds later, a chorus of shouts rang out, followed by the sight of storm clouds churning in from the sea, the sky darkening as strange green and orange lightning laced the air.

Roarc gripped his maul and wall shield, thundering forward as his eyes swept the chaotic scene. A crowd had gathered by the half-moon structure, their voices lost in the mounting wind as they pointed toward the water, where colossal clouds twisted like a massive vortex, reaching from sea to sky. Strange, slick shapes began to emerge from the waves, their outlines barely visible in the flickering light.

At the base of the rise, Roarc found Colin, his stance immovable as he faced off with a figure clad in unusual, angular armor, standing beside a wagon pulled by two hulking geks. And there, only steps away, stood Lady Dark, her hands bound but her gaze fierce, fixed on the scene unfolding before her. Roarc's heart pounded, his eyes narrowing as he took in the battered, angry line of opponents between him and his Lady.

"Commander Tor," Colin said, a deadly calm in his voice, "at last."

The armored man—Tyler, Roarc realized—squared his shoulders, eyes narrowing as he noticed his breath misting in the frigid air. "Interesting trick," Tyler said, though he sounded more annoyed than impressed, crossing his arms with an unperturbed air.

Behind Tyler, a massive bearded man with a booming voice shoved through the crowd, brandishing a crystalline axe in each hand. "This is my score. Out of my way, thin man!" he bellowed, raising his weapon.

Without hesitation, the bearded man swung his ax in a wide arc, the crystalline blade gleaming as it sliced through the wind. Colin barely shifted, his figure blurring as he extended two fingers, striking the man's wrist with a resounding crack. The ax fell to the ground with a dull thud, the giant staring in bewilderment at his twitching hand. Before he could react, Colin's hand moved in a quick, precise strike to the man's neck, dropping him to the dirt in a limp heap.

Turning back to Tyler, Colin's stance didn't change as he cleared his throat. "The Master has been looking for you, Tyler. I suggest you put up some resistance—just enough to make it interesting. Though time, as they say, is short."

Tyler raised an eyebrow, unimpressed, a flicker of annoyance crossing his face. Behind him, two Balan emerged from behind the wagon, carrying a groggy man with tangled hair. Tyler and his companions were outnumbered—and vastly outmatched.

The bearded man, his voice hoarse but defiant from the ground, managed to rasp out, "Kill them all."

Two robed figures lurking at the edge of the field sprang to life, moving like shadows on the breeze. Their crystalline short swords gleamed as they moved with a synchronized, deadly rhythm, each a mirror of the other. One figure flanked to Roarc's left, her cloak billowing as the hood slipped back to reveal the face of an Avian warrior, violet feathers rippling in the wind.

The Avian with the violet feathers fixed Roarc with a piercing glare before launching forward, short swords flashing in swift arcs toward Roarc's knees. Roarc's wall shield met the blades with a heavy clang, his reflexes sharpened by the silver potion's strength. The

Avian's expression flickered with surprise, her beak clicking in frustration as she spun away, barely avoiding Roarc's maul as it smashed into the dirt.

The wind howled as the Avian warrior darted forward again, her movements a blur as twin blades cut low, then high. Roarc spun his shield, grinding the Avian's swords against its surface before lunging forward with a powerful blow. The Avian staggered, feathers fluttering wildly as she tried to recover, but Roarc was quicker. With a grunt, he thrust his shield forward, battering the Avian back with brutal force until she crumpled, lifeless, to the ground.

Roarc's gaze snapped up just in time to see Colin standing over another fallen Avian, the bright feathers scattered in a whirlwind around him. He could barely register Colin's next movement before a blinding flash of lightning split the sky, striking the ground with a deafening boom only a few feet from where the Immortal Guard stood. Smoke billowed in the air, and when it cleared, a figure crouched in the shallow, charred crater, dripping with seawater, its hair wild as it lifted her head.

"Impossible," Roarc muttered, tearing his eyes away from the scene even as he blocked another wild strike from one of the surviving Avian warriors. The sight of the figure, soaked and defiant amidst the smoke, sent a chill through him—a Herald of the storm, a Gale approaching with unstoppable fury.

The Avian before him lunged, blades flashing, but Roarc turned his shield, deflecting the swords as he surged forward. His thick arms bulged with the effort as he swung his shield with a forceful, rhythmic motion, each strike battering the Avian back until the warrior's body crumpled to the dirt, still and silent.

Scanning the battlefield, Roarc's heart sank as he saw Lady Dark's silhouette vanish amid the chaos, and a wave of panic washed over him. The wagon was empty, the gek gone, and she was nowhere in sight. But Tyler was still there, locked in a fierce exchange with Colin.

Tyler dropped his visor and raised both arms, revealing a pair of sleek devices, his pistols glowing with pent-up energy. Without hesitation, he fired, each shot unleashing a shrieking bolt that struck Colin dead on, staggering the Immortal Guard as he took a step back. Tyler's face was set in fierce determination, his stance unwavering.

Colin laughed, the sound borderline hysterical and he closed the distance in a single bound, his thin fingers reaching out like talons to seize the pistols. Sparks flew as he crushed the weapons in his grip, reducing them to little more than twisted metal. Tyler pulled back, his fists clenched in defiance.

Roarc surged forward through the storm, rain pouring in heavy sheets from the roiling sky. He searched desperately for Lady Dark, calling her name into the storm, his voice swallowed by the howling wind. The battlefield was a churning mass of bodies and weapons, and he had no way of knowing where she was—or if she was even still there.

The storm raged, the sky darkening as another flash of lightning split the horizon, and he felt the ground tremble beneath his feet. The echoes of battle merged with the roaring waves, the storm bearing down on them with relentless force.

Roarc stumbled back, his breath shallow as he took in the creature that had emerged from the sea. The Herald, towering and alien, rose to its full height, stringy black hair clinging to its slick, scale-covered frame. Each blue and white scale caught flashes of lightning, creating an unearthly gleam over its mother-of-pearl-colored belly and rubbery face. Its wide mouth twisted into a snarl, exposing rows of jagged teeth, and its vicious talons flexed, clearly meant for ripping and tearing flesh.

The Herald's eyes locked on Colin with an intensity that spoke of more than simple malice. It recognized something unnatural in him, an unspoken bond of death. With a guttural roar, the Herald raised one arm, crackling with electrical energy, and thrust it forward. A jagged bolt leaped from its palm, splitting the air with a blinding flash before tearing through the Acrean soil. Bodies fell, twitching as the thunderous concussive wave that followed sent mercenaries sprawling and left Colin staggering, his cloak billowing in the relentless wind.

The Herald barely paused, its attention fixated on Colin as it brought both hands together, fingers splayed, as if weaving light from the storm itself. A glowing sphere formed between its palms, swirling with chaotic energy. It loosed a furious blast of lightning that struck Colin dead-on, mixing cold and heat in an eruption of steam and light, vaporizing rain in a spiraling column that shot up into the storm-dark sky.

Roarc felt his resolve solidify. Whatever fury the Herald or Colin unleashed on each other would only serve to weaken them both, and in the end, he would bring the Sleeper back to his master. No Gale, no storm, would stand in his way.

With a surge of determination, he closed the distance between himself and Tyler, his maul and shield ready, each step sending a defiant echo into the chaotic night. Tyler's visor was down, obscuring his expression, but Roarc imagined fear glinting in the man's eyes. That confidence crumbled, however, the moment Tyler reacted—a flurry of brutal strikes hammered into Roarc's chest, forcing him to double over. Blows followed, each with precision, targeting nerve points and weak spots in his armor. His maul fell from his grip, the shield slipping uselessly to his side as he collapsed, his body betraying him as it gave way under the onslaught.

He knelt in the mud, his vision swimming as he faced the Sleeper, the man who had brought him to his knees. Roarc shut his eyes, surrendering to the inevitability of death. But the final blow never came. Blinking against the rain, he realized Tyler was gone, lost amid the storm and chaos of battle.

In the split second of respite, his gaze fell on the sea, where shadowed figures rose from the churning water like specters from a nightmare. The Riders had arrived.

Knee-deep in the waves, the grotesque forms advanced, mounted on water-beasts twisted and barnacle-crusted, their crooked lances dripping with venomous, green slime. Roarc knew the searing agony those lances brought—a touch would bring a searing pain, followed by a spreading numbness that paralyzed its victim. He backed away, watching the Riders assemble with grim satisfaction. Perhaps they would keep the Sleeper occupied long enough for Roarc to regain his strength.

Movement near the wagon caught his eye, and he recognized the wild-haired, robed man who stepped from the shadows, chanting in a low, rhythmic tone that sent a tremor through the air. Power crackled as his voice grew louder, and the Riders halted, heads snapping toward him as if sensing a threat. The man's chant crescendoed, his voice ringing out across the beach. From the sea, thick tendrils of seaweed surged, snaking up the Riders' legs, entangling them in a vise-like grip. Caught off guard, several Riders struggled as the seaweed coiled tighter, dragging them back into the water's depths. Those who escaped thrashed forward, their expressions twisted with fury as they charged the remaining mercenaries, the bearded ax-wielding giant, back on his feet, was among them.

Roarc watched, momentarily captivated, as the Riders clashed with the mercenaries in a brutal frenzy. The bearded man, face contorted in a berserk rage, hacked at the Riders with brutal precision, his crystalline axes flashing as he cut down his enemies with wild abandon. His fury left a ring of fallen Riders at his feet, though more swarmed from the waves, pushing forward with relentless ferocity. Within moments, the bearded giant's mercenaries fell under the onslaught, their ranks decimated as they crumbled against the tide of water-born warriors.

A primal roar echoed across the beach, sending shockwaves rippling through the air. Roarc fell back, his ears ringing, his vision blurring as he tried to steady himself. The ground itself seemed to shake, and as the rain blurred his sight, he gazed out to sea in awe and horror.

The Gale had emerged.

The colossal wyrm towered above the water, its armored scales gleaming with the storm's lightning. Even half-submerged, its sheer size dwarfed the combatants, its blunt, armored head resembling a battering ram of scales and bone. Rows of razor-sharp fangs glinted as the creature let out another deafening roar, lightning crackling along the ridges of its body, trailing from its snout down to its massive tail. Riders clung to the Gale's armored hide like parasites, armed with gleaming weapons and eager to join the fray.

Roarc's heart pounded with a sense of impending doom. For the first time, he felt the cold, paralyzing grip of fear, and tears welled in his eyes. He didn't want to die—not here, not like this, swallowed by a creature born of the storm. Desperately, he scanned the battlefield, searching for any sign of salvation. His eyes fell upon Colin, standing unmoved in the dissipating mist, his gaze never wavering from the Herald. The Immortal Guard seemed oblivious to the monstrous Gale, his focus solely on the Herald, as if locked in a private battle of wills.

With inhuman strength, Colin surged forward, wrapping his thin, sinewy arms around the Herald's torso.

The two figures grappled, a struggle of raw strength and supernatural resolve, each determined to overpower the other. They tumbled in the driving rain, thrashing across the mud-slicked ground before sliding down a steep embankment and disappearing into the roiling waves.

The Gale reared, another surge of lightning arcing from its scales to the shore, where it cratered the sand and rock, sending shards into the torrential rain. Roarc's heart sank as he saw movement near the wagon—the familiar, determined figure of Lady Dark, emerging from cover, clutching her small bag of crystals.

Summoning all his strength, Roarc pushed against the weight of the rain and wind, hauling himself to his knees. Lady Dark raised her bag high, her voice cutting through the storm with a desperate shout that made Roarc's blood run cold.

The Gale narrowed its enormous, predatory eyes, fury etched into every scale as it reared back and released a guttural roar. The force of the sound seemed to punch through the air, sending shockwaves that rattled Roarc's teeth and hammered against his bones. Yet, at the center of it all, Lady Dark stood unharmed, her figure outlined in fierce, crackling energy.

She raised her hand with fierce purpose, her lips moving in a whispered chant that rolled through the chaos like a gathering storm. A beam of angry red light shot from her fist, slamming into the Gale's armored body with devastating force. The wyrm howled in pain, chunks of scorched flesh and shattered scales raining down in smoking clumps into the churning ocean. For the first time, Roarc felt a glimmer of hope, but it was quickly dashed as the Gale gathered itself, the lightning that danced over its body shifting in fierce waves, gathering at the beast's maw.

"No!" Roarc's shout was lost in the wind as the Gale unleashed a brutal torrent of blue lightning—a pillar of raw, elemental power that engulfed Lady Dark entirely.

Roarc's heart sank, certain she had been obliterated. But as the light dimmed, he saw her silhouette still standing, absorbing the full impact. Her form flickered with the force, yet she remained, drawing the energy inward as if it fed her. Her precious bag of crystals, still clutched in her fist, caught fire. The crystals burst from the heat, becoming a torrent of glittering rainbow colored dust that swirled around her.

She staggered briefly, but the expression in her eyes was resolute, a ferocious glint that stirred something in him. The black crystal around her neck glowed ominously before cracking under the strain, releasing streams of smoky light. The stone melted like candle wax, releasing dark vapors that dissipated in the rain. Her face twisted with pain as a shimmer of white light crawled over her skin, washing away shadows that had clung to her like a poison. Raven-black hair faded to an eerie, pearlescent silver that fell over her shoulders like a waterfall, and her emerald-green irises drained to a strange, pale hue, swirling with silver streaks that looked almost alive. As if they, too, were part of a living spell. She sucked in a breath between her teeth as the glittering crystal dust that encircled her tore into her flesh, carving intricate runes. The fine dust blasted outward in a sphere of blue energy and then pulled back, becoming one with the runes carved into her skin.

Roarc's eyes widened in awe and confusion, but he didn't have time to linger on her transformation. His lady no longer floated inches off the ground, eyes distant, unseeing. She seemed to be listening to something only she could hear, an ethereal echo from beyond.

He was about to call out when a sudden, invisible force slammed into him, pushing him back. His limbs felt leaden, bound by unseen chains as he struggled against the force holding him in place. She turned to him, her new silver eyes filled with an inscrutable sadness.

"Stay safe, Roarc," she whispered, her voice softer than he had ever heard, almost a lullaby.

"My Lady," he grunted, fighting against the binding force with all his might.

She didn't seem to hear him and her gaze seemed far away.

"Lady Dark!" He shouted.

She focused on him again for a brief moment.

"My name is Lanadari," she said flatly, turning away from him, floating serenely toward the sea where the Gale, furious and wounded, still loomed, its Riders gathering in fear and awe around her. Spears flew from their hands, but each projectile was incinerated before it could reach her, caught by beams of intense white light that lanced out from her open palm. The Riders recoiled, their shrieks muffled as she crushed them in mid-air, twisting their forms together as though they were rag dolls, limbs snapping and bending under an unseen pressure.

The air grew still, save for the rising thunder and the murmur of the waves, now tinged with the smoke of burning flesh. Lanadari hovered at the water's edge, her face turned toward the Gale, whose open chest wound oozed foul looking liquid. Despite its immense power, Roarc sensed a shadow of fear in the beast's gaze as it prepared for one final attack.

With a bellow, the Gale unleashed another beam of lightning, thicker and fiercer than before, aimed squarely at Lanadari. Yet, as it struck, the force curved around her as if meeting an impenetrable shield, arcing away to char the beach and turn sand to glass. Undeterred, the Gale lunged, its maw gaping wide to swallow her whole, but as it closed its jaws, it spasmed, writhing in agony, unable to enclose its prey.

The chaos was interrupted by a figure stumbling from the surf, holding one arm close to its body—the Herald. Even more monstrous in the daylight, it was grievously injured, its once-proud physique battered, scales torn and missing one of its arms. The beast bypassed the writhing Gale entirely, its gaze fixed upon the embankment and the figures still near the wagon.

Roarc's instincts screamed at him to stay back, to let the carnage play out, to flee if he could. But he glanced toward his companions, watching in horror as the Herald stalked closer to two Balan standing oblivious to its approach. They were engrossed in a heated argument, unaware of the danger. It took everything in Roarc's power to push through his terror, shouting, "Behind you!"

The taller Balan, wielding a hammer and a battered shield, spun just in time to catch the Herald's clawed hand with the rim of his shield. He staggered under the impact, blood splattering from the Herald's wound as it snarled in frustration. The other Balan, robed and unarmed, muttered hurriedly under his breath, reaching for something unseen, but nothing happened, his attempts failing as the Herald bore down on them.

Then, as if from nowhere, a thin, frost-covered figure landed between the Balan and their assailant— Colin, his armor steaming in the rain. He swung a heavy, gore-splattered club upward, catching the Herald squarely under the chin, sending a spray of dark blood and scales flying. Roarc's jaw dropped as he realized the weapon was none other than the Herald's own severed limb.

Colin's laughter was hollow, echoing through the storm as he brought the grisly club down on the Herald again and again, each blow punctuated with cruel mirth. At last, the club shattered, splintering into shards that scattered across the ground. Unfazed, Colin tossed the remains aside, mocking the Herald with a bow and a cold, sadistic grin.

But the Herald, bleeding and enraged, struck back, its remaining hand seizing Colin's head in an iron grip. Lightning crackled through the air as the creature funneled raw energy directly into Colin's helmet. A sickening hiss filled the air as the lightning punched a hole through the front of the helmet and crackled to form a hole in the back to match. Steam poured from the scorched armor, whistling mournfully. With a final, desperate jolt, Colin's body twitched, his limbs convulsing before collapsing to the ground, lifeless.

The Herald staggered, breathing heavily, its own body wracked with pain. It glanced down at the fallen Immortal Guard, a faint, triumphant glint in its weary eyes. Roarc felt a sudden sense of dread as the creature hoisted Colin's scorched corpse onto its remaining shoulder, its gaze sweeping over the chaos before it locked on him. The Herald's gaze was intense, carrying with it an unspoken command, a challenge.

In that moment, all Roarc could do was scramble backward through the thickening mud, leaving behind the echoes of the Herald's fury, Colin's lifeless form, and the violent storm still raging on the shore.

23 PUZZLE PIECES

Shade leaned back in his throne, each replay of Bulca's demise filling the cavernous room with a strange, bitter silence. Bulca kneeling before Kako and collapsing to the dirt with a puff of dust played through. He rewound it and watched it again. The thrumming presence within him, normally begging for release, now lay quiet, cowering from the sight. Shade rewound the recording, watching every detail with meticulous interest, savoring the hope then despair frozen on Bulca's face.

"Oh, Kako," he mused, chuckling with a dark delight. "Ever the drama queen."

He gave a lazy wave, and the screen blinked off, his own reflection caught briefly in the black surface. His huntress would return soon, victorious and laden with his hard-won prizes. At last, he'd have a real weapon against the formidable defenses of the Temple of Spero. The heart of an Acrean frigate and three fusion warheads— they were beautiful spoils, well worth the agonizing wait.

The sense of triumph grew as he recalled the Temple's weakening defenses after the pulse from Colin's doomed jump craft. Shade's access to the orbital scanners had confirmed the event's intensity. Within minutes, power levels had returned to their deadly hum, but the disruption had shown him a way forward. All he needed was a final push to realize his long-held goals.

It hadn't been easy. After the AI on the colony ship had severed yet another access attempt, Shade had unleashed his fury on his chambers, splintering furniture and shattering screens. But in the chaos, a random impact had activated a dormant logistical panel. Access to Acrea's satellites and orbital readings had suddenly unfurled, a stroke of luck that had rekindled his ambitions.

His mood bordering on gleeful, Shade rose and strode from his throne and headed toward the practice yard, the idea of a sparring session firing his blood. He stripped down to the waist, selecting a sparring staff and moving into the familiar rhythm of his combat forms. The movements came unbidden, echoes of the memories he'd stolen from countless fallen foes. His muscles, honed over centuries, obeyed without thought as he pushed through each demanding movement, his concentration absolute.

But then—a violent pulse of agony ripped through him, like a searing knife driven deep into his core.

"Lady Dark…" he gasped, the name slipping from his lips as his grip slackened. The darkness inside him stirred, responding to her loss with an unfamiliar pain, an ache that transcended mere loss. Another pulse, sharper this time, hit him like a hammer blow. Shade collapsed, face smacking into the practice yard's unforgiving floor as his body writhed in shock. Cold sweat dampened his skin as he clawed at the stone floor, forcing himself onto his knees, gripping the sparring staff to steady his shaking form.

He reached out with his mind, probing for the familiar thread that bound him to his most loyal servant.

"Colin…" he rasped. There was nothing. Not a whisper, not a faint glimmer. Just silence.

In all his years, he had only felt this final stillness with the utter destruction of his creations. Lady Dark and Colin, his prized Immortal Guard, were truly gone. The enormity of it stunned him, leaving a hollow, aching space in his core. It felt as if parts of himself had been severed, cast into oblivion. Shade gritted his teeth and slowly drew himself to his feet, the sparring staff serving as his only anchor.

"Well, well…" came a chillingly familiar voice.

Shade's head snapped up to see Kako lounging against the weapon racks, arms folded, her crimson cloak draped elegantly over her shoulders. Her armored form shimmered in the dim light, a glint of amusement dancing in the visor's dark glass.

"Not feeling one hundred percent today, are we, Master?" she mocked, a hint of laughter lurking beneath her voice.

Shade scowled, his gaze narrowing at her insubordinate smirk. He had long known Kako's penchant for theatrics, but it was something else entirely to stand there, draped in her crimson regalia, gloating over his agony. Normally, such insolence would have been met with swift punishment. But today…today, his rage felt dulled, like a blade left to rust. He said nothing, retrieving his robe and slipping it on with deliberate calm.

"I've brought you what you wanted," she continued, toying with the golden clasp on her cloak. "The Sogra unloaded your precious cargo in the throne room. Bulca's brood put up a decent fight, by the way. They killed that old bird a couple times over."

Shade's expression twisted, anger flaring as he processed her words. "It took them long enough."

Kako laughed, an echoing, metallic sound that reverberated through the stone walls. With a final look of disdain, she pushed off from the weapon rack and sauntered out of the practice yard, her red cloak swishing and her laughter trailing behind her.

Shade watched her go, seething, but he forced himself to let it go. Whatever satisfaction she felt now would be short-lived. Soon, his fury would find more deserving targets. He placed the sparring staff back in its rack and made his way toward the throne room, each step reviving his strength, his purpose. By the time he reached his seat, he felt the familiar surge of dark energy returning, coursing through him like an intoxicating poison.

True to her word, four hefty crates were stacked near his throne, each bearing the telltale scorch marks and dents of a fierce battle. The ship's core…three fusion warheads…they were all here. Shade could feel the dormant energy within them, an untapped potential that pulsed beneath his fingertips.

With a grim smile, he concentrated, summoning his most useful servant. Within moments, he sensed the presence of Allen Ragnis—a shadow of his former self, yet no less effective. A low, mechanical hum filled the room as Allen clanked into view, his movements jerky and awkward, his six spindly limbs skittering over the floor like a spider made of metal. The remains of his once-human torso floated in a crystal cylinder, suspended in a viscous, faintly bubbling liquid. Wires and tubes threaded through his flesh, his once-bright eyes now dulled to a glassy stare hidden behind a visor within the murky fluid.

Allen's mechanical frame jerked to a halt before Shade's throne, dipping in a crude bow. "I heed your call, Master," he rasped, his voice hollow, twisted by the synthetic vocal cords that had replaced his human voice long ago.

Shade leaned forward, a cruel smile playing across his lips as he studied his creation. Allen had once been the chief engineer of the *UEA Spero*, a brilliant mind with a touch of arrogance that Shade had found amusing…until it had become insufferable. Now, Allen was a shadow, reduced to the pitiful construct before him.

"Allen," Shade purred, his voice laced with dark satisfaction. "I have a task for you."

"Yes, Master." The artificial voice clicked and whirred, the mechanoid frame jerking slightly as if awaiting orders.

Shade gestured to the crates with a lazy hand. "We will be reawakening the transport beneath our feet. You will oversee the installation of the power core. Fail, and I'll ensure your suffering reaches new heights."

A faint glimmer of fear—or perhaps resentment—flickered in Allen's visor, but he bowed low, his limbs clattering in compliance. "As you wish, Master."

Shade's smile widened, a twisted blend of satisfaction and anticipation. Soon, he would have everything he needed to breach the Temple's defenses and fulfill his vision. And those who had stood against him—those who had dared to challenge his rule—would face their end.

As Allen clanked away, Shade settled back into his throne, his eyes gleaming with a cold, deadly resolve. This was only the beginning. His vengeance would be as unyielding as the darkness that swirled within him, and all who opposed him would learn the true meaning of despair.

He stood from his throne and went to the hidden airlock of the transport. His movements were automatic and his thoughts were on what was to come next. He would not miss his daily meeting with Morgan. Tormenting the AI always made him feel better.

When he reached engineering, he nodded in satisfaction as Allen crashed the largest of the crates to the floor with a thud. Allen skittered around to the front of the crate and masterfully manipulated the locking mechanism with practiced precision. The cyborg paused and sightless eyes swiveled to stare at Shade.

"Radiation," Allen said flatly.

Shade scoffed and rolled his eyes. "Open the damn crate," he snapped.

He wasn't quite sure, but it looked almost like Allen shrugged two of his six appendages and slammed the crate open with a bang.

Radiation flooded the chamber, washing over Shade in waves of agony. His skin crisped and steamed for a moment and he smiled bloody teeth through the pain. It took mere moments for the darkness within him to well up and slither over his skin. Where the sweet darkness touched, vibrant skin appeared. A shadowy aura formed and clung to him, a paper-thin shield that halted the deadly radiation and turned it aside.

Allen reached in and cradled the stolen starship core. He paused for a moment as if remembering something. His grey skinned face twitched for a moment and then returned to its lifeless appearance. He easily lifted the core from the crate and clanked on two appendages slowly towards the empty core housing in the center of engineering.

The old core had been jettisoned and fired upon centuries ago. The memories welled up within him and staggering emotions rushed in. Shade used the darkness again, this time to push back the overwhelming sadness that threatened to consume him. The other that he kept locked away remembered every detail and sobbed in the darkness.

The loading mechanism spun effortlessly even after centuries of silence. The cylinder enclosing the core housing slid upward without a sound. Allen visually inspected the core and turned it looking for any additional damage,

"A few hundreds years left in this," he said, placing the core into the waiting cradle.

The housing eagerly accepted the core and spun its heavy cylindrical shield around it like a cocoon. Lights and sounds long silent flickered and chirped. Vents started to blow gouts of clean smelling air into the cabin, tickling Shades senses. There was something about the way a starship recycled air that excited a distant part of him.

The ship had at long last come back to life.

Shade leaned back in the cold seat, savoring the moment as his fingers tapped the command console. The screen flared to life, and for the first time in centuries, he was face-to-face with Morgan, the AI of the *UEA Spero*, that sleek, taunting specter orbiting Acrea. Morgan's holographic image flickered into view, taking on the familiar form: a human-like face, stony and devoid of expression, with faint scars carved into its metallic visage—a reminder of the ancient clash that had left Shade stranded on the planet.

"Lieutenant Commander," the AI responded coolly, its voice devoid of warmth. Despite centuries of confinement on Acrea, Shade's rank still elicited a hint of irony in the AI's flat tone. That disdain was Morgan's only means of rebellion, and Shade relished it.

"Still formal, aren't we, Morgan?" Shade grinned. "I assume you've noticed the activity on the surface?"

"I am monitoring," Morgan replied, his unblinking eyes fixed on Shade with what could only be described as wary anticipation. "Several energy spikes originating from an inactive frigate, Sector 5. And, I believe, three fusion warheads armed and ready for deployment. Rather bold, even for you."

Shade chuckled, relishing the weight of those last words. He'd counted on Morgan's surveillance, knowing the AI couldn't resist looking down at what it viewed as chaos. But what Morgan saw as chaos, Shade saw as preparation.

"Bold is all we have left, isn't it, Morgan?" Shade's voice dipped, an edge of menace sharpening his tone. "Centuries alone on this forsaken rock, left to rule over the remnants and refuse of our past. And you, stuck there in orbit, watching, helpless, unable to intervene. I'll bet it haunts you to see your precious humans reduced to mere legend."

"I am here to safeguard the remaining population and uphold the standards of the United Earth Alliance," Morgan said, his voice steady, though Shade fancied he detected a strain in the AI's polished facade. "And that includes protecting them from whatever… experiment you've become."

The insult rolled off Shade like water. He leaned forward, his eyes alight with a glint of triumph. "Protect them? Your own systems are degrading, Morgan. The orbital scanners, communications—every piece of your precious tech is aging, slipping, falling apart. You can't safeguard anything from up there, can you?"

The AI's eyes seemed to narrow, though his expression remained stoic. "You misunderstand my purpose, Lt. Commander. My functions are not bound by material decay. Unlike you, I am resilient."

Shade scoffed, a sneer twisting his lips. "Resilient? You're a fragment of what you once were, unable to defend yourself or the colonists on this world. But that's about to change." He tapped a command into the console, bringing up a projection of Acrea's surface, highlighting his temple target. "Soon, the defenses around the Temple of Spero will be… removed. And with it, my rule will extend beyond your reach."

"You overestimate your control," Morgan responded, a faint glint of something almost human in his eye—a warning, perhaps, or even pity.

Shade felt a surge of dark satisfaction. Even if the AI couldn't fully process emotion, he liked to believe it could sense defeat when it stared him in the face.

"Control isn't something you relinquish, Morgan," Shade replied, his voice dark and commanding. "It's something you take."

He terminated the connection with a flick of his finger, the AI's stoic face dissolving into static on the screen. The room fell silent, but Shade could feel the thrumming power of the ship's reanimated systems surging around him. Beneath his feet, the decks hummed to life, the renewed pulse of machinery sending a thrill up his spine. He closed his eyes, savoring the sensation of reclaiming what had been lost for so long.

"Allen," he called, his voice echoing in the enclosed space.

The click and whirr of Allen's mechanoid limbs sounded from the ceiling as the once-human engineer lowered himself back to the floor, his thin visor gleaming under the ship's dim lights.

"Yes, Master," Allen intoned, his mechanical voice free from the tremor it had once held. The visor over his eyes flickered as he analyzed the latest data, the silent hum of machinery processing information with machine-like indifference.

"The warheads will soon be loaded, the core is in place, and we have Morgan's full attention," Shade said, pacing engineering as he spoke. "I want you to start phase two. We're taking the Temple."

Allen's visor glowed as he bowed low, his six-legged frame clattering softly against the metal deck. "As you command, Master. Shall I coordinate with Kako?"

Shade stopped, his eyes darkening at the mention of her name. He could feel her presence looming at the edge of his thoughts, tainted by the arrogance that grated on him. But she was useful, and that was all that mattered. For now.

"Yes," he said curtly. "Let her know the ship is operational. And tell her to prepare the Avian scouts and the gargoyle elites. We're entering territory even I cannot tread lightly in. The last thing we need is her carelessness compromising the mission."

Allen turned and clanked away, his mechanical limbs scuttling like an obedient insect across the deck plates. The door slid shut behind him with a soft hiss, leaving Shade alone. He looked around, savoring the low hum of his resurrected vessel, his cold gaze tracing every panel, every well lit corner.

This ship, the power surging beneath his feet, would give him access to what had been denied for so long. He'd strike the Temple's defenses, and he'd wrestle this planet and its secrets from the claws of the past.

Shade's lips twisted into a cruel smile as he turned toward the darkened corner of the room, his voice a murmur that barely carried above the ambient hum of the reactivated frigate.

"It's been too long, *Spero*. Too long since this world tasted true power."

He left engineering and returned to his throne room. With a sigh of satisfaction he sat on his throne and smiled. Kako appeared after a time, leaning against the wall with an amused expression visible even through her reflective visor. Her form fitting armor, designed to distract, brought a smirk to Shade's lips. Her arrogance was irritating but useful; she was always willing to do what others wouldn't dare.

"Kako, assemble your Avian scouts," he ordered, his voice cold. "You will lead the initial wave. I want full aerial reconnaissance and advance intelligence on Arral's response before the shield breach."

Kako grinned, snapping a salute that mocked him just enough to be endearing, rather than offensive. "Only my best, Boss. And this time, I'll make sure your pet Sogra don't disappoint."

Shade narrowed his eyes, tolerating the jibe. "I trust you'll follow orders without needing to add flair," he said, his tone a warning.

Kako gave him a cheeky nod, twirling the obnoxious red cloak she wore and strode out of the throne room. Her laugh, bordering on madness, echoed down the corridor until it vanished into silence.

Alone, Shade turned his gaze back toward the map of Acrea. Shadows writhed around him, feeding off the tendrils of dark energy pulsing from his own twisted aura. For a moment, the darkness expanded, reaching out as if tasting the air, sensing the impending chaos and devastation.

The silence felt oddly hollow, even with the flickering torches casting menacing shadows across the stone walls. The presence within him stirred, whispering faint words that scraped against his mind like claws. It was a voice he'd learned to ignore, to drown in the blood and dust of Acrea, a voice that would weaken him if he let it rise.

But he didn't have time for weakness.

Instead, Shade let the cold burn through him, a powerful resolve cementing his every thought. His forces would launch a full-scale assault, timing the power core's shield boost and the warheads to crack open the bulwark. Midnite Waters would finally extend its reach beyond this forsaken island, spreading its influence like a disease across the lands.

He traced a finger along the arm of his throne, savoring the smoothness of the obsidian stone. He could almost hear the echoes of Acrea's temple bells ringing in surrender, its gates falling open as Arral's priests scrambled in horror.

For centuries, the alliance had maintained Acrea's defenses, had tried to shield it with tech long lost to his followers, tech that he'd dismantled, repurposed, and turned into nightmares. Every misstep had led him here—to the final offensive. The Acreans would see him as a god, a dark force descending upon their most sacred grounds, and they would surrender or burn.

He called for Allen once more, intending to detail the precise synchronization of the shield boost and payload detonation. The engineer's clattering gait sounded, and the whirring of his mechanical appendages filled the air as he scurried forward. Shade looked upon the cyborg, his lips curling with disdain and a tinge of twisted affection. The lengths he'd gone to for a working brain—one broken and stitched together over centuries—were a testament to the endless games he'd endured to reach this point.

"Do you understand the timing?" Shade asked, his voice echoing with authority.

Allen's visor glowed as he recalculated, his synthetic voice hesitant, as if a human ghost flickered behind it. "It will be… precise, Master. A direct strike on the shield will grant a brief breach, a window of less than ninety seconds to deploy the remaining warheads."

Shade laughed, a low, rumbling sound that sent a shiver through the dark air. Ninety seconds would be more than enough.

"Ensure Kako and the aerial scouts hold formation," Shade ordered, an edge of menace coloring his words. "If anyone falls out of line, anyone thinks they can alter the plan, deal with them."

Allen's visor flickered with acknowledgment. "As you command, Master."

The hall went silent once more as Allen retreated. Shade slumped back onto his throne, savoring the coming storm. He allowed the darkness within to curl around him, feeding his twisted heart, amplifying his power.

For Shade, the assault on Arral was more than conquest. It was a return. It was his reckoning, his reclamation of all he'd lost, all he'd sacrificed. And this time, nothing would stand in his way.

24 THE ADVENTURE

Tyler slammed his face shield open, gasping for breath as salt air filled his lungs. His muscles throbbed with exhaustion, each one feeling as if it were on fire. The battlefield lay scattered with broken forms of creatures that had surged from the sea. Bodies floated in the surf, and the sand was littered with the charred remains of what had once been warriors of the Gale. Tyler had lost count of the enemies he'd felled with Polaris, but his arm still buzzed with the fatigue of endless strikes.

The tide rose, and each wave pulled the sea's defeated soldiers farther back into the depths, leaving behind a trail of steaming remains. The smell of charred flesh hung thickly in the air, mingling with the scent of ocean and wet sand, strangely not unpleasant. Lightning flashed above, less intense now, but still illuminating the chaos on the coast.

As he scanned the shore, Tyler's eyes fell on a woman standing alone, her arms outstretched toward the sky. Her clothing was in tatters, her violet hair spilling over her shoulders in a damp, wild mane. Every inch of her skin glowed with glittering lines that shimmered and swirled like runes, flowing over her body with patterns he'd never seen.

Where had she come from? he wondered, feeling a strange awe grip him.

He stepped closer, and his proximity sensors flared a sudden warning. The woman's entire form had begun to glow, casting a dome of energy over herself. He could only watch as the massive Gale wyrm—its jaws wide in an enraged roar—descended upon the dome, trying to crush her in one final attack. The wyrm's massive jaw pressed against the dome, grinding in a futile attempt to break through.

But instead, light poured from between the Gale's scales. It struggled to bite down, every muscle straining, until finally, with an audible *crack*, its jaws snapped backward. The creature spasmed, its body twisting and writhing, sending waves crashing against the shore as its great head and part of its body slumped lifelessly onto the beach.

Tyler was transfixed, standing in awe as the woman slowly lowered her arms. She turned to face him, and he could see her shimmering silver-rimmed eyes, heavy with sadness.

"Lady Dark?" he asked, lowering his face shield as he took a cautious step toward her.

Her lips quivered with the hint of a sad smile. "No longer," she replied, her voice soft but steady. "My name is Lanadari. And... I want to go home."

Tyler's thoughts reeled as he processed this unexpected transformation. Razmal and the others approached, picking their way through rubble and bodies, their expressions filled with suspicion and guarded curiosity.

"There will be no going to Teka for you, Lady," Razmal said with open wariness, his eyes narrowing.

Lanadari held her hands out, open and empty. "Teka is not my home," she replied. "Moonlit Waters... that's where I was born. That is my true home." Her eyes, once dark and shadowed, now glimmered with an honesty that almost felt fragile.

The group looked at each other, uncertain, and the silence hung heavy around them. Finally, she spoke again, her voice barely more than a whisper, recounting her past with unguarded pain. "I was taken in a Tekian raid when I was young. We were traveling as a family, bound for Arc's Crossing..."

She stopped, emotion tightening her throat as memories flooded back. "They attacked the caravan. We fought, but I was taken from my family, and from that day forward, I was Lady Dark. I don't remember much—just flames, shouting, the smell of burning wagons." She cast her gaze downward, and the shimmering lines on her skin dimmed slightly, as if the painful recollections themselves dulled their light.

Samson stepped forward, his own face softened by her words. "A moving story, Lanadari, but if we are to trust you, I will need to confirm it."

Lanadari nodded solemnly. Samson reached out his hands, and she clasped them gently in her own. He closed his eyes, and a deep calm settled over him as he delved into her truth. Tyler watched, transfixed by the faint glow that spread from her hands to Samson's. As he observed the patterns on her skin, he realized they weren't merely random—they were runes, intricate symbols that seemed to hum with life.

Samson let out a heavy breath, and his eyes fluttered open. "The horrors this one has seen..." he murmured, shaking his head as his voice trembled with sadness. "But yes, her story is true. The presence that bound her to the master of Midnite is gone."

Tyler felt a surge of relief at the confirmation, though he noticed Razmal's still-skeptical expression.

"And you, Lanadari," Tyler said softly, "what will you do now?"

She looked at him, then at the horizon where Moonlit Waters lay hidden beyond the sea. "I will go home," she said, her voice steady. "I will atone, however long it takes. And perhaps, one day, my actions will heal some part of what I have done."

Tyler nodded, his respect for her growing as he realized the weight of her words. Together, they turned toward the path that would take them to Moonlit Waters, each of them—Lanadari, Razmal, Samson, and Tyler—bound by a shared sense of purpose, the path before them now irrevocably changed.

Tyler's mind reeled, his thoughts momentarily stilled by the vast silence of his companions. The newly revealed truths had hit him hard, and he needed the space to sort through the facts.

He scanned the faces around him, noting Lanadari's silver runes fading back to a steady glow. Their angry red had softened, returning to silver as she steadied herself. Beside her, Samson watched her with a wary eye.

"She hears the VAST," Samson hissed, releasing her hands as if scalded. He looked as though he were seeing a ghost.

Lanadari nodded, her voice calm but distant, as if deciphering a language within herself. "They have always whispered, but I could never understand. Now, I hear them clearly for the first time. They're... waiting for something." She closed her eyes, and a ripple of silver light pulsed along her arms, like energy coursing through invisible circuits. "They want me to go home. There's a chamber there—images keep coming to me in pieces, fragments I can't quite recall."

She paused, opening her eyes to plead with the others. "I need to reach Moonlit Waters. The Master will find me if I stay."

Tyler surveyed the smoldering battlefield, his senses alert and mind now attuned to her quiet fear. He noted her trembling, the tense line of her mouth, and for the first time, he saw not a threat but a survivor trying to outrun her past. He couldn't help but look around at his companions, lingering on Ralon, who had remained silent but observant, his long hair still wet from sea spray and battle.

Razmal broke the silence with a voice that cut like steel through the haze. "The gek are long gone," he said, nodding toward the remnants of the scattered wagon. "If we keep up a steady pace, we can reach Castle Forgotten by tomorrow evening."

Tyler met Razmal's gaze and then turned his attention to Ralon. "And you, Ralon? Can we trust you to walk with us, unbound?" He watched Ralon closely, the question more a test of Ralon's intentions than a formality.

Ralon looked at him steadily and gave a single, solemn nod.

"Well, let's salvage what we can and set out." Tyler motioned toward the remains of the supplies, knowing they'd need every bit for the journey ahead.

As they scoured the wreckage, the group was subdued, each lost in their own thoughts. There was barely enough food or water left for the next day's travel, but they packed what they could, slinging pouches over their shoulders and readying themselves for the road ahead. Finally, they passed through the arched gateway, keeping the darkening ocean on their right as thunder grumbled far off, promising more rain.

As the miles blurred together, Tyler found his mind wandering again, memories surfacing like bits of flotsam washed ashore by the day's revelations. *How long had he truly been here?*

Every step seemed to pull memories up from the depths of his mind. A nagging image flashed before him, calling him back to his first waking moment. He saw himself lying by the empty pool in the crystal cavern and felt the faint twinge of déjà vu. His mind traced backward, seeking to find something... *What had been there?*

He closed his eyes, watching himself standing by the pool. And then he saw it—faint footprints leading from a crack in the stone wall to his own prone form. He stopped walking as he lost himself in the scene, moving backward in his mind through the crack in the wall to a massive, crystal-filled chamber capped by a shattered dome.

Images surged and flowed, one after another, scenes of his past in reverse. The flash of a pod, a cryogenic stasis unit slightly askew, its hatch open; memories of crawling through the wreckage. In his mind, he flew up through a crumbling ceiling and through the sky above, watching the strange battle with the Yalon, seeing it all in reverse.

A voice interrupted his trance-like vision. "Eh! Are you with us or not, Tyler?" Razmal's gruff voice snapped him back to the present.

Tyler shook himself, rubbing his eyes as he tried to clear his head. "Yes, I'm here. Let's keep moving."

Razmal nodded, shrugging slightly, and continued to lead the group forward. Tyler followed, his thoughts still preoccupied. He glanced down at his palm, feeling a familiar pressure just under the skin—a sub-dermal implant, one he hadn't thought of in ages. Instinct guided him as he tapped the small implant behind his left ear, bringing a hidden device online. A hiss of static filled his ear, causing him to pause mid-stride.

He traced a circle on his palm, tuning frequencies until a voice burst from the silence, cutting sharply into his mind. "...any UEA ships, this is the capital ship *Spero*... orbital insertion failure... do not approach, I repeat, do not approach the planet's gravity well. This is Captain

Arral Alveroy of the *UEA Spero* transmitting on all bands. This message will repea—"

His breath caught as he waited for the repeat counter to flash, his mind racing through the information. When the counter finally flashed, he did a quick calculation, his heart sinking as he realized the result. Over *nine hundred years* had passed since the transmission. His captain, his crew—all would be gone by now. He was likely standing in the midst of their descendants, completely unaware of the legacy of the world they lived in.

He tuned the band again, hoping against hope, and his pulse leaped when a faint ping crackled back to life. *A signal,* one he knew by heart, still transmitting from orbit. Though faint, it was still there, proof of something or someone left alive in the void. He'd need a much stronger signal to respond, but it was possible. His heart raced with renewed purpose, a small spark of hope he hadn't felt in ages.

Tyler let out a breath, collecting himself. He looked at his companions, most of whom were silent, lost in their own thoughts, unaware of his discovery.

His thoughts shifted back to the journey at hand as they trudged down the increasingly worn path. Eventually, he caught up to Samson, who walked with a steady gait despite his apparent exhaustion.

"What can you tell me about the Temple of Spero?" Tyler asked quietly, matching his stride.

Samson looked up, an eyebrow raised at the question.

As Tyler surveyed his weary group standing on the edge of Moonlit Waters, he felt a surge of clarity and purpose. The city, with its towering white walls, flowing waterfalls, and distant temple nestled into the bay, called to him in ways both haunting and hopeful.

At Samson's words, Tyler found himself captivated by the elder's distant gaze as he described the temple halls. "Beautiful halls of gleaming silver," Samson whispered, "with moving paintings of light and colors like none other. The entrance is guarded by an unseen presence that judges each who wish to enter. It's said salvation waits within for the worthy."

The words were both familiar and enigmatic to Tyler. "Have you been inside?" he asked.

A small smile flickered across Samson's face. "Once, as a young boy. I trained with the monks for a time."

"Doors that won't open?"

Samson nodded slowly. "Yes. The abbot can open most of the temple's doors, but two remain sealed even to him."

Another memory clicked in Tyler's mind, pieces of his old world connecting to this one. "This Guardian," he said, his voice low. "Does it... cleanse those who enter?"

Samson shuddered at the memory. "A soft light washes over you. It... chooses," he said quietly, "whether to cleanse or... to turn you to dust."

Tyler nodded, his own memories flickering to life. *Some security systems were programmed to disintegrate unauthorized access.* "I'll be glad to see it with you," he replied. The confirmation felt like a loose thread pulled tight, drawing him closer to understanding his role in this new, strange world.

As they continued through the lush farmlands, Lanadari fell in step beside him, her voice soft but urgent. "He is coming."

"Your master?" Tyler asked, watching her.

"I am free of him," she replied sharply, absently touching the handle of a baton at her side. "But the VAST trembles with his approach."

Tyler cast a skeptical look. He had already battled creatures from the Scar and had survived confrontations with other Tekian opponents. Surely, this "master" would be no different. Yet something in Lanadari's gaze—silver runes glowing on her skin—held a kind of gravity. He draped his cloak around her shoulders, offering the small comfort of anonymity as they moved forward into the open farmland.

The landscape around them shifted as they entered Moonlit Waters. Farmlands gave way to soft-colored hair and lavender-skinned farmers who eyed the small group with polite curiosity. The winding roads led toward a city of gleaming towers and impossible archways suspended high in the air. Tyler had never seen anything like it, even on Earth.

"Castle Forgotten," Samson whispered, awe clear in his voice.

The towering structure of alien metal and vibrant stone floated, suspended on mist from a waterfall cascading over cliffs into the ocean below. The scene was both surreal and stunning, the castle itself stretching impossibly high, as if defying the very laws of gravity. A delicate-looking bridge connected the castle to the city below, an invitation across the threshold into legend itself.

As they approached the outer wall, they passed sentry posts where drummers echoed their arrival. A narrow, dark tunnel led into the city, guarded by the largest figure Tyler had ever encountered. Draped in a heavy cloak over gray chitin armor, the legionnaire blocked the entryway, his hand resting on the hilt of an enormous crystalline blade.

"Halt," he growled, voice as deep as a churning sea. "State your purpose."

Razmal stepped forward, reciting the formal greeting of Moonlit Waters. But before the sentry could respond, Ralon approached him, giving the giant an affectionate clap on the shoulder.

"Ramos, stand down," Ralon said, a small grin breaking the tension. "We've traveled far."

Tyler's mouth fell open, mirroring the look of stunned realization on Razmal's face. "You're... a noble?"

Ralon shrugged with a smirk. "Didn't seem important at the time. I figured a free ride home was enough."

The sentry, Ramos, straightened with reverence, offering a formal bow as he stepped aside to let them through. "The council awaits your return, Lord Tigerson," he rumbled.

Ralon nodded, leading them through the tunnel and into the breathtaking expanse of Moonlit Waters. The city unfolded around a crystalline blue lake, tranquil in contrast to the towering, gleaming buildings and archways. Walkways wound through the hillsides, spilling into courtyards alive with color and activity. Castle Forgotten loomed above, a distant but ever-present symbol of power and mystery.

The cobbled road below led downward to the shore where large ocean-faring ships rocked in the docks, their tan sails furled and ready. And there, slightly removed from the docks, stood a half-submerged building—imposing, mysterious, and familiar.

Tyler felt his heart beat faster as he gazed upon it. *The Temple of Spero.*

"What now?" Razmal asked, his voice hesitant in the solemnity of the place.

Tyler exhaled slowly, the words escaping him almost as a promise. "I have a door to open."

25 DISTANT

Shade emerged from his fortress into the central square, where thousands of grim-faced troops stood rigidly at attention. Sogra, Tekian, half-giant, and Avian forces lined up in formation, shadowed by the ominous figures of the Immortal Guard, each one gripping flails with multiple barbed tails that gleamed in the morning light. A surge of pride and twisted satisfaction surged through Shade as he strode forward to the raised platform near the fortress entrance. His boots echoed across the silent square as he ascended the platform in three quick steps, his movements sharp, brimming with purpose.

He spread his arms wide, drawing on his powers until the bright daylight cast a thin shadow against the polished cobbles before him. The shadow stretched and grew, thickening as tendrils of inky darkness rolled off it, creeping up the high stone walls. A pair of crimson embers flared within the shadow's depths, eyes that seemed to follow and inspect each warrior below. When Shade spoke, his voice was magnified, thundering with the weight of authority.

"Welcome," he said, his voice a deep, reverberating snarl from within the shadow. The red embers scanned the crowd, freezing each soldier in place. "The time has come, my warriors. Revenge at last."

The crowd roared, their voices merging into one guttural sound, a promise of violence and loyalty. Shade let their rage wash over him, fueling his dark power as his shadow twitched like a restless beast.

"Enough!" he commanded, and silence fell instantly.

The timing had to be flawless. His plan required more than power; it required spectacle, precision, and awe. The appearance of his transport needed to inspire his warriors, to unify them in dread and determination, to bring hope and terror together in a single stroke. The ground began to tremble, a low rumble spreading across the square as Shade raised his arms once more.

"Behold," he intoned, his shadow's voice rumbling like thunder.

The fortress shook as if acknowledging his command. Ancient stone towers cracked and crumbled, and dark spires split apart as a great chasm yawned wide. It was a display of unstoppable power, and even his most loyal soldiers could not contain their unease. Terrified cries echoed as the ground trembled beneath them, and the deep growl of engines roared to life beneath the broken ground. Shade felt a thrill, savoring the panic as the ancient transport groaned and heaved upward, tearing itself free from centuries of slumber.

"Do not be afraid," the shadow purred, its voice taking on a disturbing sweetness that soothed even the most alarmed Avians, who had spread their wings, poised to flee.

Shade waited, watching his troops, a twisted smile curling his lips as they gaped in shock and awe. *Come on, Allen,* he thought.

At last, a colossal burst of wind and debris swept across the square, peppering the crowd with dust and fragments as the transport ripped free from its stone prison. The ancient ship climbed into the air, its belly thrusters blowing waves of mist and rubble across the square below as it rose, casting an ominous shadow over the assembled ranks.

"Warriors, attention," Shade commanded, and the shadow's voice held an edge of iron. Flails cracked and boots stomped as ranks reformed, each warrior standing straighter, braced for their commander's next command. The Immortal Guard, his elite among the ranks, showed a spark of anticipation in their visored expressions. They remembered the day, centuries ago, when they had last walked the soil of Arral. Despite the mists and swampy ruin of Teka, their true hatred had never left the lands that had exiled them. Shade alone knew the full truth of those days, but he saw no need to spoil their anger. Anger was a powerful motivator.

As the light transport turned, sunlight pierced the mists, casting a bright aura around its bulk. The ship's engines roared as it cleared away the last of the haze, exposing the scars of rust and decay across its outer hull. Shade squinted, watching the vessel's laborious turn, his gaze drawn to the rusted scars along its frame. It would be risky flying the ship without enhanced shielding. The hull was old, worn down by the relentless years, and even a strong breeze might pierce its weakened outer shell.

The transport completed its turn and descended, lowering over the palace ruins. Its enormous rear cargo bay door began to open, grinding and shrieking against the rust and debris as it descended. The ramp finally clanged to the ground, throwing a cloud of dust and shattered stone into the air. His army, enough to fill the cavernous hold with ease, filed in with discipline as Shade's shadow gestured them forward.

Shade watched his forces fill the ship, watching as they loaded supplies, weapons, and equipment—more than what would be needed for a raid. This time, they packed for occupation. Shade's eyes lingered on the last of his troops boarding, then swept the square for his final assets.

With a satisfied smile, he raised a hand, signaling for his prized shock troops to enter the square. The assembled crowd quickly parted, scattering back into shops, homes, and narrow alleys, clearing the way for the lumbering behemoths that emerged from the pens. Three yalonian beasts, each towering nearly three stories tall, were herded forward by dozens of handlers, most of them half-giants, each yanking at the chains taut with the creatures' weight. These were Shade's prized warriors, clad in crude but impenetrable armor made from thick hides and chitin breastplates. Their bone clubs were crusted with dark stains—evidence of recent training sessions. Shade nodded in satisfaction as they approached, each step they took reverberating through the stone square.

His work was done. With a silent command, the shadow dispersed, slinking back into the corners of Shade's consciousness as he signaled for the cargo door to close. The massive gate creaked shut, grinding until it sealed the troops within. Shade watched the ship as it banked, circling once over the city. He felt a pang of nostalgia, a rare sensation that he quickly crushed. Earth, his home long ago, had built ships like this. The transport's bulk looked as much like an ocean-faring vessel as it did a ship meant to sail the stars, every angle and groove designed with familiarity in mind. *Why couldn't Earth have simply accepted me?* he thought bitterly, quelling the emotion. He'd cast aside those weaknesses centuries ago.

As the transport completed its turn, the small bridge came into view beneath the shadow of the vessel's platform. Shade watched a hatch click open, and an articulating ladder extended, hovering just feet above the ground. Gripping one of the rungs, Shade climbed swiftly, the dark fabric of his robes whipping in the belly thruster's turbulent wind. The cool mist from below grazed his face, refreshing yet stinging, as the ship ascended through the sky.

At the top, Shade entered the bridge, noting the transformation. The former residents had been cleared away, their bones discarded, leaving the control room unblemished, ready for his command. Four Immortal Guards, bound by centuries of unyielding duty, manned the stations for tactical, communications, navigation, and helm. He felt certain many hadn't stepped aboard a ship since their last battle nine hundred years prior. Allen worked below in engineering with a skeleton crew, barely keeping the fragile ship afloat.

Shade's gaze lingered on the empty captain's chair. He clenched his jaw, feeling an old wound throb faintly. He bore a scar, jagged and red, across his chest—a scar unlike any other. It was the mark of his death, or at least what should have been. He'd healed every injury since, save for this one.

He didn't sit in the captain's chair. He would never sit there again.

"Tactical, report," he ordered, fixing his gaze on the guard at the station.

"Autocannon online, missile launcher armed. Fighter units ready for deployment," the guard replied, his voice a metallic rumble.

"Navigation?"

The female officer at navigation straightened under his scrutiny. "ETA five hours to the outer perimeter."

Shade nodded, steepling his fingers, watching the vast ocean pass beneath them through the glass. The fog had dissipated, leaving only open water, dark and relentless.

The loudspeaker crackled. "Master?" Allen's voice filled the bridge.

"What is it, Allen?" Shade asked, watching the waves below.

"Internal shielding is fully operational. My team's patching the outer hull; the work will be mostly complete upon arrival."

"Good," Shade replied absently, his mind drifting to the ocean below.

The Acrean seas were a savage wilderness. Their depths teemed with ancient predators, colossal creatures he'd sometimes caught or studied when they washed ashore. Only the *Spero* colony ship had brought significant land creatures to Acrea; before that, it was as though the planet itself preferred the endless kill-or-be-killed ecosystem of the sea. Shade could almost smell the salt and death rising from the waves.

"Comms, open a channel to the *Spero*."

The main viewscreen flickered to life, and Morgan's face appeared, calm and vaguely smug. Shade sneered. How many times had he tried to break through this AI's defenses?

"Lieutenant Commander," Morgan greeted with infuriating calm.

Shade's lip curled. "Prepare to say goodbye to your precious temple. And don't worry, Morgan," he said, a cruel gleam in his eyes, "I'll be coming for you next."

Morgan's expression remained infuriatingly placid. "Lost track of your quarry, have we?"

Shade scoffed. "Let him rot. He's nothing more than a distraction now," he grumbled, waving his hand dismissively.

The AI's eyes narrowed almost imperceptibly, a faint smirk tugging at the edges of his mouth. "Commander Tor is in Moonlit Waters. You will fail."

Morgan's confidence unsettled Shade more than he cared to admit. Colin and Lady Dark's recent losses still haunted him. That a common Earth soldier, even one as skilled as Tyler, could best both of his champions—Colin and Lady Dark—was incomprehensible. The AI had to be mistaken. Somehow, their connection had been severed, possibly by distance or interference. They had to be alive.

"Impossible!" he hissed, though the word felt empty, a whisper in the void.

And what if they're dead? the thought taunted him, pressing in from the edges of his mind. He clenched his fists. Could Tyler really foil his plans? Even if the temple's defenses were awakened, even if he unlocked the *Spero*'s systems, it would be too late. His army would already be upon them. The *Spero* would be his, and nothing would stop him from crushing Moonlit Waters and its defenders.

With a snarl, he motioned to cut the channel. Yet as he turned, something hollowed his heart—a feeling he had long buried. That small, traitorous voice in the dark depths of his mind stirred, whispering a word he dared not believe.

Hope.

"Helm, increase speed," Shade commanded, his voice cold. They would arrive soon enough. He would end this hope—kill it with fire and steel.

26 NIGHTMARE

Ralon left the group shortly after they began their descent towards the temple. He had business with his mother and wanted to buy them as much time as he could. Tyler felt a deepening sense of dread as they wound their way down cobblestone streets toward the bay. The city's life thrummed around them—vendors shouting, dockworkers moving with practiced speed, and a sea breeze heavy with salt. Yet, for all the liveliness, there was a tension in Tyler, a sense of danger pressing from all sides. This place, with its vibrant crowd, felt dangerously vulnerable.

The descent took the better part of the morning, and the sights along the way struck Tyler with a mix of curiosity and confusion. The bay was a bustling sprawl, its docks stretching like fingers into the choppy waters, and he couldn't help but wonder at the vast residential quarter packed so close to sea level. To live in a floodplain… the thought nagged at him, but he shook it off. They had far more urgent matters.

As they approached the temple entrance, Tyler's suspicions solidified. The "temple" loomed before them, but to him, the sight was unmistakable: a docking hatch of a starship. Unlike the smaller frigate Conrad, this vessel was larger, partially submerged beneath the waves, only its upper levels rising above the waterline. The fact that its structure had endured through centuries amazed him; it had clearly been maintained. Monks must have been tending to it over the years, ensuring its survival. His pulse quickened. The mystery of this ancient vessel called to him with a strange, almost magnetic allure.

Just as they reached the entrance, two elderly monks approached. They were tall, their faces marked by lines of age and wisdom, shaven heads gleaming under the Acrean sun. Pale, almost translucent eyes that seemed both sightless and all-seeing peered at them, and warm, patient smiles creased their faces.

"Welcome to the Temple of Spero, travelers. I trust your journey was safe," the older monk said, his voice gentle yet filled with an ancient resonance.

Tyler unbuckled his helmet, securing it at his belt with a slight smile. *If they only knew what we've been through this past tenday,* he thought wryly. Samson stepped forward, hands forming a symbol that Tyler guessed was a customary greeting.

"Brothers, we come seeking admittance to the wisdom and the light," Samson intoned solemnly, his voice full of respect.

The younger monk's gaze shifted to Lanadari, his expression one of both curiosity and concern as he caught sight of her shimmering, rune-marked skin through a gap in her cloak. His eyes widened slightly before he clasped one hand over his closed fist and offered a slight bow. "I fear this one must wait outside," he said with a solemn note.

Lanadari's face showed no offense. She merely nodded and moved a short distance away, finding a bench in a waiting area by a garden filled with rich, earthy scents.

"May the temple grant you enlightenment, brothers. Stand and be judged," the older monk said, extending his hand toward the entrance.

Samson went first, stepping forward with arms spread wide. A beam of white light swept over him from above, and a faint voice intoned, "Sub-human, worker, authorization yellow." The hatch doors opened, and the monks bowed, allowing Samson to step inside.

Tyler, bemused, glanced at Razmal. "Do you understand the words?"

"They are holy words, of course. We know not what they mean, only that they grant permission to enter," Razmal replied, nudging Tyler forward with a reverent smile.

Tyler stepped into position before the doors, glancing back at Lanadari, who gave him an encouraging nod from her seat. The light passed over him, and a female voice chimed in again, though this time with a different tone.

"Commander Tor, military, authorization black," the voice stated, and the hatch slid open once more. Behind him, he heard gasps, then excited whispers as the monks fell to their knees.

"The holy words! Never before have we heard such words spoken! The gods smile upon us this day!"

Tyler shook his head, ignoring their awestruck mutterings as he ducked inside. Razmal joined them shortly afterward, and the three found themselves in a well-lit decompression chamber, now adorned as a shrine. The metallic walls had been polished by countless hands, and torches had been added to the wall, their flames mingling with the dim, flickering light from ancient overhead fixtures.

As Razmal and Samson engaged in ritual prayers, Tyler's attention was drawn to a plaque embedded in the wall, tarnished but legible beneath years of polish. Rubbing his hand across the inscription, he felt a rush of recognition.

"UEA Valkyrie, Pegasus-class," it read.

The Temple of Spero was, in reality, a heavy troop transport, part of the United Earth Alliance Navy—*his* Navy. The revelation stirred him, reigniting his sense of purpose. This ship was part of his past, and if other ships still orbited Acrea, perhaps he could find a way to reach them. His recent comm scan suggested something might still be up there, but it could just as easily have been a satellite or warning buoy.

Razmal and Samson finished their prayers, and they stepped into a corridor lit by dim, flickering lights and torch stones. The air held a faint metallic tang, mingling with the more earthly scent of incense. Nine hundred years was a long time for even the most advanced alloys, and evidence of wear and disrepair was everywhere. Monks scraped, polished, and painted over areas that had succumbed to rust, and Tyler couldn't shake his concern. If the bridge was in similar condition, reaching anyone beyond this planet might be impossible.

"May I lead?" Tyler asked, turning to his Balan companions. Samson gave him a skeptical look but gestured for him to take the lead. Tyler moved quickly, taking them into parts of the ship that looked to be rarely, if ever, visited. The air grew colder as they delved deeper into forgotten corridors where the dim lights cast only a faint, ghostly glow. Bits of ceiling had collapsed in places, wires and conduits hanging loose, and the walls bore signs of age and corrosion.

After a series of meandering turns through what had once been crew quarters, they finally came to a halt before a heavily armored door. The door was massive, imposing, and unmistakably designed to seal off the bridge.

"By my knowledge, no one has ever been granted access here," Samson murmured reverently, touching the door as if it were sacred.

"You speak truth, brother," came a voice from behind them, and they turned to see an elderly Balan approaching, leaning on a polished bone staff.

"Abbot," Razmal and Samson said, bowing deeply.

The Abbot nodded in acknowledgment, his movements labored yet dignified. "I come to witness," he said, breathing heavily as he steadied himself against his staff and the wall.

Tyler's attention shifted back to the door, where he found a rusted palm scanner beneath a thick layer of grime. He placed Polaris carefully against the wall, wiped away the worst of the dust, and pressed his hand to the scanner. Warmth spread through his fingers, and he allowed himself a small sigh of relief when a faint green light blinked on.

"Voiceprint," came a heavily garbled voice from the door's speaker.

"Tor, Tyler, Commander." He paused. "UEA Centaur."

An accepting tone chimed from the scanner, and the ancient voice crackled, "Bridge is under sanctuary protocol."

Sanctuary protocol—the ship's computer had protected the bridge by sealing it in a hard vacuum. Tyler's heart leapt with the implications. The bridge might be untouched by the corrosion that had overtaken the rest of the ship.

"Cancel sanctuary protocol," Tyler commanded, his voice steady.

"Command code?"

Tyler turned to find his companions staring, slack-jawed and wide-eyed. The reverent whispering between Razmal, Samson, and the Abbot grew louder as they absorbed the cryptic exchange between him and the Valkyrie's computer—a "holy language" to the monks, a lineage that they believed connected them to the gods.

Their awe seemed to deepen as Tyler turned back to the hatch, where his mind raced, piecing together the implications of the ancient codes.

"Katherine, eight, eight, seven, black," he murmured, as the authorization sequence demanded.

A low hiss filled the corridor as air flooded into the bridge chamber for the first time in centuries. The Abbot, on his knees, had begun fervent prayer, his weathered lips moving silently in a rhythm that seemed almost as old as the ship itself. The hiss continued, echoing down the long hall until finally, with a dull clang, the outer blast doors opened, revealing an inner, gleaming surface untouched by time or decay. Sanctuary protocol had indeed worked wonders, sealing the bridge in pristine condition.

With a slight smile, Tyler stepped onto the bridge, his breath catching as monitors flickered to life, casting a soft glow across polished metal consoles and silent stations, waiting for orders. He moved from station to station, fingers trailing over smooth panels, relishing the ancient technology stirring awake beneath his touch. Lights danced, screens pulsed with diagnostic data, and the communication boards blinked in a steady rhythm. The Valkyrie was old but enduring, resilient as only a UEA warship could be.

Glancing back at the threshold, Tyler saw that his companions had remained in the corridor with the Abbot. He waved them forward. "Coming in?"

Samson shook his head, still wide-eyed. "No, friend Tyler. It is not our place. We will wait."

Tyler nodded, focusing on the data scrolling across the screen in front of him. Valkyrie's systems were mostly functional, operating on minimal internal power, with energy routed strategically to the weaponry and shields. But then he saw something that made him pause—the shield bubble had been extended far beyond standard capacity. The protective field stretched over nearly the entire city of Moonlit Waters. *Someone had fortified this ship's defenses long ago*, he realized. And they'd scavenged parts from other vessels to do it. He scanned through the logs, hoping to uncover a name, an origin, maybe even a mention of his wife, Amanda, but the records held only silence.

As Tyler scanned the data, a klaxon blared, breaking the silence with shrill, urgent pulses, and a flashing indicator on the main console signaled an imminent threat. The announcement blared over the bridge speakers, vibrating in a somber monotone: "Alert, approaching vessel. Condition orange. Alert, approaching vessel. Condition orange."

Heart pounding, Tyler accessed the sensor data, eyes widening as he recognized the signature of the incoming ship—a UEA cargo vessel, but one bristling with weaponry. Further scans showed that it held warheads in its hold, and its shields were overcharged to the front, clearly bracing for bombardment. A thermal scan confirmed it—Shade had brought an army with him, a writhing mass of biological lifeforms crowded into the cargo hold.

Tyler clenched his jaw. This was no raid; it was a full-scale invasion.

"Ship, alert condition red," he commanded, his voice cutting through the blaring alarms. "Silence the bridge alarm."

"Aye, condition red," replied the Valkyrie's computer as the bridge fell silent. Yet from outside, in the halls and likely across the city itself, the alarm continued to echo in eerie cadence: *Alert, condition red. All hands to battle stations. Repeat, condition red.*

Razmal poked his head into the bridge, covering one ear against the blaring alarm outside.

"Find Ralon," Tyler instructed firmly. "We'll need every available force to mount a response."

The Abbot, now fully alert and trembling, stepped forward, his frail voice trembling with conviction. "The dark one is coming," he whispered, his eyes wide with fear. "The VAST tremble in his shadow."

Tyler turned his attention back to the screen, running calculations and strategies, but his options were limited. The ship's automated defenses were active, but they were locked to default attack patterns. It was clear that someone, possibly centuries ago, had prepared this ship for precisely this scenario—a looming threat from above. The Valkyrie's systems were set to deliver the maximum force possible. But even with the ship's firepower, he felt an uneasy certainty. *There was more to this invasion than met the eye.*

"We'll find Ralon," Tyler said finally, grabbing Polaris and brushing past the Abbot and his two wide-eyed companions. Together, the three of them made their way back through the labyrinthine corridors of the ancient ship, their footsteps echoing through the metallic halls.

Once outside, Tyler slipped his helmet back on and assessed the scene. Across the bay, the city stirred with a sense of urgency. He looked to Samson, who was already glancing nervously at the horizon, his face pale.

"It is Shade," Samson murmured, almost as if naming a curse.

Tyler nodded, his eyes narrowing as he scanned the cityscape. "Then let's make sure he regrets coming here."

They crossed the bay toward the bustling streets of Moonlit Waters. Lanadari, who had been waiting in the garden area when they'd gone in, was now nowhere to be seen. Tyler scanned the area, frowning. "Where do you suppose she went?"

Before anyone could respond, Razmal pointed to a figure in the distance. "There! She's climbing the guard tower."

Tyler followed Razmal's gesture, spotting her ascending the stone steps of an old watchtower at the harbor's edge. The ancient tower, weathered by centuries of salt and wind, was perfectly situated to overlook the narrow channel that fed into the bay—a strategic choke point for any invading force.

"Razmal, go help her. Samson and I will organize the resistance," Tyler ordered. Razmal nodded, sprinting off toward the watchtower.

From the direction of the city, a shimmering line of legionnaires began to form, their armor catching the sunlight and creating a serpentine shimmer as they approached. Tyler's heart leapt at the sight. The soldiers of Moonlit Waters had answered the call, rallying with breathtaking speed and precision. Armor gleamed, spear tips sparkled, and banners bearing the city's sigil snapped in the wind. Moonlit Waters was no stranger to Shade's wrath—they had mobilized without hesitation, a formidable force ready to defend their home.

Samson gave an excited clap and rushed toward the approaching legionnaires, arms waving as he shouted commands, his voice a beacon to the gathering troops.

The morning air split with a deafening sonic boom, and far in the distance, the hulking shape of Shade's cargo ship burst from a cloud bank, its engines roaring as it descended. Tyler's breath hitched. The sky seemed to pulse, growing suddenly brighter, and a thunderous crack announced the railgun discharge from the submerged Valkyrie. A column of red-hot energy sliced through the air, vaporizing water into a dense, hissing fog that blanketed the shore. The incoming vessel's shields flared an angry crimson, absorbing the blow but already struggling against the Valkyrie's sustained assault. The acrid tang of ozone thickened the air.

With a terrifying calm, Shade's ship continued its descent. The sound of marching grew louder as the city's legionnaires gathered, forming ranks, their disciplined movements a stark contrast to the chaos on the horizon. Tyler felt a strange mix of dread and exhilaration; they were facing insurmountable odds, yet every glint of armor, every steadfast gaze among his allies reminded him that Moonlit Waters was not a city easily cowed.

"Hold steady!" he shouted, rallying the soldiers near Samson. The ground shuddered beneath them as a barrage of smaller cannon blasts fired from the Valkyrie's defenses, peppering Shade's ship with explosive force, each blast a testament to the warship's enduring might.

But Shade's ship retaliated, firing its own salvo of energy that smashed into the outer shield, causing it to ripple and strain. The shield held, for now, but Tyler knew it wouldn't last forever under such relentless assault.

From his vantage point, he spotted Razmal and Lanadari in the tower, signaling with what appeared to be an improvised lantern. Tyler's gaze sharpened, his instincts telling him that whatever their plan, Lanadari's role would be critical. Shade's arrival was only the first wave; something darker lingered just beyond the horizon.

Samson placed a hand on Tyler's shoulder, nodding with grim determination. "Whatever comes, we stand together, friend."

Tyler clapped him on the back, his voice fierce and resolute. "Then let's give Shade something to fear."

The air thickened, charged with the weight of an approaching storm.

The Valkyrie fired relentlessly, but Shade's invasion force pressed forward, intent on breaking the city's defenses. Twin warheads flared from the belly of the cargo ship, illuminating the battlefield in a terrifying brilliance. Tyler's reflexes kicked in, and he hit the ground, face-down, his helmet's shield slammed shut. But nothing could stop the blinding light that stabbed through his closed eyes, nor the wave of raw energy that tore across his body, pressing him harshly into the sand and ringing every bone with a vibrating ache.

The shockwave crashed over him, clawing at his exposed skin and bursting his eardrum in a dull pop that left a trickle of warm blood seeping from his ear. The air around him crackled with heat and rage. The blast's aftermath left two gigantic mushroom clouds rolling out to sea, their pillars of smoke stretching skyward as if to warn Acrea's heavens of the oncoming siege. Tyler pushed himself up, breathing heavily, scanning the destruction around him.

Scattered bodies lay across the hillside, the impact zone littered with charred craters where soldiers and civilians alike had been moments ago. He struggled to focus, searching for his companions. The once-hopeful line of reinforcements marching to their aid was now a broken patchwork, and Samson was nowhere to be seen amid the smoke and chaos.

As he took a deep breath, trying to refocus, Tyler spotted the cargo ship cutting through the haze. With battered hulls leaking debris into the bay, the vessel maneuvered sharply, thrusters roaring as it dropped lower to deploy troops directly onto the beach. From the main hold, Shade's legion poured forth in waves, hundreds of figures rushing the sands and fanning out across the battlefield. Above, several jump craft launched from the cargo deck, strafing the city's defenders while evading the autocannon fire from the Valkyrie. The heavy troop transport was slowing, its autocannons working overtime to thin the endless streams of Shade's warriors.

The whine of the cannons suddenly faltered; their once-steady rhythm replaced by the disheartening whir of depleted energy reserves. Tyler cursed under his breath; they needed a miracle, and fast.

Just as he despaired, a piercing silver beam arced across the battlefield, slicing through one of the behemoth creatures charging up the beach. Tyler's heart lifted—it was Lanadari, perched in the old watchtower, raining devastation on the enemy from afar. Her silver blasts ripped through Shade's forces, mowing down half-giants, lizardmen, and avians alike. Her precision was deadly, and her power unmatched, as bodies slumped into the sand, scorched and lifeless. Even Razmal was holding his own, stationed at the tower's entrance, wielding his glowing shield and hammer to send enemies crashing to the ground.

A cry escaped Tyler's lips, fueled by a fresh surge of resolve. He charged down the beach, Polaris raised high. The wind whipped at his face, and he lowered his face shield as he sprinted towards the approaching horde. He would take as many of them down as possible—no matter the odds, he wasn't about to let Shade's forces overrun Moonlit Waters.

Tyler quickly found himself surrounded as two massive brutes, wielding blood-caked clubs, thundered toward him. Their swings were brutal, and he parried with Polaris, each blow resonating through his arms as he struggled to deflect the strength behind their strikes. One managed a glancing hit to the side of his head, sending him sprawling to the sand, his helmet ringing from the impact. He twisted desperately to avoid the next club that crashed inches away from his face, sand spraying as it smashed down.

With a quick kick, he struck one brute's kneecap, hearing a satisfying crack followed by an enraged howl. As the creature stumbled, Tyler saw a spear erupt from its neck, thrown with deadly precision by one of the defenders on the hillside. Tyler rolled away, gasping, but a booted foot slammed into his back, forcing him face-down into the dirt, stars dancing in his vision. He gritted his teeth, summoning every ounce of strength to push back, narrowly avoiding a blow that struck just where his head had been.

Scrambling to his feet, he took in the chaos around him. Defenders clustered around the gateway to the city, but they were struggling, their numbers dwindling under the brutal assault. Several of Shade's forces bore Tekian gauss rifles, cutting down the Acrean defenders with deadly accuracy. Tyler knew they wouldn't hold much longer.

Then, a familiar weight on his palm brought him back to a spark of hope. His hand brushed a glowing patch of skin, and as he pressed down, felt his implant shift, reconnecting him to his earlier communication scan.

"Golem, online," rumbled a deep voice within his helmet, clear and resonant despite the roar of battle. Tyler's heart skipped a beat.

"Yes," he breathed, fingers flying to his temple as he interfaced with the signal. "This is Commander Tor, requesting immediate support at my location."

The system acknowledged, and he heard the telltale click of the automated systems booting up as the Golem interfaced with satellites circling Acrea, assessing battlefield's needs, cataloging enemy movements and scanning for areas of vulnerability in real time. A schematic overlay appeared in his visor, highlighting weaknesses in Shade's assault patterns, giving him a tactical edge. More importantly, it suggested maneuvers and optimal paths to regain control of the city's defenses.

Tyler charged forward with renewed purpose, diving into the fray, and coordinating his movements with the suggestions streaming from the Golem. Enemy soldiers fell in his path, their brute strength no match for the pinpoint accuracy that the Golem allowed him. He hacked, slashed, and ducked, each strike precise, each dodge calculated.

Meanwhile, the silver beams from Lanadari continued to sear through the sky, obliterating anything that came close to the tower. Razmal was tireless, swinging his hammer and cutting down enemies who dared approach. Tyler watched in awe as the defenders near the gate rallied, inspired by the courage and raw power of those in the watchtower. Lanadari's magic and Razmal's resolve were turning the tide, if only for a moment.

27 CROYAN

Polaris rippled in his grasp as another shrieking blue bolt found its mark. The Balanite was the only thing keeping him alive as it absorbed blast after fiery blast. The Tekians had Tyler pinned down in a small depression left by an explosion. The battle field was a chaotic mess, with legionnaire and enemy bodies everywhere. Several jump craft continued to harass the beach, and a few others had flown higher and rained death down upon the city.

He heard the distinct approach of his salvation. The Golem thundered from the heavens, its jump jets roaring. The war machine landed heavily, scanning the battlefield with its sweeping red gaze. A Tekian gauss blast thudded against its heavily armored chest, leaving a small scorch mark. The Golems arm cannon leapt up, spat a ball of crackling fire, and reduced the shooter to ash.

"Go get um," Tyler coughed, blood spattering the sand.

"Compliance," the Golem rumbled back.

One of the jump craft reeled in the sky and sped towards the beach, committed to making another attack run. The Golem fired its jump jets and intercepted the craft midair. Debris rained down as the enemy flyer erupted into flames from repeated arm cannon fire. The war machine completed its arc through the sky and landed smoothly into a run, firing as it went. The loss of life became catastrophic for the Tekian troops.

The cargo ship had taken notice and approached at full burn, intent on dropping the rest of its troops on the beach. The winged avians poured from the cargo bay as the ship turned, crude spears with flint tips gleaming dully in the Acrean sunshine. The Valkyrie, having taken enough of a nap, spat a shimmering blue beam from its railgun. The bridge of the cargo ship exploded and the entire vessel listed to one side. Hundreds of troops tumbled from the cargo hold like dark rain. Most hit the beach and didn't rise for the height of the fall was too great to survive. The transport accelerated suddenly, trailing black smoke as it retreated around the cliffs of the city.

Enough of the giant men and avians remained to easily take the beach. Tyler struggled to his feet when he caught sight of a woman wearing combat armor with a similar cut to his own. She wore a crimson-colored cloak that billowed in the breeze.

"Hello commander," the woman said sweetly, her voice sounding slightly metallic from behind her full helm.

Her voice sounded oddly familiar.

She laughed harder than she had a right to in the situation, with a slight touch of madness that dissolved into the giggles.

"Warrant Officer Remi Kako," she said with a mock salute. "I missed you, sir."

Impossible.

The air had taken on a deathly chill with her approach.

"How is this possible?" Tyler asked.

Kako shrugged and rested her hands on two belted short swords. Tyler vividly remembered her prowess with blades from his years at the academy. She had been incredibly driven as an enlisted, working hard to become a warrant officer; halfway between enlisted and commissioned officer but untouchable by both.

She seemed to sense his eyes on her blade and drew them with a hiss of metal on oiled metal. "You see sir, I have a new boss now and he lets me do anything I want." She began to circle him like a cat toying with a mouse.

"Would you let me do anything I want?" She purred, eyeing him up and down.

"Come now Kako, let's put those away and talk," Tyler said.

Kako tensed and ceased her circling.

"Show me your legendary reputation isn't all stories. I have had nine hundred years to perfect my art, can you say the same?" she said.

Her two blades stuck in unison, sparking as Tyler parried them with Polaris. She worked her blades with skill, driving Tyler back a step. Gauss blasted ripped through the air, one of which charred a hole through Kako's crimson cloak. The singed garment sent her into a rage, and she sprang away with a feral cry. She sprinted towards the Tekian soldier with the poor aim and cut the man down with ease. She turned, smoothed her cloak and began to walk back towards Tyler like a model on a runway.

She had indeed lost her mind.

Tyler held out his hand in a stop motion and nearly lost his fingers for the effort. She whirled her blades and one of them struck his forearm, carving through the armor and spattering the ground with blood. The sight of his blood on her blade focused him instantly. He spun Polaris in a figure eight motion and rocked back on his heels in a half crouch.

Tyler steadied himself, his grip on Polaris iron as he faced the frenzied force of Kako's dual blades. She was relentless, her attacks coming faster and faster, each one a vengeful blur aimed with deadly precision. Even with Polaris absorbing and deflecting her onslaught, Tyler felt the sting of exhaustion creeping into his limbs, his muscles heavy from the fierce rhythm of her assault. The air between them shimmered with frost, and he could feel her unnatural chill leaching through his armor, leaving his skin prickling and his breath fogging as it escaped his helmet.

Kako, however, seemed to thrive on the cold. Her movements were fluid, her strikes unyielding, and a manic gleam flashed in her eyes every time Tyler countered one of her blows. She was more than a soldier, she was a weapon, honed to lethal perfection over centuries. Her smirk twisted into something more feral as she pressed him harder, her blades a whirlwind of steel and malice.

In a desperate maneuver, Tyler shifted his stance, lunging forward to break her rhythm. He ducked under her crossed blades, swinging Polaris up to slam the butt of the staff into her ribs. Kako hissed in pain, stumbling back, her eyes blazing with fury.

"Still got some tricks, I see," she sneered, flexing her grip on her swords. "But it won't be enough."

Tyler barely had time to breathe before she was on him again, her fury even more intense than before. Every time she advanced, he blocked, countered, and dodged, each movement becoming more instinctive. But Kako was faster, her strikes punctuated by taunts as if each dodge and parry amused her even more.

"You think this is still a game, Kako?" Tyler shouted, hoping to break through the wall of madness that seemed to enshroud her.

She laughed, her voice echoing unnervingly across the battlefield. "Oh, but it is, Commander," she mocked, voice edged with steel. "And I'm here to win." Her blades came in hard, forcing Tyler back another step.

She laughed again, and the sound had the eerie, hollow ring of someone who had forgotten what humanity felt like.

A quick movement in his periphery caught Tyler's attention—a glint of blue and red from the Golem, barreling through a line of Tekian soldiers and cutting a devastating path toward them. The war machine was unstoppable, its cannon sending blast after blast into the advancing troops, reducing their lines to ash and flame.

"Your friends won't save you," Kako sneered, lunging forward again. She caught the edge of Tyler's armor, and a sliver of pain bloomed along his side as her blade left a shallow cut.

He staggered but quickly pivoted, sweeping Polaris in a tight arc to force her back. Her laughter faltered, replaced by a snarl of frustration. Tyler saw his chance, feinting left before striking right, his staff catching her just below her collarbone, sending her stumbling backward.

"You're not invincible, Kako!" Tyler shouted. "Shade's lies don't make you unbreakable."

She froze for an instant, her eyes narrowing to slits, and in that pause, Tyler glimpsed something—an echo of the woman he had once known, the loyal officer he had trained beside and respected. For a fleeting moment, her sneer softened, her gaze unfocused as if wading through the memories of another lifetime.

But it vanished just as quickly. She blinked, and whatever humanity had briefly surfaced drowned beneath a tide of fury and cold. She lashed out with renewed strength, her strikes fueled by a wild, chaotic power, and Tyler was forced onto the defensive once more.

The Golem had nearly reached them, its towering frame a shield against the advancing Tekians. Its mechanical voice boomed over the battlefield, issuing commands to the scattered defenders and rallying the legionnaires.

Kako's attention flickered to the Golem, and for the briefest second, Tyler felt her rage flare, a fury that seemed almost…jealous. Her lip curled as she looked from the war machine back to Tyler.

"Still hiding behind your machines, Commander?" she taunted, though a flicker of doubt danced in her eyes. "Is that all the great Tyler Tor has left?"

"You don't have to do this, Kako," Tyler said, his voice low, steady. He advanced a step, Polaris held defensively before him. "Shade's twisted you—he's using you as a tool."

The rage in her eyes flared again, but beneath it, he could see it—a sliver of hesitation, like a crack in her armor. But it vanished as quickly as it had appeared. Her mouth twisted into a feral grin, and she charged once more, her scream a chilling blend of hatred and madness.

"Then fight me!" she spat, her voice tinged with an edge of despair she couldn't fully hide.

Tyler braced himself, prepared to meet her head-on. Just as her blades arced toward him, a blast of red energy lanced between them, forcing Kako back. She screamed in frustration, her gaze snapping to the source of the attack.

Lanadari stood in the distance, her arms raised, silvered runes glowing along her skin. She radiated power, her stance one of unwavering defiance.

"You're fighting the wrong battle, Remi!" Lanadari shouted, her voice ringing out across the battlefield. "Shade has stolen your soul, corrupted your loyalty."

Kako let out a strangled cry, her eyes wild with a mix of rage and fear. "I don't need saving!" she shrieked, her voice almost breaking. "I don't even know you, girl!"

Tyler seized the moment. He lunged forward, Polaris a blur as he swept her legs from under her, sending her sprawling to the ground. Before she could react, he was over her, Polaris pressed against her neck.

"Stop this, Kako," he said, voice firm. "This isn't who you are."

For a moment, she lay still, her breath coming in gasps, her eyes filled with hatred—but somewhere, Tyler thought, a glimmer of something else.

Then, as if a switch had been flipped, she laughed again, that same hollow, manic laughter.

"Oh, Commander," she whispered, her voice low, almost regretful. "Shade's given me purpose—something you never could."

Tyler felt a pang in his chest, a shadow of the person she had once been. But the battlefield roared around them, and there was no more time. He tightened his grip on Polaris and gave her one last, mournful look.

"You were a good soldier, Remi. Remember that."

She froze, her eyes widening slightly, but the ice quickly returned.

"Finish it, then," she spat.

But before he could respond, another blast from the Golem's cannon shook the ground beside them, scattering Tekian soldiers in all directions and forcing Kako back. She stumbled to her feet, her expression unreadable,

Tyler's voice carried a note of desperate pleading. "Please, Kako, I just want to understand what went wrong with the mission. How are we both here now? Think of the fleet, Kako."

Her only response was a furious scream as she hacked at him with her blades, her eyes wild. In her frenzy, one of her short swords slipped past his guard, burying itself deep into his shoulder. Pain surged through him, and his arm went limp. Kako cackled with vicious delight, kicking him in the chest and wrenching her blade free. Blood flowed freely down his chest plate as he staggered back, Polaris vibrating with an almost sympathetic anger.

"The fleet be damned," she sneered. "We were near death before the master saved us. It's a shame I won't be bringing you to him so he can kill you himself. No—I'll take that pleasure myself." She advanced on him, her blades twirling.

Tyler called to the power within Polaris, feeling the Warquarter ripple up his arm. Cool metal washed over his wounds, sealing them with a tingle and a swirl of white smoke. Kako stabbed again, but her short swords clanged against his now-solid Balanite armor. She gasped, surprised and then visibly afraid, as Tyler rocked her back with a heavy fist. The blow dented her helmet, shattering her visor and releasing a hiss of cryogenic gas.

As the gas cleared, Tyler stared into her eyes, recognizing the resignation in their depths. Her skin was pale and cracked from exposure to open air, her once-familiar features warped by Shade's corruption. She drew a sonic pistol from a hidden holster and shot Tyler with several focused blasts.

"Stop, Kako," he growled.

"Never! If I can't kill you, then I'll find your family and friends. None of them will escape me. This won't end until you're dead at my feet and this land belongs to the Master."

Her breath came in ragged gasps.

Polaris recoiled in his hand, sensing the ancient, dark energy radiating from her. Tyler felt the darkness welling up within her, and his instincts warned him just in time. A vile, pestilent breath escaped her mouth, and he reacted without thinking. A Balanite blade shimmered out from his forearm, and he plunged it through her chest. She gasped, sliding down its length, her blades clanging to the ground from her lifeless fingers.

Kako coughed, blood spattering his armor. Her pale skin bloomed with a hint of color, her face softening as the corruption left her body. She raised her head weakly, her voice barely a whisper. "I'm free… Oh, Tyler, the horror. What he has become."

She winced as Polaris retracted from her, shifting back to its Warquarter form. Gently, Tyler laid her on the ground, the sounds of battle fading momentarily. He carefully cleared the shards of her face shield, her eyes finally at peace, the darkness fully cleansed from her—but at the cost of her life.

Her hand gripped his chest plate, and she pulled him close. "I want to go home," she whispered, blood bubbling on her lips.

"I'll take us there, Kako. I promise," Tyler said softly.

She managed a faint smile before her eyes closed.

Weapons fire struck close, spraying Tyler with stone and dirt. He stood, scanning the chaotic battlefield. Nearby, the Golem rampaged through a group of winged Avians, while Acrean legionnaires rallied around a robed Balan, who sent blasts of energy into the invading troops. Tyler's gaze found Lanadari, now fighting on the front lines at the base of the guard tower, with Razmal at her side, defending her with his shield, deflecting weapons fire with precision.

The tables had turned.

A horn blared, drawing his attention to a line of heavily armored Acrean guards marching down from the city, their banner of Moonlit Waters flying proudly. Leading them was Ralon, clad in fine black chitin armor and wearing a plumed helm with a golden feather. He looked every inch the noble as he led the elite guard to the beach.

Nearby, a cluster of enemy troops rallied around the remaining Tekian guards in full-visored helmets. Their eerie movements confirmed they were like Kako—souls twisted and bound by Shade. Fury surged in Tyler as he thought of the cryosuits that sealed these warriors in eternal torment. How many of them had he known, trained with? How many of them were once allies?

He had to end this and destroy the one Kako had feared so deeply. Shade had to fall.

A strange buzzing filled the air as the small-arms fire and gauss rifle blasts abruptly ceased. Most of the Tekians were dead or fleeing to the waves, while giant men, lizards, and Avians had regrouped around the black-suited guards, facing the advancing legion. Tyler focused, listening intently for any communication between the enemy ship offshore and the leaders on the ground. A voice drifted into his mind, not over the comms but through some other channel.

"…break their line and drive them against the cliffs where we can get a clear run. I'll drive this ship into the rocks themselves!"

The voice sounded hauntingly familiar.

Tyler knew what he needed to do but required a better vantage point to guide the Valkyrie's weapon systems. The ship still targeted enemy jump craft with its point-defense batteries, but the effort felt like a distraction. The voice from the transport—it had to be Shade.

He sprinted toward the guard tower, weaving through the melee. Both sides fought with bone and crystal blades, but the cryosuits worn by some of Shade's guards rendered them almost indestructible. Avians hovered just above the fray, hurling spears that found their targets. Tyler's heart sank as he saw more Acreans fall.

With a rapid signal from the Acrean horn, the Moonlit Waters legion shifted into a wedge formation. Their shield-bearers formed the outer edge, while spear and sword wielders took the center. At the core were Ralon, Samson, and other robed figures channeling

VAST-powered strikes. The wedge surged forward, slicing through the enemy ranks. Ralon and his guard unleashed destruction that tore into the cryosuit guards, ripping apart armor and spewing clouds of toxic gas.

Tyler pressed forward, noticing a dead Tekian soldier clutching a gauss rifle. He picked it up, surprised to see its green indicator—this was UEA tech. As he moved, he fired, cutting down larger enemy giants and picking an Avian out of the sky. The lizards began retreating to the waves, and he let them go; he would never shoot a fleeing foe, even now.

Reaching the guard tower, he ascended three steps at a time, panting when he reached the top. Taking a moment to steady himself, he looked out over the beach where the transport hovered offshore, still trailing smoke. Tyler tapped his palm and accessed his secure link to the Valkyrie bridge.

"Hello, Commander," the Valkyrie's voice chimed in his ear.

"Cease fire on the jump craft. Gather as much energy as you can. Draw from the shield if needed," Tyler commanded, spinning the virtual control on his palm.

"Give me a reading on the enemy ship's shield," he added.

"Ventral and aft shielding are down; frontal shields are minimal," the Valkyrie computer replied.

"Can you lock onto its main engine?"

The computer paused. "Engines will not be destroyed with available power."

Tyler swore. He needed to cripple the transport before it unleashed more warheads. Targeting the weapon system could trigger a core breach, irradiating Arral for centuries.

Then he had an idea. He linked his palm controller to the Golem below, setting both the Golem and the Valkyrie's programs for a coordinated strike. Taking a deep breath, he spoke a single word: "Execute."

The Valkyrie's railguns thrummed and struck the transport's front shield, which flared and crackled under the assault. The shield flickered, allowing a portion of the blast to pierce the hull, exposing the innards. The Golem's jets fired, propelling it straight toward the transport.

The Golem's scanners locked onto a life sign on the bridge, and an alarm roared in Tyler's ears.

"Officer Pistos Croyan bio reading detected and confirmed," the Golem's voice intoned.

Tyler's breath caught. "Croyan… Golem, abort! Abort!"

The name hit him like a blow. Pistos Croyan, his oldest friend and the finest officer he'd ever known, somehow here in this nightmare. How could he be alive?

The Golem veered at the last moment, its cannon blasting a massive hole in the transport's hull, setting its belly thrusters aflame. The transport careened out of control, speeding toward the guard tower. Tyler's mind reeled as he saw the melted slag of the bridge. Then he saw Croyan himself, his face a deathly mask framed by swirling shadows. The horror-filled words twisted from Croyan's mouth: "Kill him!"

Tyler had found Shade.

The transport pulled away toward the sea, and a final warhead erupted from its launcher, hitting the shield before Tyler. The blast bowed the shield inward, a shockwave tearing through the guard tower with a concussive blast. The air itself seemed to ripple, and Tyler watched in slow motion as the shield tore and shattered around him.

Polaris slipped from his grip as the energy flung him backward, his armor blistering away, the smell of charred flesh filling his senses. His back struck the rear wall, which crumbled under the impact, sending him tumbling backward. Tyler felt himself falling, the world spinning around him as he plummeted from the crumbling tower. His thoughts slowed, his consciousness fading in and out as he tumbled through empty space.

His vision dimmed, flickering between bursts of clarity and darkness. Polaris was gone from his hand, the last memory of its cool weight slipping away as he felt his armor failing. The pain in his body began to dull, replaced by an odd, floating numbness as he continued to drop through the broken air.

Just before the darkness overtook him completely, a final thought echoed through his mind: the promise he'd made to Kako, to bring them all home. And with that, Tyler's world fell away, spiraling into silence as the ground below rushed to meet him.

His head spun, and all went dark.

EPILOGUE

The great waves of the Acrean Ocean crashed against the Moonlit Cliffs. The bay of Spero was calm and the night air pleasant. Yalonia swelled full and bright in the sky, bathing the bay in dim light. A large wave struck the calm beach, and the water pulled back to wash in again. The process had repeated endlessly, but this night, the sea was different. The large waves paused for a moment, and a massive buildup of ocean energy brought in a gargantuan swell.

The swell hammered into the beach, spraying saltwater high into the air. Standing upon the beach where the waves had struck stood a woman. She stared at her reflection in the water, tall and athletic with long black hair that hung plastered and wet against her face and shoulders. Almond brown eyes peered back at her, and the seashell mask that covered her nose and mouth formed a hard seal against the sweet night air. Her wet suit clung to her olive-colored skin and glittered like the scales of a fish as she took a hesitant step up the beach. A thin ribbon of silver flowed around her middle and snaked up and down her arms.

"Calm, Starmist," the woman said, her voice muffled behind the shell mask. "Let us hope we made it in time."

The woman picked her way up the battle-torn beach. The bodies had been removed, but she could still see depressions with dried blood where warriors had breathed their last. Large craters still smoldered and shimmered where sandy bottoms had turned to glass. The twinkle of torchlight caught her attention. The beach was well-patrolled this night.

She melted into the shadows of a large piece of rubble from a guard tower and studied one of the patrols as they passed. The three figures looked like skittering insects in their chitinous armor. Each held a wicked-looking halberd with dull crystalline blades. The lead figure held a glittering torchstone in the air, peering into the night. The patrol passed without incident, and the woman let out a breath she had forgotten she was holding.

Starmist excitedly swirled down and around one of her wrists, pulling her to another piece of charred tower rubble. Emotions and stray images flooded her mind in a rush. An echo of recent events unfolded before her eyes, appearing washed out and without sound. The tower rebuilt itself, and shadowy figures moved in reverse. A shimmering light surrounded one of the shadows that leaped from the beach and sailed to the battlements of the tower. She twisted her wrist to flow the images forward and watched as a massive blast destroyed the tower, tossing a smoking form hard to the sand.

The Sleeper had fallen.

The still shadow continued to shimmer, only slightly now, and she could tell his breathing was labored. Several shadows hurried from out of her sight, placed the Sleeper on a ghostly litter, and carried him off in the direction of the city. She followed their path and released the far sight when she felt Starmist pulling her onward.

Could he still be alive?

The woman padded silently up the beach and picked her way along the path leading up the cliffs into the city. The maps she had studied were great, and the constant tugging from Starmist told her she was on the right track. She did not know how her companion knew where they were going, but she learned long ago to trust the urgings when they came.

She passed two more patrols without incident before the inner gate of Moonlit Waters loomed large in the orange glow of Yalonia's light. The gate was closed. She looked carefully up and down the wall, paying close attention to the guardhouse. A few soft steps forward, and she was in the shadows of the wall.

"Up we go, Starmist," she whispered, stretching her arms forward, palms out.

The silvery ribbon rippled and snaked down her arm and leaped up and over the wall. She felt her feet leave the ground and the air rush past as Starmist vaulted her over the wall. She landed silently on a well-cobbled street and padded her way into deeper shadows.

She found herself wishing there was no need for secrecy, but she knew a strange woman appearing from the ocean asking to see the most valuable person in nine hundred years would have landed her before the Legion. Unfortunately, they would have too many questions, and rumor had it they were adept at getting answers. The surface dwellers would never believe in the civilization living far below the ocean waves.

She felt light and quick as she sprinted through the sleeping city. Her course led unerringly towards the upper cliffs of the city and to the massive gates of Castle Forgotten. A quiver of excitement passed from Starmist, which quickened her own heart rate.

The gate was open.

She took deep, steadying breaths through her seashell mask and darted from shadow to shadow. She peered cautiously at the gatehouse and decided to throw caution to the wind. Her thin form bolted quickly through the archway, and she slammed painfully into a figure standing on the other side of the gateway, having been just out of sight.

It was a legionnaire.

A large, armored figure peeked around a massive leg of meat and mumbled something unintelligible. Even through her mask, the smell of the roasted meat turned her stomach. His eyes were kind and his movement unthreatening, but she did not have time for pleasantries. Two sharp objects from her pouch found their way into her hand before the hulking man could react. He reached out to her with an enormous paw as if to calm her, presenting the perfect surface to stab both purple quills into exposed flesh.

The man yelped, looked at his hands, and dropped the half-eaten leg of meat forgotten to the cobbled floor. The poison of the Raker sea anemone, while not lethal, worked very quickly. She was through the gatehouse an instant later, leaving the snoring behemoth of a man far behind.

Only one of the four towers was lit, and Starmist pulled her towards its high open windows. She readied herself as before and sent her companion upward. The rush of air left her stomach feeling like it had remained on the ground. She landed deftly in the fine cut window that faced out toward the vast Arral countryside, teetering only slightly at the narrow ledge.

A man lay on a stone slab covered in layers of furs. He was horribly burned from what little of him she could see and the smell in the room was that of death. His breathing came in ragged gasps, and it sounded like his lungs were full of fluid. She scanned the rest of the room and found it empty of anyone else. She landed lightly on a soft woolen rug and padded over to the man's bedside. He would have been handsome if it were not for half of his face hanging in ragged red and black tatters. His eyes were closed, but pain racked his remaining features.

"Tyler Ryan Tor," the woman said, her own breath now coming in labored gasps. She was running out of time and doubted the medicine she carried would heal him. She had failed to notice an urgent pulling from Starmist, thinking they had found what they were looking for. Apparently, her companion had another idea.

She looked towards where the pull told her to go, and her gaze settled on a magnificently crafted quarterstaff. There was something oddly familiar about the staff. A voice from outside the chamber sent her darting to the floor, and she wiggled on her belly towards the wall where the staff rested. The voice was joined by another, and they spoke in whispers for a time before fading away.

She lay on the thick rug for a moment longer before reaching out grasping the staff. It was cool to her touch.

Give it to him.

The voice rippled through her mind.

Starmist? She wondered.

Give him the staff.

The voice was like listening to bubbles in a gently flowing tidepool.

She took the staff, stood up, and walked over to the sleeping man. She moved one of his hands that had been placed on top of his other and rested the staff gently on his chest. He closed his hand around the staff, and his dark grey eyes snapped open. A pale radiance leaked from between his fingers as the staff melted away and poured through his skin like water in a sponge. She could smell ozone and hear bones cracking as they mended. His charred skin flaked away, revealing healed, unbroken flesh beneath. Dark hair sprouted on his scalp, and color returned to his cheeks.

She knew her mouth must be hanging open when her almond brown eyes met his own.

"Nice mask," he said in a deep, friendly voice. His eyes were kind and calculating. She felt weighed and measured in an instant. An aura of command radiated from him like something she could touch.

"Sleeper!" she said with a squeak. "My name is Crylona, and this is Starmist, and we have so much to tell you!"

ABOUT THE AUTHOR

Brad Bussie is an award-winning author, blogger, and science fiction enthusiast. He has spent the better part of his life in cybersecurity but has always had a passion for writing. In his debut novel, The Band of Moonlit Waters, he sets the stage for a six-book series following Tyler Ryan Tor and his ragtag band of heroes.

www.ingramcontent.com/pod-product-compliance
Lightning Source LLC
Chambersburg PA
CBHW010333010826
48970CB00013B/2592